Camille's Dilemma

By

D.C. Johnson

This book is a work of fiction. Places, events, and situations in this story are purely fictional. Any resemblance to actual persons, living or dead, is coincidental.

© 2004 by D.C. Johnson. All rights reserved.

No part of this book may be reproduced, stored in a retrieval system, or transmitted by any means, electronic, mechanical, photocopying, recording, or otherwise, without written permission from the author.

ISBN: 1-4140-2594-7 (e-book)
ISBN: 1-4140-2595-5 (Paperback)

This book is printed on acid free paper.

1stBooks - rev. 05/27/04

Chapter 1
Come Home, Cynthia

You know it's going to be a hot day when you wake up sweating. Just looking out the window, the outside seems to have taken on the look of a desert, dry and still. I spend most of my time in this window. I sit here all day and tell other folks' business to myself. I've been all around the world. I settled here in Chicago a few years ago. There's not much left for me to do but look out this window. I'm eighty-five years old. I love to look over there in the Jenkins' house. They're my favorite family to watch. Them kids over there always getting popped in the mouth for saying something smart. Camille's my favorite. I reckon she's about eleven years old with her pretty little self. She's the third born in that family of four children.

I wonder what was wrong with the mama naming all them with Cs. Let me see, you got the oldest, Chester, then there's Cynthia, then

Camille, and then that baby boy, Clifford. Even got an aunt named Cathy!

From what I done seen so far, that Jenkins family is getting ready to go through some real troubled times, especially Camille. Now, that can only be Camille's sister, Cynthia, knocking on that bathroom door. (I reckon I'll talk to you later. Bye.)

"Hurry up, girl! You're not the only one that has to use the bathroom. I have to pee."

"Well, you just have to wait till I come out!"

"Open the door, Camille."

"No, because you're going to stay in here if I open the door. You just want to get in here so you can wash up first."

"Camille, girl, you're gon' make me pee on myself."

"Well, pee on down the stairs and get the mop!"

"You two better get on down here," Ms. Jenkins shouted from the bottom of the steps.

"Mama…Camille won't let me use the bathroom."

"Camille, come on out of there and let your sister use the bathroom."

"Mama, you know Cynthia's always faking." Camille unlocked the bathroom door, keeping one foot pressed against it. She opened the door slowly to look straight into her sister's face. She wanted Cynthia's expression to be one of urgency; if not, she was going to shut the door and take her bath, ignoring what her mama had just said. I guess Cynthia won her over because Camille grabbed her robe off the hook on the back of the door and slowly walked out with her face

Camille's Dilemma

knotted up. Cynthia walked in. As she was shutting the door, she licked her tongue out at Camille. Camille knew it would be twenty minutes before she'd get back into that bathroom.

Everyone was finished eating by the time Camille came down for breakfast. She stood with her hands on her hips looking around at the deserted kitchen. Chester and Cynthia had gone outside to play. Clifford had gone over to the babysitter's house, and Ms. Jenkins was in the laundry room sorting dirty clothes.

After eating her breakfast, she gulped down a glass of milk then headed outside to play with her friends.

While in the middle of playing, Camille heard her mama calling out to her and her siblings. It was embarrassing—at least it was to Camille. Ms. Jenkins would stand with the screen door wide open and holler out the names she gave to them from the top of her lungs. All the kids in the neighborhood already think they're from the country, because Cynthia calls everybody by the name of boy or girl.

"Mama, do you always have to call us in the house?" Camille asked, shutting the screen door. "Can't you just give us a certain time to be in? People are always making fun of us. It's the middle of the day, and you're standing with the screen door wide open, shouting out our names. They be mocking you, Ma."

Ms. Jenkins put her hands on her narrow hips and asked, "Well, for one thing, how will you know what time it is? Neither one of you have a watch. Is the sun going to tell y'all what time it is? Second," she said, bending in a little closer to Camille, "if you did what you were told to do, you wouldn't have to come in the house in the middle of the day. Now, get on up there and get that room clean."

"It is clean! My side and Cynthia's side of the room is clean. It's Chester and Clifford's side of the room that's messed up," Camille pouted.

"You know the rules. I want the whole room cleaned up, not just one side. And where are Chester and Cynthia?"

"They coming," said Camille with her face twisted up, mad.

"Camille, I don't know why you feel you have to always clean up by yourself. And where is Clifford?"

"You sent him to the babysitter's already." Camille stood at the bedroom door staring at the imaginary line that separated the boys' side of the room from the girls'. The girls' side was clean. So Camille did what she always does: sweep everything under Clifford and Chester's bunk bed. Ms. Jenkins never looked under the beds. She would assume it was clean and would let them go back outside to play.

"Cynthia! Chester! Camille!" Ms. Jenkins was calling them again, only this time it was to come in for the night. Dusk was covering the projects. The only time Camille and her siblings got to go out after dark was when they had to look for Cynthia; she always took her time coming in.

Chester and Camille had washed up for dinner and raced down to the kitchen. There, bologna, bread, and cheese lay on the kitchen table awaiting their presence.

Camille's Dilemma

Camille stared in disgust at the cold cuts for dinner. She mumbled to herself, "Bologna again—that's all we ever have," rolling her eyes at it.

"Where is Cynthia?" Ms. Jenkins asked as she poured a glass of RC Cola from a sweating, sixteen-ounce bottle.

Chester said, as he searched the kitchen drawer for a butter knife, "I don't know." Ms. Jenkins went into the half-furnished living room and stood at the bottom of the step. She called out to Cynthia. No answer. She called out again. Still no answer. She walked back into the kitchen and just stood there with her hands on her hips.

"Mama, can I have some of your pop?" Camille asked.

"Drink some milk," she said, staring down at the floor.

"Well, can I go down to Mrs. Griffin's house when I finish eating this brick...I mean, this sandwich?"

Chester quickly sprouted out, "Mama, I left my baseball cap in the yard. Can I go get it?"

"Chester, you always trying to find some way to get back outside. If you go back outside, I'm going, too," Camille huffed.

"Hush, both of you. Neither one of you are going back outside."

Ms. Jenkins went to the back door and called out to Cynthia.

"Chester, go outside and tell Cynthia I said to get her butt in here right now. I'm gon' tear her butt up when she gets in here." Chester pretended like he didn't hear his mama because he didn't want to go look for Cynthia.

"Chester! Boy, why are you still sitting there when I told you to go look for your sister?"

5

"Why do I always have to go get her? She knows good and well she's supposed to be in the house. I'm hungry. I wanna eat," he said, frowning and crossing his arms over his chest.

"Since when did you start craving for bologna and cheese, Chester? You just don't want to go look for Cynthia," Camille said, licking the mayonnaise from the rim of her sandwich.

"I'm tired of always having to be the one to look for Cynthia. Why can't Camille go look? Shoo! That's just what Cynthia wants. She wants somebody to come looking for her so she can be out longer. She makes me sick." Ms. Jenkins stood fast and stared into Chester's face with pursed lips and piercing eyes.

"Boy, if you don't hush up with all that fussing, you gon' have to look for your head, 'cause I'm gon' knock it off.

"Camille, go out there and see if you can find Cynthia. Tell her I said to get her butt in here right now. Chester, boy, don't you move an inch! You think you too big for your own britches."

Chester didn't say a word. He knew he went too far.

"And don't you be out there messing around. You hear me, girl? You bring your butt right back. Don't let me have to come get you, too."

"I'm coming right back."

Camille thought to herself as she walked out of the kitchen, "Now I know why Cynthia calls everybody boy or girl. She got it from Mama."

Camille ran up the stairs in twos to put what she had on earlier over her pajamas. She grabbed onto the wooden banister and galloped back down the stairs. As she was closing the front door, she heard her mama say, "Chester, since you think you're too good to look for Cynthia, you stay in the house for the rest of the week."

Being outside alone in the dark was spooky to Camille. She would always look up into the midnight blue, speckled sky. Every time she looked up there she felt a gracious connection. She also felt angels watched over her. But she still feared walking alone in the dark. She sprinted everywhere she went. If anyone were going to grab her, they would have to catch her first.

Camille went to look over at the recreational center. The recreational center stayed open until 9:00 PM every night, except Saturday and Sunday. It would be closing in any minute. If Cynthia were in there, Camille would see her when she came out. Just as she walked up to the door of the center, Mr. Patton, the man in charge, was about to snap the lock on the door. Camille shouted out, "Wait! Mr. Patton, I think my sister Cynthia is still in there." Mr. Patton knew every kid in the projects by their first and last name.

"If Cynthia Jenkins is in here, she'll still be tomorrow," he said flatly as he locked the door to the center. Cynthia was not in the center. Mr. Patton may look mean, but he wasn't.

Camille strolled over to Cynthia's friend Vanessa's house. She stood on her tiptoes to ring Vanessa's doorbell. It startled her to see a tall, Fig Newton-brown-skinned girl with bumps on her face quietly staring down at her.

"Is Cynthia here?" Camille asked, looking into the dusty screen door.

"Do you see her, with yo' big-eyed self?" the girl asked, turning her nose up at Camille.

Camille frowned at her and said, "Your mama, you big wench. That's why you tall as a tree and got them big bumps in yo' face." The Fig Newton-skinned girl kicked at the screen door, scaring Camille off.

Camille didn't know where else to look, except for that graveyard. And there was no way she was going over there without a shadow. The graveyard was a creepy dumpsite that housed old, beat-up cars. So she headed back home the same way she went, sprinting. She figured she had to have been outside awhile, at least half an hour. Maybe Cynthia would be home when she got back. Cynthia was no fool. But she'd come in that house as much as an hour late after her mama had called them in for the night. Ms. Jenkins could care less about whipping their butts in they yard in front of folks. Cynthia would just grin and bear it. Camille, she wasn't about to be ridiculed in front of folks. She would run in the house. It didn't make Chester any difference, and Mama wouldn't dare spank her precious Clifford.

Camille asked out of breath, shutting the door, "Mama, is she here? 'Cause I couldn't find her."

"What do you mean you couldn't find her? As long as it took, you should have found something. Did you check over that girl's house she plays with?"

"Yeah."

"Yeah, well, was she there?" Ms. Jenkins asked, looking profoundly at Camille.

Camille's Dilemma

"I don't think so."

"Girl, what do you mean, you don't think so?"

"I asked this tree…I mean, her sister if she was there, and she looked at me all smart and asked me if I saw her. Then she kicked the screen door at me."

"You know, you two are about to get on my nerves." Ms. Jenkins walked over to the back door.

"What, Mama? I didn't do nothing," Camille said on the defense.

Ms. Jenkins mumbled, as she looked out the door, "I don't believe this. I'm gon' whip her butt when she gets in here. Camille, who else does she play with? What's that child's name that lives on the hill?"

"Angela. Mama, I know she's not over there because they ain't friends no more."

"Ain't. What did I tell you about using that word? Ain't, ain't no word. Now you got me using a word that's not a word."

"Maybe Cynthia and Vanessa went on Thirty-fifth Street."

"Thirty-fifth street!" Ms. Jenkins said, quickly looking at Camille, surprised, because that was near her workplace.

"Yeah, to the White Sox Park. They always like to wait for the players to come out to get their autographs. Or she could've gone over to them other projects."

"Now, she know she don't have no business way over there."

"They be sneaking over there all the time, Mama. Even though it may sound like it, I'm not trying to tell on Cynthia. I know you looking for her right now. Yep, they have friends that go to Thornbird School. I know because my friend, Michelle, and me wanted to go

9

with them one day, and they wouldn't let us. So we followed them, and that's where they went, to them other projects. They be going in them high-rise buildings, too." Ms. Jenkins stood with her hands on her hips, gawking at Camille through the mirror while Camille continued to run off at the mouth.

"Go on in the kitchen and finish eating," Ms. Jenkins said, sweeping her hand in the direction of the kitchen.

She then told Chester to keep an eye on things while she went to search outside for Cynthia. Camille licked her tongue out at Chester when her mama turned her back.

Chester loved to feel like he was in command because he was the oldest, but Cynthia and Camille would rule right over him soon as the door was shut.

A few minutes later, Ms. Jenkins returned, but with no Cynthia.

"You couldn't find her either, Mama?" Camille asked.

"You two go on to bed."

"Bed!" Chester expounded. "Mama, it's only eight thirty! Why we got to go to bed so early? It's not even ten o'clock yet! You making us go to bed because Cynthia's not here. That's not fair!"

"Chester, boy, you better get out of my face and do what I just told you to do. I'm in no mood for your nonsense. And you better not turn on that TV."

"Dang!" Chester mouthed, walking away. "All 'cause she don't know how to bring her butt in the house, we have to go to bed early." Chester just didn't know when to shut up; pop went the weasel. Ms.

10

Camille's Dilemma

Jenkins took off her house shoe, threw it, and hit Chester in the back of his head with it.

"Go get me the belt," she said, looking over at Camille.

"You gon' get your butt whipped," Camille said, pointing and laughing with silly expressions at Chester. Ms. Jenkins had to be in another world. When Camille handed her that belt, she took it and laid it on the couch next to her, disappointing Camille.

Chapter 2

Stop Crying, Mama

An hour had passed and Cynthia still hadn't come home. Ms. Jenkins started walking around the house announcing to whoever was listening. "She better hope she broke a leg, or I'm going to break it for her. Where is that girl? Just wait. Just wait till she gets here. She thinks she's smart; I'll teach her."

It was now ten o'clock. Darkness had flooded the projects. Ms. Jenkins started calling everyone she knew on the telephone, asking if they had seen Cynthia. She even went searching outside again—still no Cynthia.

It was now ten thirty. Curfew was in effect, and Ms. Jenkins' anger and worry had turned into anxiety. Chester had turned the TV on when he knew his mama told him not to. He thought he was being smart by turning the volume down and closing the bedroom door. He would give himself away by laughing at something that was funny.

His mama knew he wasn't crazy, so he had to be laughing at something on TV. When he got caught, it was oops up side the head or the weasel got popped.

Camille crept quietly down the stairs in her sister's hand-me-down pajamas—couldn't make the cartoon characters out on them, they were worn so badly. She sat on the bottom step and rested her chin on top of her knees, hugging her ankles. She wanted to hear what her mama was babbling about. She intently listened.

"Where is she? She knows she should be in this house by now. Where could she be this late?"

Every few seconds, Camille would peek around the corner and watch her mama be a grownup.

"God, where is she?" Ms. Jenkins shouted out. Camille thought for sure that Cynthia would come falling through the ceiling. Her mama was talking to God, something she's never seen or heard her do before.

"Lord, where is she?"

This was really serious, Camille thought, because now her mama was talking to God's Father.

"Lord, where can my baby be? Please send her home," Ms. Jenkins asked Him, with her hands on her chest.

A sudden chill came over Camille. She felt Cynthia was okay, but was in harm's way. She closed her eyes real tight and tried to push her angels to wherever Cynthia was. But the crown of light would stay orbited over Camille.

14

Camille's Dilemma

Ms. Jenkins started to look worried. These new expressions on her face were scaring Camille.

"Maybe she ran away," Camille said, loud enough for her mama to hear.

"Ran away! Where are you? Come in here, Camille." Camille walked slowly toward her mama.

"What did you just say?"

Stuttering a little, Camille said it again. "Maybe she ran away."

"What would make you say something like that? Cynthia don't have a reason to run away."

"She's ain't...I mean, she's not here."

"Just because she's not here, Camille, doesn't mean she ran away. She could be anywhere. Did you two have a fight?"

"Nope," Camille replied, shaking her head back and forth.

"I don't understand. Why would she want to run away? Is that what she told you she was going to do?" Ms. Jenkins jerked both of Camille's arms toward her.

Camille stared down at the un-waxed floor.

"Think! Did she tell you she was going to run away?" Again, she jerked Camille's arms toward her. Camille shrugged her shoulders, looking into her mama's watery eyes. Ms. Jenkins covered her sad face with her hands and told Camille to go back upstairs. She knew that a lot of times when Camille said something she was just being honest and wasn't trying to be smart. She felt she had a very direct and sensitive child on her hands. Camille didn't intentionally say things to hurt people's feelings. She just spoke her mind. Like one

15

time she told her aunt Cathy that her breath smelled bad. Her aunt Cathy had bought Camille an Easy-Bake Oven. When they were taking the little cakes out the oven, Aunt Cathy said, smiling in Camille's face, "See, I told you it really works." Camille had scrunch up her face and said, "Aunt Cathy, yo' breath stinks, eat some of that cake," she said, pointing at it. Aunt Cathy was taken aback by the serious look on Camille's face.

Anyway, Camille wanted to stay downstairs with her mama. "Mama, I want to stay down here with you."

"Go on now." She gently pushed Camille away.

"But I want to stay down here with you," Camille said, puckering up her lips.

"I need to think, Camille. Go on now. I don't have time for this." Ms. Jenkins' hands started to shake, and it frightened Camille. Camille grabbed at her shaking hands, but was rejected.

"I'm not going to say anything. I'm going to be quiet."

"Camille, if I tell you to go one more time." Ms. Jenkins looked defenseless as she held back her tears. Camille slowly turned around and walked away. Her tears fell down to the floor. Camille didn't go far; she patted her feet on the bottom step to make it sound like she went upstairs and sat quietly on the same step she sat on before.

"Hello, I want to report a missing child."

"Ooooh!" Camille whispered, covering her mouth with one hand. "Mama's calling the police."

"Well, she's usually home by now. It's after ten, and she's not here…I don't know where she could have gone…Twenty-four hours!

Camille's Dilemma

What do you mean twenty-four hours! I haven't seen her since four o'clock this afternoon, and it's after ten o'clock!" Ms. Jenkins slammed the telephone receiver down. Camille jumped up and ran up the stairs. Her mama had frightened her.

Chester was sitting in front of the television sucking his thumb when Camille burst into the room. It didn't faze him one bit that his sister was missing. He was mad because he was on punishment. The thought of not being able to go outside tomorrow disgusted that boy. Whatever he was looking at on TV was not as important to Camille as her big sister being missing. She paced the room, wondering where Cynthia could be. Sometimes she would walk right in front of the TV while Chester was looking at it. He'd look up at her and shake his head.

Camille wanted Cynthia home so her mama wouldn't be sad. She went into the closet and wrote "Come Home Cynthia" on the wall ten times with her big, black crayon. The closet was where Camille went to escape. In there was a little, brown bench she could sit down on. Camille would close her eyes, slipping inside of natural darkness. There, she would let the warm shadows embrace her. It felt different from the darkness outside. This darkness was a place where evil had no being, where it couldn't sleep. A place Camille's heart could pulsate in peace. Sometimes she took her Close-N-Play in there with her. That was a record player you can carry around with you. She would sit on her bench and dance away. Or, she would talk to her spirit friend, Louise, in there.

17

Her siblings could never conjure up enough nerve to stand in it, let alone find peace of mind in the dark closet. If they had something to put into that closet, they would open the door and throw it in there real fast. They had been spooked by their friends and would never be alone in the dark. Their friends told them a story about a lady named Mary. They say that if you stand in a dark room and say "Mary" five times, you would come out all bloody with scratches on your face. I guess they thought the same to be true of the closet. Camille felt she had angels watching over her all the time, so she wasn't afraid. If Mary wanted to join her and her angels, it was okay with Camille. There was plenty of room in there for a myth.

And let me tell you, Camille spent a lot of time in that closet. She would run for that closet every time her mama's man friend came over to visit. One day Camille looked him straight in the eyes and twitched her nose at him the same way Tabitha did on the TV show *Bewitched*. Then she ran in her closet and wrote over and over on the wall, "DON'T SHOW ME THAT NO MORE." She asked her angels if they could make him go away. He did. I believe it was the way Camille looked at him that really made him leave her alone. Louise could probably tell you better than I can.

That's right, I can. I don' come a part of Camille. We talk; she tells me just about everything. When it would get too dark to see, Camille ran to me. I guess she feel like she knocking on heaven's door when she comes here.

Camille's Dilemma

I remember the first time she ran in her closet. They were living in them projects. She must have been 'bout seven years old. She ran in her bedroom closet hiding from her mama's friend. She knew he was gon' want to pick her up and rub on her and make her do nasty things to him. One day while she was in her closet, she started letting all her hate for him out. She shouted, "I hate you! Why don't you leave my mama alone and go away, you black mustafucker. When I grow up I'm gon' look for you, and I gon' hurt you, hurt you, hurt you! Nasty man." Then she peeked out her closet to see where he might be. She heard him ask her mama where all the kids at when he already knew where they at. The two oldest kids were in school. He was trying to find out where Camille was. I don't remember whether or not that youngest boy was born yet. If he was, he was probably down at the babysitter's house. Anyway, Camille continue to rumble off to me 'bout that man and how she wished he would leave. Then the mama called out to Camille 'cause she wanted her to do something for her. She called Camille 'bout three times before Camille came out the closet and went to see what she wanted. "There my sweet little girl is," said the mama's friend. Camille run right on pass him and to her mama to see what she wanted. She wanted Camille to take the toys laying around to they bedroom, so her house don't look junky in front of her company. Reckon she didn't want him falling over none of them toys. By the time Camille finished putting all the toys away, the mama had fallen asleep. That's when the mama's friend would mess with Camille. After her mama fall asleep. He picked Camille up and held her tight to him. Moving her all around on him, just about squeezing that poor child to death. He put his hand over her mouth so she couldn't make any noise. When he put her down, he held on to her little wrist real tight, pointed his big finger in her face, looked real mean at her, and said, "Don't you tell your mama." Then he gave her a dollar. Camille ran upstairs with it. First, she jumped in her bed. Then she jumped out of it. Then she hid under her bed. Then she came from under the bed with that dollar balled up in her hand, and she ran in the closet. Went way in the back of it and sat down on a little bench that was in there. She cried and she cried. She tore that dollar up in little pieces. She felt around for the corner in her closet and pushed the little pieces in it. While she pushed the little pieces of dollar in the corner, she also felt a little hole in the corner wall. She chipped and chipped at that hole in the wall with her finger till it was big enough for her to put her little fist through. Then she put the pieces of dollars into it. This went on for a while. Camille was now getting tired of him messing with her, 'cause he started doing more than just squeezing her to him. He just flat out started molesting the child. And that made the dollar turned into two dollars. They went in the same hole in the closet the one dollar went in. I guess that's when it got to be too much for Camille. She was ready to hurt her mama's friend so he couldn't hurt her no more.

A lot of times, Camille's mama's friend would fall asleep smoking on one of his cigarettes. Camille told him one day when he was almost sleep, "You gon' burn yourself up while you sleep one day. Look, Mama, he dropped his cigarette, and it's still burning."

Camille's Dilemma

One day he was asleep in the chair. Sho' nuff he done fell asleep with one of his cigarettes, again, right after the mama had fallen asleep up in her bedroom, and he had messed with Camille. Camille was gon' set him on fire. She got herself a rag. Tore up one of Chester's T-shirts. Now, her mama warned her 'bout playing in the yard while the leaves was burning. 'Cause she almost burned herself up once before playing with them leaves. She went out there with her rage and held the T-shirt over the burning leaves 'til it caught on fire. Soon as that rag was burning good, Camille tiptoed back to the house to set him on fire. But the rag was burning too fast. It burned so fast that it caught the sleeve of her little white cotton blouse on fire. Camille dropped the rag. She was too busy stomping on the rag that fell to the ground to realize her sleeve was still burning. When she did, she patted and patted and patted till she put the burning sleeve out. Then she ran to the bathroom. She took her white cotton blouse off, and her arm had burned real bad. It was what they call a third-degree burn 'cause it was white and pink. Camille started blowing on it 'cause it burned so bad. But when she blew it, it made it hurt more. She wanted to cry loud, but she cried soft to herself. She knew she was not to play in them leaves. She couldn't tell her mama she was gon' set that man on fire, and that's how she burned her arm. So she took another one of Chester's T-shirts and wrapped her arm up in it. She went to her closet, sat on her bench, and cried. Then she started talking. This time when she talked, she heard somebody talk back to her. It was me. I'm the one she talks to in her closet. I help keep little ole Camille sane. That's why I pop in and out her story.

D.C. Johnson

I told Camille she gon' be able to see some things too and wasn't nothing she could do 'bout it. It's funny how you can know something gon' happen to other people and don't know when something gon' happen to yourself. Let me tell you this before we get back to telling you Camille's story. It might be important. I used to have a closet. It's been a long time since I ran in that closet. I only go in it now 'cause Camille goes in it. When I was a little girl, I got messed with, too. Sho' did. I must have been 'round eleven, twelve years old. It was my master that messed with me. Master Clayton. Ain't gon' never forget his name. Master Clayton thought I was too pretty of a nigger girl to be working in them fields with the other black folks, some of which was my kin. So, I worked in the master's house. Made sure his house stay neat and clean. Sometimes I set the dinner table for his family to eat.

At nights, the master come in my room. I told you I was a special nigger child, so he made sure I had my own room. Anyway, he come in my room and do his thing. Leaving me with stain sheet and tears. He hurt me so bad one time after doing his thing that after he left, I went inside my closet. I'd sit in there on the cold floor and cry, just like Camille used to do. Then one day I came out that closet with my plan. I say the next time he hurt me, I was gon' hurt him. And he did. After he hurt me, he demanded I bring him a cold glass of water to his room. I went and got my master his cold glass of water. I tapped on his door. When I went in I said, "Here's your water, Master Clayton." He took himself a sip and asked me why I was still standing there. I say I got something else for you. He watched me reach in my apron

22

Camille's Dilemma

pocket. I pulled out one of his guns and shot him, and I shot him, and I shot him. Shot him till wasn't no more bullets in that gun. All the white folks came running to the master's room. I drop the gun, turn around, and run to my closet. The master's son ran in my closet and shot me. Sho' did. Shot me dead, in my closet. I died, just wasn't put to rest. I said I was eighty-five 'cause I'm not sure, probably a whole lot older. I know there gon' come a time when I'm gon' be put to rest. That's all I'm gon' say 'bout that 'cause if I keep going, the book gon' be too big to read. Now, back to Camille's story. I'll talk to you later, bye.

Still, nobody knew where Cynthia was and Camille, pursuing her mama around the house, was getting in the way of her thinking. Ms. Jenkins wanted to be left alone. Camille didn't want her to be left alone because it made her feel totally unwanted. She already felt like she got the least amount of attention from her mama. Now, with Cynthia being missing, maybe her mama would notice her and want to show her some affection. Divided by her mama's bedroom door, Camille sat quietly listening to her mama prattle about her second born being missing. Camille got up and went downstairs. She looked into an empty closet. Maybe she was expecting Cynthia to be in there. She then pulled a kitchen chair up to the back door and looked out of the door window. It was as still outside as it was in their house. Camille went back upstairs to her mama's room.

"I'm scared, Mama," Camille said, climbing into her mama's bed and snuggling up next to her. She couldn't snuggle long because her mama rose up crying and yearning for Cynthia. Camille stood up and endured the pain with her, nestling her head into her mama's back. She wanted to give her as much comfort as she possibly could before her mama remembered she was there.

Here it was, way past curfew, and Cynthia was nowhere to be found. She was lost. She was milk-carton missing. All because she wanted some candy. Cynthia had been sitting on a stoop in the playground waiting for Vanessa to come out and play, when a man drove up and called out her name. Cynthia walked over to the car and asked him who he was. He told her that he knew her mama. Told her what her mama's name was. Even told her he knew her sister and brothers. Told her what they names was, too. He got out with a smile and walked around to the passenger side of the car. He then handed Cynthia a bar of candy. Smiling, she reached for it, and when she did, he grabbed her, covering her mouth so she couldn't scream. He pushed Cynthia into his car, which didn't have any door handles in the inside, and drove away.

He drove her to his house where he had about ten other girls locked inside a room. All the girls in there was about the same age as Cynthia, twelve. The windows in the room were boarded and painted a tar black. Cynthia couldn't believe her eyes. She watched, frightened, as some of the girls slowly roamed the room. None of the girls smiled or talked to one another. Some sat around in their own worlds, coloring in books, reading, or looking at television. One, the only white one, was writing over and over on the wall with a tiny pencil, "Let me out." Cynthia shouted out, "Who are you?" The girls all looked at Cynthia then quickly looked away like they were afraid to talk to one another. Cynthia knew how she got there, so she figured they probably got there the same way she did. Cynthia began to cry, thinking of a way out. She looked at the black painted window again and cried harder.

Every day the girls would be forced to bathe and eat together. The man went so far as to knock the wall down between the bathroom and the room he kept them in to keep them together. When it was time for them to clean his house, they all cleaned in the same room before going to clean the others, with him trailing, watching and smiling sardonically at them.

After about an hour, Cynthia got one of the girls to talk to her. The girl talked about how the man treated them, believing they were his kids. Even made them call him Daddy. Said he went so far as to give each one of them a new name. She said her real name was Evelyn, but he called her Ebony. Said she's been there for twenty days. Said she know it's been twenty days because every day she wakes up, she draw one line on the wall so she would know how long she's been there. Cynthia went by the name of Serenity.

Ms. Jenkins continued to sob over her missing daughter.

"Mama, she gon' come home. Watch, soon she'll be here."

"But she's not here. Where can she be? Lord, where is she," Ms. Jenkins cried out, driving her head into her pillow.

"I'm your baby, Ma. You got me. Mama, I'm here. Chester and Clifford are here, too, even though Clifford is over to the babysitter's house. You still got us, Mama."

"I know, but I want Cynthia to come home, that's all…Lord, please bring her home."

"Mama, stop crying for Cynthia. She gon' come home. Chester said she'll be here, too."

Ms. Jenkins looked at Camille and cried some more.

"Please, Mama, don't cry for Cynthia."

"Oh, somebody please bring her home. Please bring my baby home. God, find her for me. I want my baby home."

"You stop crying for Cynthia, you hear me, Mama!" Camille demanded, standing in front of her mama's bed with her hands on her little hips. "I'm here. I'm your baby, too. You still got me, Clifford, and Chester. Stop crying for her! We're here. You have us left. Ain't that why you had all of us—in case something happened to one, you'd have the others?"

"Baby, you don't understand; she's gone."

Camille pounded her fists into her mama's bed. "No, Mama, you don't understand that she's going to come back! I know she gon' come back! You think the white people got her, Mama? Y'all say the white people don't like us. I bet Cynthia went and played in their white park," she said, folding her arms across her chest. "They probably just holding her for a while, punishing her for playing over there. They not gon' keep her because they don't like black people,

Camille's Dilemma

right, Mama? They don't want no black girl; she'll be back just like Chester and me said."

Camille slid down to the side of her mama's bed and sat with her head in her lap. She was exhausted. She resisted shedding any more tears. Suddenly, she yelled and hammered her fists on the bed because her mama started to cry again. She thought she had calmed her down.

"You still got me, Chester, and Clifford. Look at me, Mama! You stop crying for Cynthia, stop crying for her!" Camille started crying nonstop.

"I can't…I want my baby to come home."

Camille got mad at her mama. She felt if Cynthia didn't come home, her mama didn't want her or the rest of her children. She went back to her closet. She no longer cared that Cynthia was missing. All she wanted was for her mama to stop crying. She wanted her mama to say she was glad Chester, Clifford, and she was still there, but she wouldn't. She got down on her knees and prayed that Cynthia would come home so her mama would want the rest of them again.

Somewhere between praying and crying, Camille fell asleep, only to be awakened minutes later by the ring of the telephone. She ran out of her closet and into her mama's bedroom. Ms. Jenkins quickly raised up from her bed and hurried over to the rings coming from atop her dresser. She knocked her small, white lamp to the floor reaching for the phone. It was one of Ms. Jenkins' friends checking to see if Cynthia had made it home. Camille wished the phone had never rung. Ms. Jenkins was crying all over again. She sobbed into the telephone for five minutes before she hung it up.

27

D.C. Johnson

Every time Camille wiped the tears from her mama's eyes, she cried more. Camille didn't have any strength left in her little body to battle with her mama. She went to bed.

For the next five days, Camille and her mama cried and paced the floor, Camille still trying to fill the void Cynthia left behind, still irate that she wasn't being shown any attention. Chester did what he did best: sucked his thumb and watched TV.

It was now the morning of the sixth day that Cynthia was missing. The Jenkinses were all sitting at the kitchen table. Chester sat gulping down a glass of milk. Camille was reading the cereal box ingredients, with one foot up in the chair. Clifford was being the baby he was, whining because he wanted to go over to the babysitter's house. Ms. Jenkins stood up to pour herself another cup of coffee when there was a light tap on the door. Chester ran to the door to see who it was. He thought that anytime someone knocked on the door, the knock was for him.

"You better ask who it is before you open that door," Ms. Jenkins said, stirring a teaspoon of sugar into her coffee.

"Who is it?" asked Chester, too short to look out of the diamond-shaped window on the door. "Who?" he said again. He stood on his tiptoes, trying to get a glimpse of the unknown.

"Mama, whoever it is won't answer." Ms. Jenkins sat her coffee cup down on the kitchen table and went to the door.

She looked out of the window, and a second later, she shouted, "Oh my God! Cynthia." She energetically snatched open the door.

28

Camille's Dilemma

Cynthia stood still, staring down at the floor. She wouldn't look at anybody. It was as if she was ashamed of having been missing. Ms. Jenkins was ecstatic, thrilled to see her baby. She dropped down to her knees and hugged the child that she cried and yearned for one day short of a week. Chester sat back down at the breakfast table and drank the rest of his milk. Then he looked hard at Cynthia and said heartlessly, "It's about time you came home. I had to stay in the house all week because of you. I told y'all she was going to come back." He rose up wearing a milk mustache and marched out of the kitchen.

Camille walked over with a smile to welcome her sister back home. She patted Cynthia on the top of her little, black Afro, the only part of her body her mama didn't have embraced.

For the next couple of days, everywhere Cynthia went in that house she went with her head down. And just like the policeman said, Cynthia would come around to talking. She did. But she only told her mama what had happened to her. The news was so ugly that Ms. Jenkins didn't want to share it with the rest of her children. She told them to never go with strangers, grilling them as she told them. She grilled them so much, when they knew she was going to say it again, they said it for her, "Never go with strangers," bobbing their heads up and down as they said it.

Ms. Jenkins would whisper into the telephone to tell her friends what happened to Cynthia. Camille would sit on the step to listen; she didn't hear much, just bits and pieces about how the man lured Cynthia into his car by offering her some candy and telling her he knew her mama. Said they got away because the man forgot to lock

29

the door to the room he kept them in, and when he went to check for his mail, they all went running out behind him.

From here on out, Camille would protect her big sister. She wouldn't let her out of her sight. Would follow her all around the house. She mostly followed Cynthia because she knew her mama was going to hug Cynthia just about every time she saw her. So it was Camille's way of getting in on the embrace. Where Cynthia went, Camille went. Where Cynthia played, Camille played. Camille would guard the bathroom door when Cynthia had to use the bathroom. Would walk to and from the store with her. Camille was her bodyguard, her convoy, and her savior. At least that's what she thought she was. She was a nuisance, a pest, and annoying. She was on Cynthia's last nerve.

Then one day, Cynthia turned around and yelled at Camille, saying, "Will you stop following me everywhere I go…shoo. I'm getting tired of you following me all around. I don't need a shadow; got my own, girl."

"Forget you then," Camille said, twisting her fingers up at Cynthia. Camille freed her sister.

Chapter 3
Moving On

Things really started changing for the worse in these here projects. It was no longer a nice place to live. People didn't feel safe no more. And it wasn't just because that Jenkins kid came up missing; it was just turning out to be a terrible place to live. The color red could now be found on the streets. There would be trails of blood in places you least expect, like right in front of your house. The last time a family fell asleep without locking their doors, they got the surprise of their life. An unknown man walked into this lady's house while she was sleeping. He hit her in the head and walked out of there with her only television. Sho' did. Not long after that, a man was robbed as he walked across the bridge, in broad daylight. Then the robbers went so far as to reach down a lady's bra to steal her money. Maybe it was her fault he stole it that way. When he first snatched her purse, she laughed at him as he was running away with it. She then shouted,

"You ain't got nothing, you thief! I keep my money down my buzzim." He turned around, ran back, knocked the lady to the ground, reached down her buzzim, and took her money.

I reckon the worst was when Camille witnessed a man stab his girlfriend in the stomach. The lady came running out of her house in her bathrobe nearly tripping over her own guts, yelling for help! Camille ran home hysterical. Ran right to her closet. She knew that man saw her see him, and she thought he might come looking for her. She didn't go back outside for three days.

It wasn't just these projects taking on a change. Them Jenkins kids were starting to mature. Peach fuzz started to sprout from underneath Chester's chin; Cynthia and Camille looked as if they were hiding Brussels sprouts underneath their blouses. Clifford was getting too big for a babysitter, and the mama was getting sick and tired of living in a two-bedroom apartment with four children. So, the mama applied to the government for a low-income home. She got one too, a brand new one at that. The Jenkins kids was happy as slapsticks, telling all they friends about the new house and how many rooms it was gon' have.

When the mama got a ride, she and her kids would go and watch they new house being built. They were all excited because it was something they could call their own.

One day, on a trip to their new home, Camille smiled out, "Mama, now we really free." Cynthia would walk up and down the new block in wonderment. Chester was mad because he learned he had to get on a bus to go to high school. In the projects, the high school was in

32

walking distance. Plus, he didn't want to leave the few friends he just made there. I don't think Clifford, that youngest boy that stayed down to the babysitter's all the time, I don't think he knew he wouldn't see them anymore. He sure clowned about a week after they moved into their new house. See, Clifford was used to getting his way; all he got now was his butt whipped by Chester, Cynthia, and Camille. They were responsible for babysitting him now. Told him he was spoiled and wouldn't give him his way.

The new home had four bedrooms, a living room, a dining room, a kitchen, a basement, and one and a half baths. Sure was a lot more space than what they were leaving behind. Camille wanted to know what a half bath was. Said the essential, like a toilet and a sink, were in both. Then she wanted to know why the new neighborhood kids tease them and call their house a Cracker Jack box. Camille would say, "If it's a Cracker Jack box, then we must be the prize." It didn't matter to them what people called it; it was the Jenkins' house.

Soon as the mama opened the door to their new home, they met a welcome mat that Camille ran right over, rushing to claim her spread in the basement. The fourth bedroom and half bath were down there. She knew it was there because the house they built next door was its fraternal twin. Built just two months before theirs. The builders let them go in and take a look at what they house was going to look like. The only difference was someone had broke into that one and stole all the fixings.

It didn't take long for Camille to make friends because of the witty personality she possessed. She was as amazing as they come.

No telling what was going to come out of that child's mouth. She showed off the first day of school, only minutes after being introduced to the class.

The teacher left the classroom and just about every child in that room started clowning around. They began beating out tunes on their desks. Camille decided to join them and started pounding on her desk. She was off into in her own world jamming to the beat of James Brown's song "Get on the Good Foot." Camille closed her eyes and was beating up a storm. "Uh boom boom, Uh boom boom, Uh boom boom, babada boom, bop, boom bop." Snapping her head back and forth in the middle of a bop, she opened her eyes to see her teacher and two other teachers standing in the doorway looking baffled at her.

"Camille! What on earth! You come here, young lady!" Her teacher said, wagging her index finger at Camille, "Do you have a problem, young lady?" Camille stood in front of her teacher, Mrs. Wilson, with her hands entwined behind her back and her head down in shame. Mrs. Wilson grabbed Camille and pulled her out into the hall. She asked with her arms crossed, "What on earth would possess you to carry on like that? Are you out of your mind?" Camille looked up at her teacher, begging for forgiveness with her eyes. "Talk to me, young lady. Why were you pounding on that desk like that?" Then Camille looked back into the classroom, and everyone appeared quiet. "Look at me when I'm talking to you! I must admit you had a good beat going, but we don't pound on desks here at Cooper school."

"Where do you pound on desks?" Camille said in a low tone.

"What did you just say?" Mrs. Wilson asked, looking confused at what she knew she heard. "I know you didn't say what I think you said," she said, bending down to Camille's level.

"Nothing. I guess I sort of lost my mind...but I'll find it... Sometimes I talk in my sleep," Camille said, smiling up at her. Mrs. Wilson called out to the Lord.

"Lord, what do I have here? You've lost your mind all right." She shook her finger in Camille's face and said, "I will not tolerate any acting up in my class. If this happens again, I will have a talk with your mother. Do you understand me, Camille Jenkins?"

"Yes, Mrs. Wilson." Camille stood there staring at the run in Mrs. Wilson's off-black pantyhose until she told her to return to the classroom.

All was well, at least for the next two weeks. Camille was possessed again, only this time it was the Staple Singers taking her there. Mrs. Wilson bawled Camille out right in front of the class, and if she was looking for her to be ashamed this time, she had another thing coming. You see, Camille had learned a lot about her teacher in the last two weeks. Found out that Mrs. Wilson lived on the same block she did and that her teacher's mother lived two blocks over on May Street.

"Well, it looks like I'm going to have to walk across the street and tell your mother on you, Camille."

"And I'll walk on May Street and tell your mother on you," she said, catching Mrs. Wilson by surprise. That whole class busted up laughing at Camille being smart. Camille had an audience, and it made her feel good.

"Will you never." Mrs. Wilson snatched Camille up out of her seat, pushing her out into the hall. Camille stood in the hall with her arms folded across her chest staring up at her teacher, unaffected by the tone in her voice. Camille was suspended three days for insubordination.

In September, Camille would be going on to Theodore High School. Chester and Cynthia thought they'd warn Camille about all the bad things that was happening there. Said the teachers and students at the school were real prejudiced. It sounded more like Alcatraz than a high school, the way Camille was warned. Said the kids at that school would riot for foolish reasons. Said they wanted their study halls to be eliminated and wanted to be able to smoke cigarettes in their classrooms. Mind you, this was the white kids that wanted these things. They also wanted beer coming out of the water fountains. They would start fires in the garbage cans, thinking it would get they silly points across. At any given moment, them white kids would start rioting. They'd be running through the school tearing up things, throwing chairs, sticking bubble gum everywhere. Go in the washrooms and wet balls of tissue, throwing it up to the ceiling for it to stay up there.

Chester told Camille to never take the seven-three street bus to school; said she was better off taking the seven-eight bus because she wouldn't have to run so far to school when she got off the bus.

Camille's Dilemma

You had to be a fool to walk down what they believed was they streets. White folks would chase the black folks yelling, "You niggers! Get your asses out of here! Go back to Africa, you black motherfuckers! We don't want yous coming down our block tearing up our school! Get the hell out of here!" Throwing anything they could get their evil little hands on.

"I'm not running from nobody when I get to high school. I'm going to walk down them white streets or whatever color they are when I get there, proud as I can be. Ain't nobody going to make me run to school, forget them white people." Camille forgot she made that comment. The first time she stepped foot off that bus and saw all them white folks eagerly waiting, you know what, she too ran nonstop to school. She ran so fast most of the time the white folks didn't even bother to chase her. They knew they couldn't catch her; that was the real reason. The white people, young and old, would be in they yards laughing at Camille saying, "Look at that nigger run! Run, nigger, run!" Others would say, "Now, that's a fast nigger running there. I ain't seen no nigger run like that since that boy got his foot cut off... what's his name, Kunta Kinta. Ha! Ha! Ha! Must be some kin to him, huh."

It was much worse for them black kids coming home from school. The police would have to escort them to the bus stop. Not that they wanted to; they had to. Them kids knew the police wasn't on they side because their chalky faces spoke for themselves. It said, "Why don't yous take your asses somewhere else. You see you're not wanted here." Camille sometimes felt the police wanted to take their clubs out and hit them in the head with it, to help them on their way.

Anyway, having escorts didn't stop the white people from attacking and chasing blacks to a more colorful side of town. They'd be hiding a few blocks ahead under the viaduct like them kids were trophies. As the bus came near the viaduct, everyone on that bus would hit the floor, seeking whatever cover they could. Some of the kids would be on the floor even before the bus took off, seeking cover, using each other as shields. The white students and some grown ones, too, threw bricks, bottles, and rocks at the bus. Whatever their violent-stricken hands could lift went crashing through the bus windows. Though most of the injuries were minor, their attempts to paralyze them scared children were enormous. White conduct made headlines and breaking news. Sho' is a shame. It made Camille go home and write a poem.

Us

I foresee a time when we
Will rise from the pit to eternity
Without struggle, we will prosper
Every second, minute, hour thereafter
Left behind are those who juggle
The missing piece to life's big puzzle

Camille Jenkins

Chapter 4
Ooh! Mr.

Camille was now a sophomore at Theodore High. She didn't worry so much about the white people acting foolish any more 'cause they were coming to their senses. Reckon they finally realized that black was more than a color. What really happened is some of them black kids started hitting back, and they would hit a lot harder than the white kids would.

So, instead of worrying about the white folks at her school, Camille worried about where she could get her hands on some extra cash. The mama seldom had money to give her and her siblings. When she did give them money, she gave them each a dollar for the whole week, outside of giving them exact bus fare to go to school. They would walk the two and a half miles just so they could each keep the forty cents they would have paid on the bus.

Camille wasn't selfish; she knew raising four children as a single parent was a burden to her mama. She also knew there wasn't much a teenager could do with a dollar. That's when Camille decided to take care of herself. Become independent. She was no longer going to do without money. No longer was she going to be a burden to her mama. She was sick and tired of always having to wear hand-me-downs. "Hand me down some money, Mama," she would say.

One day Camille sat on her front step and absorbed everything that was happening on the block. She watched as her next-door neighbor, Mrs. Patterson, pulled weeds from between the new flowers she planted. They grew to be some of earth's finest flowers—roses, red and yellow. Then she cast her sight on the ball of heat beaming from the sky, nearly blinding herself looking at it. She wondered just how big the sun was 'cause it looked small in the sky, but everywhere she went, the sun was there, too. Then she watched as one of Cynthia's friends came strutting up the street. Her stomach was as big and round as the sun in the sky. Camille wondered why the girl wanted to have a baby before she grew up. She shook her head at the girl as she strolled by.

"Out here by yourself today, baby?" Mrs. Patterson asked Camille, pulling herself up off of bent knees.

"Yeah…by myself."

"Baby, ain't you got no friends? Why every time I see your pretty little self, you sitting alone? That there sister of yours got all the friends, huh? Maybe she'll let you have one or two." Camille just smiled at the aging woman as she walked uneasily up her steps holding on to the weak banister.

Then she watched Mr. and her baby brother, Clifford, as they sat on his porch and bonded, wondering what they over there talking 'bout today. Camille wanted to be where her brother was. She envied the bond Mr. and her brother Clifford had built. She felt cheated. Clifford had two daddies: a real one he got to see any time he like and a play one that he was talking to now. She didn't have one. Well, she got one—we all got one—but you know what I mean. Now you see 'em, now you don't. Camille's never seen hers. If he walked by her right now, she wouldn't know that was her daddy. Can't tell you no more 'cause that's her mama's business. Wouldn't be right. Be a shame.

Mr. seemed to be a good person. May act a little strange now and then, but who don't? We all got a screw loose. I'm just afraid of the ones who screw done been stripped and don't fit no more. Folks called him Mr. 'cause he never told anybody what his real name was. "Just call me Mr.," he'd say. Mr. was a short, stocky, peanut butter-color man. Had one of them handlebar mustaches. Walked with a hunch in his back, but he got around pretty good, puffing on that old, funky cigar. He had to be in his late sixties if not seventy already. He was near bald and the little hair he did have was water gray. Always squinting his eyes whether the sun was shining or not. Kept a firm look on his face. That's what sort of made me leery 'bout him. He never smiled, just looked full of knowledge like he was thinking all the time. I wondered what he always be thinking 'bout. He lived a couple doors away from Camille and her family. The only family I think Mr. had was his son and daughter-in-law. They were the only two people that visited him. They would bring food for him when they came by, which wasn't often, maybe once a month.

Now, Mr. spent most of his time sitting on his porch with Clifford. Camille thought it would be a good idea to work for Mr., do his grocery shopping. So she asked him if she could shop for him when he needed things from the grocery store. He told her, "Yes." Camille was happy. Her mama was happier than she was. She didn't have to worry 'bout giving Camille no extra change.

Camille had been going to the neighborhood store for Mr. about two months now. Her reward of one to three dollars a trip was appreciated. It kept a smile on her face. Another month and Camille was hanging with the Joneses. She was living large. In those couple of months, she had saved nearly thirty dollars. She knew most of the times when Mr. sent her to the store, he did it just so he could pay her for going. He knew their family didn't have much 'cause Clifford asked him one time if he could buy him a pair of gym shoes to replace the ones he had worn out. He did.

Mr. asked Camille to come inside his house, said his list wasn't ready yet, and he had something he wanted her to give to Clifford. She knew that she had never been inside of his house before and wasn't sure if she should go in. Thought about what her mama said about never going with strangers. But she figured since she was older and it was okay for Clifford to go in, it be okay for her, too. So she

Camille's Dilemma

went in. (I done got tired; reckon I'll sit and let Camille tell this part of the story. Talk to you later.)

I stood quietly by the front door as Mr. disappeared into what I would call Never Land. Only my meaning of Never Land meant "I'll never land feet in here again." It was junky, and I do mean junky. Newspapers, clothes, bottles, cups, and a pair of bifocals occupied his dining room table. I don't know what it was, but something was balled up and thrown in the corner of his living room. His kitchen light was dangling from the ceiling along with the paint. It surprised me that nothing was crawling around. "Did he forget to clean up?" I thought to myself. It ought to be against the law for someone's house to look as bad as this. This is a job within itself. A blind man could tell by a quick sniff the couch was in desperate need of cleaning. If you sat down on it, you would probably end up in Oz clicking your feet saying, "There's no place like home; there's no place like home."

Mr. reappeared looking firm and quite knowledgeable as usual as he carried a brown paper bag. "Here," he said, handing the bag to me. "This is for Clifford." The bag felt mighty light. Inquisitive, I looked down inside the bag at what appeared to be three cereal boxes—three empty cereal boxes. This man sure got his nerve thinking somebody wants his leftovers. The nerve of him, it's not that bad for us. "Mama does buy full boxes of cereal," I thought to myself. As if my eyes weren't big enough, they got bigger. I looked up at Mr. wondering what in the world was wrong with him, giving me three empty boxes of cereal. Then Mr. searched his pocket and handed me a twenty-dollar bill and a note listing the things he wanted from the store. I

43

stashed the note and money into my front pants' pocket and went to the store.

When I returned from the store, Mr. was sitting on his porch looking a bit disturbed. He looked sadder than I've ever seen him. I handed him the grocery bag. He nodded for me to set it on the step he was sitting on. Then I handed him the five dollars and some change he had coming back. He waved at me to keep it. "Are you okay, Mr.?" I asked.

"Oh, Mr. ain't been feeling well lately," he said with his head down, puffing on his cigar. "But don't you worry about Mr.; Mr. gon' be just fine. Come back at the end of the week. I guess I'll be out of milk by then. Go on now." He shooed me away with his hand, and I said okay.

I didn't feel thrilled this time after being financially rewarded, even though I got to keep all his change, so I didn't go back to his house at the end of the week. Truth is, Mr. had scared me.

I started spending time over a friend's house I met in the seventh grade. Her name was Etta. She was a good friend. Etta tickled me the way she talked. She'd buck her eyes and drag her bottom lip when she talked. She talked like she always meant business. Like, don't mess with me; I'll kick your butt.

During the times when there was nothing to eat at home, Etta looked out for me; she made sure I ate. She always made grilled cheese sandwiches. I was shocked the first time I saw her bring that big, old log of cheese out of their refrigerator. I thought only the people in the projects got cheese in big rolls like that.

"Y'all po'?" I asked her, looking around the kitchen.

"Naw, we ain't po'," she said, using all her might to cut a slice of cheese.

"Well, how did y'all get that government cheese? They don't sell cheese like that in the store. You have to go down to the government office with a green card and pick it up. Y'all is po'; it's nothing to be ashamed of 'cause we po', too."

Etta bucked her eyes at me. "I'm not gon' tell you no more; we ain't po'. Everybody that eats this goddamn cheese ain't po'. It doesn't matter where the fuck it comes from." She rolled her neck around and said, "Now, you want a sandwich or not?" I never said anything else to Etta about them being poor.

"Where do you be getting all that money from? You be stealing that money from your mama, don't you?" she asked glancing over at me.

"I don't steal. I work. I got a job, honey child." I rolled my eyes as she flipped over the grilled cheese sandwiches I couldn't wait to devour.

"You ain't even old enough to have no job. People with jobs pay taxes. You paying taxes?"

"Taxes. Naw, I ain't paying taxes."

"Then you ain't got no goddamn job. Like I said, you probably be stealing that money from your mama, taking it out her pocketbook, don't you? Don't you?" she said, grilling me like that sandwich.

"I told you I don't have to steal. I work for my money. You the one probably stealing, or you wouldn't be accusing me of doing it. And why do you cuss so much?"

"Don't worry about what the hell I say. I cuss when I get good and goddamn ready to. So why you don't tell where you work, Camille? 'Cause you know you be stealing that money. And while you thinking of an answer, hand me some more butter out of the fridge," she said, pointing the spatula at me.

"Okay, I'll tell you where I work, but you better not tell nobody because they might try to take my job."

"Girl, don't nobody want your so-call job," she said, swinging her head around in a circle.

"You know that store on Lunden Street."

"Yeah."

"You know Mr. that lives on my block."

"Who?"

"Mr."

"Mr. who?"

"That's his name. People call him Mr. because they don't know his name."

"You talking about that man that always be sitting on his porch looking lost?" she asked, flipping over another sandwich.

"He's not lost. He's just lonely. He sends me to the store to do his grocery shopping, and he pays me for going."

Camille's Dilemma

"Girl, that ain't no goddamn job," she said, turning the fire off under the pan. "That's why your ass ain't paying no taxes. You just be doing him a favor because he's old."

"Well, I get paid to do it. It's a job to me. Where is your job?"

"My mama gives me money. I don't need to go to the store for people. Here," she said, handing me a grilled cheese sandwich wrapped in a paper towel, which took all of a second to soil.

"But I'm not going to the store for him no more because he scared me."

"Who scared you?"

"Mr. did."

Etta clicked off the kitchen light. "How did he scare you, Camille?" She headed to her bedroom with me following.

"Etta girl, he gave me some empty cereal boxes. He was looking crazy when he gave them to me, too."

"One," she said, turning around, pointing her finger in my face. "I just told you the man is lost. Two, he ain't got no goddamn name. Three, you need to be staying away from his ass. People don't look lost unless they are." Etta looked me up and down. "I know you don't want people to be reading about you. Girl, people crazy," she said.

After a couple of weeks, things started to become a bore. Etta never had any money, so all we did was sit in the playground, listen to music, and eat grilled cheese sandwiches. I once hinted to Etta that she could make some money selling her grilled cheese sandwiches. Everybody wanted a bite of ours when they saw us eating them. I was used to having money. It was driving me up a wall to be broke, and I sure wasn't going into my savings. I commenced to go back to the store for Mr. again. He asked me where I'd been the last couple of weeks. I told him I was busy helping my mother.

I quickly grew comfortable with going back to the store for Mr. Turns out those empty cereal boxes he gave me to give Clifford had game puzzles on the back of them. Silly me.

Outside of the usual twenty dollars and the list of things he wanted, Mr. handed me a fifty-dollar bill.

"Why are you giving me so much money for going to the store?" I asked him. He looked at me in that disturbed state he had the last time I saw him and said, "Because you are a good kid...you and your brother. I...I appreciate you two." Mr. would sometimes stutter when he talked. I didn't feel comfortable taking it, but stashed it into my pocket.

Mr. would normally be sitting on his porch when I got back from the store. This time he wasn't. I knocked on the screen door, and there was no answer. I knocked again, this time a little harder. There still was no answer. I decided to go on in and knock on the other door when I noticed a gap in the curtains. I peeked in and didn't see him. I was about to knock again when Mr. walked into his dining room butt ass naked. His personals were freely dangling and hanging to what seemed like his knees. I hadn't seen that much brown in all my life. Didn't he know he could be seen through the gap in his curtains? "Ooh! Mr.," I exclaimed. "Where are your clothes and why are you walking around butt naked?" I stood speechless as my bottom lip hung, gazing at Mr.'s ass. I had to be in shock 'cause I nearly dropped

Camille's Dilemma

the bag that I was carrying. I sure didn't want Mr. to know I just saw him in his birthday suit and that he just scared me for the second time. I sat the grocery bag down quietly by the door. I dropped his change into the bag, hit his door real hard with my fist, and flew home.

I banged on the door until someone answered. Cynthia opened the door using her most valuable word (GIRL). "Girl! What's wrong with you?" I didn't answer Cynthia. I ran and sat on the couch. I grabbed one of the pillows, smothering it to my chest. "Girl, I asked what's wrong with you, come rushing in here like that. You look like you just saw a ghost." I couldn't speak. Mr.'s ass was caught in my throat. I was afraid, afraid because I had seen his nakedness. I got up and pulled down the shade to the front room window. Cynthia stood back and stared buck-eyed at me. "Camille, girl, are you gon' tell me what's wrong with you? Why you pull the shade down? It's daytime, girl." I sat back down on the couch, this time smothering my face into the pillow. I wondered if Mr. did that on purpose. I asked myself a series of questions. Why wasn't he sitting on his porch like he always was when I got back from the store? Why didn't he answer the door after my first knock? Is Mr. bad just like mama's friend is? Was he going to make me touch him like the others? I hate men. Then I looked at Cynthia and still was lost for words. So I just stared at her. "You sit there and act crazy if you want to, Camille. I'm telling Mama." I went back to thinking. Did he leave that gap in the curtains on purpose? I didn't remember seeing it the first time I went in. I wanted to go away, and I did. In my mind, I ran all the way back to the projects to my closet. It was like running through hot coal. My intuition said all would not be well.

I did everything my conscience said I should do; I stayed away from Mr. If I went out to play, I would wait for it to turn dark before I came home, thinking by it being dark, Mr. couldn't see me coming down the street. I would leave out the back door and come in through the front. I would look from the corner of the block to see if Mr. was on his porch. If he were, I would wait until somebody else was going down the block and walk by their side. Mr. and my house were only two houses apart. I knew once I passed his house that I was home free. Mr. had to know I saw him butt naked; why else would he think I'm avoiding him? I would talk to God and my angels just before I'd take off running. I would ask them to carry me like water.

One day, against my instincts, I decided to stop running. For two days, everything was all right. On the third day, as I walked home, I heard Mr. call out to me.

"Camille!"

Startled by the robust sound of his voice, I stopped. Mr. was standing on his porch leaning over his side banister.

"Come here! What's the matter with you, Camille? Why you don't come here? I need you to go to the sto' for me. Mr. ain't got much to eat. Why you won't go to the sto' for me no mo'?"

Who did he think he was fooling, standing up there staggering like a Barcardi drunk? Something was wrong with Mr., especially if he thought I was going to see what he wanted.

50

Camille's Dilemma

"You hear what I said, gal, come here!" He waved his hand at me, and his voice suddenly went up five octaves. "I said come here!"

"What do you want, Mr.?" I said, all but screaming as I walked backwards toward home, trying to keep my eyes on him. He frowns mean at me then goes into his house. I turned and ran to my house, rang the doorbell nonstop until somebody answered.

"Girl! What you keep ringing the bell like that for? You scared me. I'm gon' tell Mama, ringing that bell like that. You play too much, Camille. You did the same thing the other week. I didn't tell then, but this time I am."

"I'm not playing, Cynthia. It's Mr. Something's wrong with him. It's something wrong with him."

"What? It's something wrong with who?"

"Mr."

"Mr.! Girl, what are you up to now? You're always getting yourself in trouble. What did you go and do? What are you talking about…Mr. That man don't mess with nobody."

Mr. was now on our porch, ringing the bell like a mad man. Cynthia headed to the door. I started shuffling my feet telling her not to open it.

"Move, girl, get off me! Who is it?" she asked, shoving me away. She then went to look out of the window.

"It's Mr. Is your mama home? I need to talk to her."

Cynthia went for the door again, and I darted in front of her.

51

"Don't open the door, Cynthia! Something's wrong with him. Don't let him in here." I held on to Cynthia's arm so she couldn't open the door.

"I told you to get off me! Girl, there's nothing wrong with him. You're losing your mind. Just wait till Mama get here."

"Cynthia, don't." I hit Cynthia hard in her arm with my fist.

"Open this door! Where is Camille? I need to talk to her," Mr. bellowed.

Cynthia eyes bucked after hearing the way Mr. asked for me.

"Who did you say was at the door?" Cynthia said, rubbing the spot on her arm where I hit her.

"Open this door!" Mr. shouted.

"Well, let me see if she's here," Cynthia said, looking scared. She then tried to put the chain on the door. But before she could get it on good, with one solid push, Mr. had forced his way into our house. Cynthia and I went flying up the stairs in threes with Cynthia leading. She ran into Mama's bedroom, slammed and locked the door. I ran into the bathroom, slammed and locked the door. From the sound of it, Cynthia had pushed Mama's dresser in front of the door. I looked around, and there was nothing in the bathroom I could use as a barricade. So I stood back by the toilet, shaking from head to toe, waiting to see what was going to happen. Mr. knew which room he wanted to get into because the next thing I know, he was banging on the bathroom door.

"Open this door! Come out. I want to talk to you!"

"What, Mr.! What!"

Camille's Dilemma

"You come out right now!" Something struck the door real hard.

"No, Mr.!"

"You come out of there right now! Right now, you hear me!" And there it went again, another strike at the door. The point of something shiny and silver pierced through the door. Then it disappeared.

"Bam!" It went again.

"What's wrong, Mr.! Why are you after me? I didn't do anything. What did I do?" He wouldn't answer.

"Bam!" It struck the door again. I knew exactly what it was, an axe making its way through. Mr. was trying to chop down the door. The next bam sent me into an uphill battle. I slammed the toilet seat down and hopped on top of it as quick as I slid the bathroom window open. With overwhelming terror, I bolted like lighting out of the bathroom window, landing on top of the roof of the house next door. I dashed nonstop from roof to roof until I was halted in my tracks by the grace of God. Had I jumped one more time, I would have gone out of the world backwards. A vacant lot was next. I stood there staring down at the dirt-paved ground, shaking like a leaf. I looked up to the sky for a split second and started dashing back from roof to roof. I felt like I was being chased. The next thing I knew, I was laying down on top of the roof of the house next door to mine, stricken with involuntary movement from the chest down. To keep from breathing aloud, I sealed my lips. Then I glanced down into our bathroom window. Mr. was still in the house. He was standing in the bathroom looking deranged in the mirror. The left side of his face was sweating. His chest was rising up and down like he had just run a race. He had

53

one hand resting on the mirror and was strongly griping his axe with the other. Definitely afflicted with madness. I had never seen anyone look so mad. What was wrong with him? Why was he trying to hurt me? Mr. turned to face the window. I put my head down and shut my eyes to disappear, drifting slowly back to a well-known place. I smiled at the face that greeted me. I opened my eyes and looked up to God's playground. It looked so peaceful up there. I wanted to be up there. I wanted to die.

The sound of police sirens was evidence that help was on the way. My body was still paralyzed; all I could do was look and listen. I tried to speak out to the red and blue lights going 'round and 'round, but all my lips did was pantomime the word *help*. I was unable to move from the roof and didn't know why. I watched as the two policemen examined the piercing of the bathroom door, shaking their heads in disbelief. Mama was somewhere in the windy city of Chicago. She had no idea that one of her children was on top of a roof being forced into hibernation.

After the policemen left and everything was calm, my ability to react to emotions returned. But I was still scared. The block I lived on was now deserted. Where was everybody? Where was Mr.? Where was Cynthia? I tried to get the attention of the people who lived in the house I was on the roof of. I used the reflection off our window and reached into the gutter, shoveling up a handful of mud filled with tiny branches. I slung it into their kitchen window, but to no avail. I knew, sooner or later, I would have to climb down. My heart began to race as I looked down at the fence that separated our house from theirs. If I

Camille's Dilemma

jumped, I was bound to fall on the fence. It was a chance I had to take. I scooted to the edge of the roof, scraping up my legs and knees. I slowly swung my body over the edge of the house. I seesawed a few seconds, trying to get my balance. The next thing I knew, I was hanging from their gutters. My hands started to tremble, so I let go. I did just what I knew I was going to do. I fell on the fence. I wasn't hurt too bad; only one of the wires stuck me in the knee. I jumped up and ran away, feeling no pain. I knew where I was running to because I spent enough time on the roof to figure out where I wanted to go. I ran to my friend Judy's house because she lived the farthest from all my friends. I also ran there because I didn't plan on being found. When I got to Judy's house, I went around to the back and tapped on her window.

"It's me, Judy, Camille, open the window."

"What!" I put my forefinger over my mouth, telling Judy to be quiet.

"Open the window," I signed to her.

"Come to the front door," she signed back.

"Please," my lips said, and she opened the window.

"What's wrong with you, Camille?" I climbed through Judy's window, landing on her unmade bed.

"This man is after me."

"WHAT?"

"Shhhhh!" I said and sat down on her bed to catch my breath.

"What man, Camille? I know you playing."

"No, I'm not. This man name Mr. was chasing me."

55

D.C. Johnson

"Yeah, right. Camille, quit playing."

"I'm not playing, Judy. He lives on my block. He was chasing me with an axe." A tear fell from my eye.

"Wait, Mr. Are you talking about that man you go to the store for?"

"Yeah, he was chasing me. How do you know him, Judy?"

"Who else? Etta. She was laughing one day, talking about you work for him. Camille, are you playing? What is that man going to chase you for?"

"I don't know. Something's wrong with him. I told Etta something was wrong with him."

She reared back. "Well, if you knew something was wrong with him, why you go to his house, Camille?"

"Judy, that's a long story. I just need you to help me right now." She went and got me a glass of water, and I told her everything that had happened.

"Do your mama know?"

"Nope."

"Well, don't you think you should call and tell her? Let her know where you are and that you're okay. If he did what you said he did, that man is crazy. Walking around the house with his thing hanging out, ugh."

Judy grabbed a brush from off her dresser and started brushing her pony-tailed hair.

"Camille, what are you going to do? You need to call your mama, your sister, somebody, and let them know where you are."

Camille's Dilemma

"I am. Where's the phone?" I was still frightened. I had no idea why Mr. had come after me the way he did.

"Wait. Let me make sure my mama and father's door is shut. Okay, come on." Judy's family had three phones. One was in the kitchen on the wall. Another was in her mother and father's room, and the third one was sitting in their hallway on a chipped nightstand, the one we were sneaking to.

We rushed into the bathroom with it. I flip the lid down on their toilet, sat, and started to call my mother. As soon as I heard the first ring, I hung the phone up. I saw visions of Mr. chasing me up the stairs. I didn't know who might answer the phone. For all I knew, he had come back.

"Camille, why you hang the phone up? I know nobody answered it that quick. Girl, you better call your mama before I do."

"Okay, okay. I got scared, Judy. I'm scared."

"Girl! Where are you?" Cynthia snapped into the phone. "The police and everybody is looking all over for you."

"I can't tell you," I said and a flow of tears ran from my eyes. "What's wrong with Mr.? Where is he? Why was he trying to kill me?"

"I don't know where he is. Don't nobody know where he is. He's probably hiding somewhere. The police had taken me with them. What did you do, Camille, to make him chase you like that? Girl, the police and everybody are looking for him. You should have seen all the police that came. The block was loaded with police cars."

"Where is Mama?" I asked, wiping at my tears.

57

D.C. Johnson

"She just came home. Now she's gone next door. Lea came over and said she heard somebody on they roof. She said it sounded like they were running. She was the only one home, and it scared her, so she ran in they basement. I told Lea that it probably was you because you ran into the bathroom. Camille, how you jump up on they roof? Girl, that's at least two feet up in the air. There's no way you could have jumped up on they roof from our bathroom. How did you get up there? Hold on, Camille, let me go get Mama."

"No, Cynthia, because I'm not coming home till they catch Mr."

"Girl, you…" I hung the phone up.

Judy put it back on the stand, and we tiptoed back to her bedroom. If she had any more doubts, they quickly disappeared after the phone call. I had also lifted up my pants' legs, and Judy frowned at the marks and dried bloodlines on my legs. She pointed and said, "That one needs some stitches. Damn, Camille, he was trying to kill your butt for real."

58

Camille's Dilemma

For the next three days, I sought refuge at Judy's house, praying each and every night that they would catch Mr. or, worse, that he would die. We would watch the ten o'clock news to see if I was going to be on as a missing person. I was not.

On the fourth day, Judy talked me into calling home again. She didn't know how much longer it would be before somebody found out I was hiding at her house. This time Mama answered the phone.

"Hello, hello."

"It's me, Mama."

"Where are you? Are you all right?"

"I'm all right...I'm just scared. Mama, I didn't do anything. He chased Cynthia and me upstairs. I don't want to come back home."

"I know, but it's okay now. They found Mr."

"They did! Who? Where? Where did they find him?"

"Come on home, Camille."

"Where is he? I'm still scared."

"He's...he's dead. He's dead, Camille."

"Dead! What happened? Did they kill him? Did the police kill him, Mama?" I asked, startled by the news.

"Come on home. We'll talk about it then."

I didn't want to go home. I felt more afraid now that he was dead. I couldn't believe he was dead. How did he die? Who killed him? Maybe Mama was just saying that so I would come home. The police must have killed him.

59

Judy insisted that I go home, or she was going to tell I was there. I agreed to go home only if she walked me to the corner of my block. She said, as we stood at the corner of my block, "When I count to three we gon' run, okay?"

"Okay."

"One, two, three." Off we went running in separate directions. While I was running, it seemed everything outside was running with me. I stumbled on a crack that landed me right in front of Mr.'s house. I fell on memory lane. I looked up at Mr.'s porch and could have sworn I saw him standing up there.

It sure wasn't déjà vu when I walked into the house. At least for Mama it wasn't. Mama just stood there with her hands on her hips, looking calmly at me. She asked if I was all right. I almost got mad. I was looking for her to run and embrace me the way she embraced Cynthia when she came home from being missing. Chester smiled a little bit. Then he turned around and went about his business.

Mr. had come back to our house the morning after he went berserk. He told Mama that he was upset because he thought I had stolen three hundred dollars from him. Said he ended up finding it behind his dresser. He apologized to Mama and told her to tell me he was sorry for coming after me the way he did. Soon as he turned his back to leave, Mr. had a heart attack and died on our living room floor.

There was something else missing in the Jenkins' house, and it wasn't Cynthia or Camille. They were a family knitted with thin

Camille's Dilemma

thread. They come together and play them games and stuff, was always together on the holidays. They lack affection. It's important that every family share that, you know. A hug has never hurt anybody. Plus, it's free. What people afraid of, I'll never know. If you standing or sitting by some member of your family, do yourself a favor, put Camille's book down for one second and give that family member a hug. All it's gon' take is a second. So what if they look at you like you crazy; they'll figure it out. It starts from inside the family in case you didn't know.

After what Mr. done, Camille was afraid to leave the house. Now all she did was play cards with Chester at they dining room table.

Even though Chester acted uncaring and like a grouch most of the time, Camille knew he had a soft heart hidden away. She didn't think it was by choice either. She also knew he preferred playing with her more than with his other siblings. You could tell there was a special bond between them. Well, at least I could.

Chester had a secret that only Camille knew. He didn't tell her his secret either; Camille sensed it from him. A secret people would shame. Camille sometimes would throw out hints to Chester that she knew his secret while they were playing cards. What she wanted to tell Chester was that she had the same secret he had. She didn't 'cause she felt he'd get mad at her and wouldn't play cards anymore. Them two would sit at that dining room table for hours playing cards.

After Chester got tired of playing cards, he would leave the house. Camille would become depressed and lock herself into her room. She would put a chair up against the door as a barricade so nobody could sneak up on her. Then she'd play her music. If she had one gift she could open up at any time, it would be the gift to sing 'cause she couldn't. But she sang anyway. Her next-door neighbors would come to her bedroom window and change the words to the song she'd be singing. That song called "Don't Ask My Neighbors," they would say "Don't hurt your neighbors, you gonna need some friends to hang around." And that popular Mother's Day song, "I'll Always Love My Mama," they would sing, "I'll always love my ear drums; I need them in this world. I'll always love my ear drums, why don't you shut up, girl." Camille with scrunched up eyes would peek out of her bedroom window and watch them mock her.

Chapter 5

Ralph

Camille, deciding to come out of her shell, started going skating with Etta on Saturdays. A lady named Mary would rent a charter bus that would take them to a skating rink in Markham, Illinois. Camille couldn't skate that well, but she did okay. She would spend most of her time watching Mary's eight-year-old son, Michael, zoom around the skating rink. She thought he was so talented on his skates. When he wasn't skating so fast, he would look at Camille when he came around the rink to where she was. Camille would wink and smile at him. He would shyly smile back, sometimes winking a cute wink back at her. Every Saturday for the next six months Camille went skating. Mary, Michael, and her had become real close. So close that Camille nearly lived with them. She was over there practically every day. (Well, I done got tired of talking. I'm gon' let Camille talk a little. She's been itching to put her two cents in. Louise gon' take a nap. See ya.)

Mary knew I got a kick out of being her babysitter and a part of her family. It benefited the both of us. I was a big help to her when she needed a babysitter, and she was a big help to me on payday.

Michael was eight and caramel brown with chestnut-colored eyes. His eyebrows were soft and silky looking. He had the cutest little dimples you ever saw. People young and old couldn't seem to talk to him without the "goo goo, gaa gaa" approach. They would pinch his face like it was a cream puff. His mama, Mary, was also caramel brown, but her eyes were of the hazel color. She was not tall but tall enough. A full-figured woman with long, fine hair. I loved Mary the first time I saw her, though I was confused about the love I had for her. I loved her like a mother, and I loved her another way, too.

I had just come back from grocery shopping with my real mother. I had about ten minutes to get over to Mary's house. I kept my skates over there because I spent most of my time there. They were in Michael's closet. Even though I stayed there most of the time, I didn't have a key to Mary's house. Mary was standing out by the bus, collecting money from the people who were going skating that week. Michael was already on the bus; I could see his head sticking out of the window.

"You made it. Where are your skates, Camille?" Mary asked me.

"They're in the house. Can I have the keys so I can get them?" Mary searched her pockets for the keys.

Camille's Dilemma

"Ralph's got them. He may be on the back porch. Hurry up, Camille! Mr. Lewis can't hold the bus; he's got some more kids to pick up. You got about ten minutes." I darted across the street to the house to see if Ralph was on the back porch. He was, smoking a cigarette.

"Ralph, can you let me in the house? The bus is getting ready to leave, and I don't have my skates."

"Mary don't have her keys?"

"No. She said to ask you."

"Well, what about Michael?" he said, swinging one leg as he sat slumped on the stairs.

"He's already on the bus. Can you just let me in so I can get my skates? I don't want to miss the bus," I said, afraid that I would miss it if he didn't hurry.

Ralph was about five-six and a lot on the chunky side. People referred to him as black because he was very dark—deep chocolate dark with straight white teeth and about twenty tiny pimples on his forehead; he was also slow-footed.

For a long time I thought he was just a friend of Mary's. That was until I heard those noises coming from her bedroom nearly every night. Whatever they were doing in there was good to the both of them. All you heard was "Oh Ralph! "Ooh, Mary!" "Oh, Ralph! "Ooh, Mary!" "Ralph!" "Mary!" and the sounds of a howling fiesta followed. I couldn't wait for Donald, who was Michael's cousin and the same age as me, to come over so we could laugh at the noises they made.

65

"Well, you just have to climb through Michael's window, 'cause I don't have my keys either."

"You don't have your keys either! Well, how am I going to get my skates?"

"I said you gon' have to climb through Michael's window, didn't I? That's the only way you gon' get in. I don't know where Mary's keys are."

I was scared even though the window was only about four feet from the ground.

"Are you going to climb through the window or just stand there? You know the bus will be leaving in a minute. Here, step into my hands, and I'll boost you up to the window."

"Ralph, why don't you climb through the window? You're taller than me," I suggested, uncomfortable with the idea.

"Now, how is your little ass gon' boost me up? If you want to go skating, you best climb your little ass on in this window." I took a deep breath, tucked my fear into my twenty-five-inch waist, rubbed my hands together, and started to climb through the window. After landing two feet onto the cold, bare, hardwood floor, I gleefully got up and jetted to the closet to retrieve my skates. I grabbed them by the strings that were tied together then closed the closet door with my foot. It sounded as if another door shut at the same time I shut mine, so I paused a second to listen. I didn't hear anything, so I ran out of Michael's bedroom into the front room, heading for the door, when I saw Ralph standing in front of it. He had his arms folded across his chest. He almost looked like Smokey the Bear, only he didn't have a

66

Camille's Dilemma

hat on. I stopped. I just missed running into him, startled to see him standing there.

"How did you get in here, Ralph? You said you didn't have a key."

"Well, I lied."

"Why did you tell me a story? Move so I can go."

Every time I tried to walk around Ralph to open the door, he would move into my way.

"Move, Ralph, you know the bus will leave if I'm not on time." He didn't say a word, just stood there with a smirk on his face and his arms folded across his chest.

"Why are you trying to make me miss the bus, Ralph? Mary and Michael are already on the bus." Ralph didn't go skating much with us because people laughed at the way he skated. He sort of dragged one leg when he skated, the slow one. I pushed at him, and he still wouldn't move away from the door. I looked out of the front window, and all I could see was the tail end of the bus. There were gray and black clouds of smoke coming from the back of it. At any minute, it would be taking off, and I would be left behind if Ralph didn't move away from the door.

"Move, Ralph! The bus is going to leave me. I want to go skating." I bellowed, disturbed that he wouldn't move out of my way, and I didn't know why. I pushed at him again then dashed back to the window to see if the bus was still there.

He said, looking coolly at me, "Looks like you gon' miss the bus."

67

"I don't want to miss going skating, Ralph. Why are you stopping me from going skating?" I said as tears attempted to blind my sight. Again I tried to push the one hundred seventy pounds of darkness out of my way, but he wouldn't budge. I thought about going out through Michael's window. I ran into his bedroom, but Ralph ran past me and slammed the window shut. I ran back into the front room, but he put his feet against the door, stopping me from opening it. Then he pushed me with his belly, forcing me backwards. I bumped into the arm of the couch.

"What are you doing, Ralph? Stop! I want to go skating. You're trying to make me miss the bus on purpose!"

"You're not going skating."

"What do you mean I'm not going skating! I'm going if you move out my way." I heard the bus pulling off and ran to the window.

"See, you made me miss the bus…what did I do that I can't go skating this week?" I slammed my skates down to the floor, just barely missing Mary's cocktail table. After I realized how close I came to breaking the glass top on Mary's table, I picked my skates up and went to put them back in the closet. Ralph started to follow me. I turned around and shouted at him.

"Why are you following me? You made me miss the bus. I'm going home."

"You thought you were going skating, didn't you?" He was smiling alien at me.

"Why did you make me miss the bus, Ralph? You know I like going skating. You did that on purpose." I threw my skates back into

68

Camille's Dilemma

the closet. I walked toward him to leave. He stood in the doorway of Michael's room and pushed at my shoulder with his hand. He wouldn't let me out of Michael's bedroom.

"Why do you keep pushing on me, Ralph? You already made me miss the bus," I said loudly, hoping Grandma Mamie would hear me. She spent most of her time upstairs looking out of her front room window. Michael's room was in the back of the house, downstairs. I knew she wouldn't be able to hear me, but I shouted anyway as I talked to him.

"You know, you pretty," he said, smiling at me.

"What! I'm not pretty—I'm mad. I wanted to go skating with Mary and Michael." I put my head down and looked around for a way out. I tried to run around him and out of the room when he gave me a real hard push backwards. He pushed me again and again until he backed me on top of Michael's bed.

"You stop pushing me, motherfucker!" I shocked myself saying that. I almost wanted to cover my mouth for disrespecting my elder. It sounded so weird coming from me. It obviously sounded funny to him too because he smiled when I said it. His smile scared me. My heart started to accelerate.

"Why are you doing this? Why are you being mean to me? What did I do?" I started to cry. I put my head in my lap to shield the pain I now knew was coming. He pushed my shoulders back and fell on top of me, grabbing both of my hands and placing them above my head.

"What are you doing, Ralph? Stop! Stop, Ralph! I'm going to tell Mary."

69

"I'll kick your ass you tell Mary…you hear me."

All I wanted to do was hurt Ralph the way he was hurting me. I began swinging my hands and kicking my feet at him.

"You little bitch," he said, jumping up. "You bit my goddamn fingers! I should slap the shit out of you!" He flung his hand down at me as if he was going to do just that.

"Get up and put your clothes on," he instructed, pointing at my pants. He picked them up and threw them at me, and then began packing away his stuff. He shook the bitten hand then looked as though he wasn't sure if he was finished with me. I was scared to move.

"Hurry up and put your damn clothes on." He looked out of Michael's window as he zipped up his pants. "Hurry up, goddamn it!" he yelled at me again. I felt something run down my lip and wiped it away. It was Ralph's blood. I was shaking so much I had a hard time putting my pants back on. Ralph then started to apologize over and over to me.

"I'm sorry, Camille. I don't know what happened. I didn't mean to hurt you. Did I hurt you? You gon' tell Mary? You better not tell her! I'll get you," he said all in one breath.

With my eyes fixated on the floor, I shook my head. "No." I couldn't look at the devil.

"Don't you tell nobody," he barked under his breath, shaking the bitten hand as I ran to the door. "I'll get you, Camille. You hear me. I'll get you if you tell."

70

Camille's Dilemma

I now knew what Kunta Kinta felt like wanting to be free, wanting to run away. I tried to run, but it hurt too much. I walked five blocks home in pain.

Fortunately, when I got home, no one was there. I grabbed clean clothes from my dresser drawer and went into the bathroom, taking a pair of scissors with me. I cut up all the clothes I was wearing and put them in a bag. I threw the bag in the garbage then went to take a shower. As I put the hot towel to my face, I stood there reflecting on what had just happened. I concluded that I should not tell anyone and never go over to Mary's house again.

Then the thought that I might be pregnant crossed my mind. They say the first time you do it you can get pregnant. But I didn't willingly do it. So I prayed to God not to make me pregnant. I said if I was going to be pregnant, I was going to kill the devil's baby.

I didn't tell anybody in my family what had happened to me when they came home. I felt ashamed. Chester said, "It's about time you came back to your real house. What they do, kick you out?" I figured that Chester couldn't help it. It wasn't his fault he was born without compassion. He probably missed me, just didn't know how to tell me. Then he gave me a look, as if he knew everything wasn't well. Like he wanted to reach out to me but decided against it. I wanted to tell him what Ralph did. But altercations did not suit Chester. I thought about the time some big boy was bothering me, and I went to get Chester to make the boy stop. Chester went strutting out of the house like the big, bad wolf. When he got to the playground and saw how big that boy was, he turned around and marched back home. That was

71

okay because the boy thought Chester was going home to get a gun. That's what somebody shouted out, and the boy took off running.

A few days later, Mary called. She knew it wasn't like me to stay away for more than a day or two at a time. I told her I went to visit my grandmother. I was defending the criminal. That's what Ralph wanted me to do when he told me not to tell. I told Mary that I would be back over in a couple of days. I guess distress was in my voice because she asked me, "You sure everything's okay?"

"Yeah, I'm fine," I said, trying to sound unconstrained.

My heart invariably ached from wanting to be with her and Michael. As far as I was concerned, Ralph could fall off the face of the earth. Even better, he could get run over by the earth itself. How dare he invade my privacy! I had the right to my privacy, not Ralph. I sat around thinking of ways to make him disappear. I could hit him in the head while he's asleep, knocking him into a coma. Or, I could torture him to death by cutting his testicles in half. Then pull each one of his pubic hairs out, one by one, replacing them with needles.

Two days later, Mary called again.

"Camille, we miss you, sugar. Are you sure everything's okay? You don't sound well. Talk to me, Camille. What's wrong?"

"Everything's fine. Mama said I should start spending more time at home with them. Chester has been complaining he's bored. Says he don't have nobody to play cards with because I'm gone all the time. Mama said I just about worn my welcome out over there."

Camille's Dilemma

"Now, she know I don't mind you being here. Is she there? Put her on the phone."

"Mama went to bingo," I blurted out.

"You sure you okay? You said that pretty fast, Camille."

"Umm-hmm, I was just about to go to the store...we're out of milk."

"You know, Michael's over here having fits about you not being here. You know he looks up to you, Camille. He thinks you're mad at him. You know Michael can be stubborn. I'll tell him you said a couple of more days. We miss you, Camille."

"I'm going to come back."

"Well, I guess a mother would miss her baby if she was gone all the time. Tell your mama to call me when she gets in. Hope to see you soon. We love you, Camille."

"I love you, too."

I hung up the phone, inhaled and exhaled to calm my nerves then burst into tears. It hurt because my real mama never said that to me. That was the first time Mary said she loved me. And I've only been a part of their family six months. It was a fact that she and Michael missed me. I walked back into my bedroom, closing the door behind me. I played Michael Jackson's "Ben" over and over again, singing it to the top of my lungs. "If you ever look behind and don't like what you find, there's something you should know, you've got a place to—" Bam! Bam! Bam!

"Turn that music down!"

73

D.C. Johnson

I opened the door, and Mama was standing there with her hands on her hips.

"Why are you playing that music as loud as it can go? Have you gone and lost your mind?" She stared at me, I guess waiting for an answer.

"I didn't know it was that loud," I said with a bit of attitude. She walked over to my stereo and turned it down to where I could barely hear it. She turned and walked away.

I put on my earphones. Music seemed to make everything okay for the time being. Whatever music I was listening to, I was able to put myself into the shoes and soul of the singer. They say that most singers sing about the things going on in their life. Right now I felt like I had lost my best friend, my two best friends. Just as Michael Jackson had lost Ben, I felt I had lost Mary and Michael.

Two weeks had passed, and I wholeheartedly missed Mary and Michael. I yearned for their company. Mary would grab and hug me like one of her own, just like Etta's mother would do. Only, Mary's hug felt more genuine. How warm-hearted that would feel. I wanted to be with Mary and Michael all the time, whether it was going to the Laundromat, the grocery store, or following them from room to room. I just liked being in their company. They liked having me around. I admired Michael's security. He never got jealous of me borrowing attention from Mary. He knew there was more than enough love to go around and that he was number one in that book. He also had a little crush on me, so that helped.

Camille's Dilemma

Growing tired of being alone, I decided to take a stand. Here I was a sophomore in high school, and I was acting and being treated like I didn't know any better. It was time for me to take control of my life.

It was pouring down rain. I put on my red windbreaker and walked the few blocks to Mary's house. Michael was glad to see me. He was real glad that I had not been mad at him. He told me to never go away and stay that long again. I didn't spend any more nights there. I would nap next to Michael's bed after he had fallen asleep. When I woke up, Michael would be cuddled underneath me, snoring away. Michael had no idea that he was my security blanket. But sometimes I would sense that Michael knew something was wrong and that Ralph had played a role in it.

After I saw how much Michael and Mary really cared about me, there was no way was I going to let Ralph rip us apart. I just stayed my distance from him. I would come over every day after school for a few hours. If Ralph dared to sit at the dinner table with us, I would take my plate and eat in Michael's room. He never sat at the table to eat with us before, wasn't any sense in him doing it now. He surely wasn't a part of the family I considered mine. I couldn't bear his presence. When Ralph did come too close to me, it was hard for me to keep my poise. I would shake a bit. He sensed the fear he had insolently thrust upon me and would move away from me. As much as I tried to hide it, it was obvious something was wrong with me, because when Mary left the house, I was one step behind her. One day, I almost took off her shoes walking so close behind her. I was her shadow. Michael said to me one time while I was tucking him into

75

bed, "You know you love my mama. Do you love your real mama like you love my mama?" I smiled down at him and gave him a big hug. Then he said, "You know you love me, too."

Ralph stopped coming around as much, which was fine with me. He would tell Mary he didn't feel good. I hoped I was making him sick. He had no right to infringe on my privacy. I would see him standing across the street staring at me whenever I went in or out of the house. Sometimes he would be looking mean, sometimes repentant.

Michael was in his room playing one night after dinner. I was cleaning up from our Kentucky Fried Chicken. I walked over to the kitchen sink to make dishwater. I never liked washing dishes at my own house but was content with washing them here. As I swished my finger around in the dishwater, at ease with my thoughts, Mary asked with reverence, "Camille, has Ralph ever tried to bother you?"

I shut and reopened my eyes, swallowing a big gulp of air as I tried to take in what she had just asked me.

"Camille, I'm talking to you. Did you hear what I said?"

"Yes," I said, staring down at the bubbles.

"Did he? Did he ever try to bother you?"

I tried to sound undisturbed. "Bother me?"

"Has he ever tried to force you to do something you didn't want to do?"

Before I could fib and say no, tears welled up in my eyes, blurring my vision. I stood looking down into the kitchen sink at what looked like one big bubble. I picked up a plate and started washing it in slow motion, looking at my shallow reflection through it. Mary came over and put a caring hand on my shoulder. I nearly collapsed right there.

"Did Ralph rape you? Did he? It's okay, Camille."

I dropped the plate back into the dishwater, turned around and hugged Mary as tight as I could. I wanted to stay tucked away in her space forever.

"Damn you, Ralph," she grumbled. I looked at the tears Ralph put in Mary's eyes. I hated Ralph more.

"Tell me what happened, Camille. I want to know everything he did to you," she said, keeping my head tilted up with her forefinger. With shaken nerves and an abundance of tears, I told her everything Ralph did. We cried together. Mary couldn't believe that Ralph, the man she cared about, the man she loved, would stoop so low as to rape her little girl.

"It's going to be okay, Camille. It'll be okay."

"Does Michael know?" I asked her.

"I don't think so. Let's just keep this between me, you, and Ralph." I hated to hear her say Ralph's monstrous name. "He won't get away with this! Why? I don't understand," she mumbled, shaking her head in disbelief.

"How did you know?" I asked her.

"Things just haven't felt the same around here. Especially after you stopped coming around. And it wasn't like you to miss going skating."

I wanted to disappear. I was scared. Ralph had said he was going to get me if I told, and I told. I had nowhere to go. I didn't want to go back home. Chester stayed away all the time. Cynthia didn't like me hanging out with her and all of her friends. Aunt Cathy only came over on Saturdays. Mama worked, and played bingo every other night. Etta and Judy willingly got to the fast point and started doing it with guys. I wasn't ready for that. I stayed away from them so I wouldn't become fast.

Mary had a plan. She called Ralph on the phone and asked him to come over. She made believe they were going to go to the movies. Ralph was hen-pecked when it came to Mary; he was at her every beck and call. I said to her, "Mary, I'm scared. Ralph said if I told, he was going to get me."

"Don't you worry about Ralph. I'll take care of Ralph. He had no right to do what he did. When he knocks on the door, I want you to go wait in the closet while we talk."

"Okay."

We sat in the living room waiting for Ralph's knock. It came. Mary hugged me with an unhappy smile, which was my cue to get into the closet. She opened the door and just like the inside of that closet, darkness entered. I closed my eyes and instantly felt the presence of Louise. I imagined she was an angel standing behind me with her wings in full bloom. I then heard Ralph say, "Hey, baby, what do you want to go see tonight? You know there's a new flick— I"

"Ralph, sit down; we need to talk."

"Sure. About what, baby?" It sounded like he had kissed her. I heard a kissy smack sound, and my nose curled up. It stayed quiet for about a minute. I pictured Mary standing by the living room window, looking out with her arms crossed, trying to figure out how she wanted to broach the subject.

"Ralph, have you noticed anything different about Camille?"

"Camille? Naw...baby, something wrong with her?" I pictured Ralph sitting back with his hands clasped behind his head and the slow foot stretched out.

"You tell me."

"Tell you. Tell you what?"

"Ralph, don't play dumb with me."

"What are you talking about, Mary...You're talking in circles," he chuckled.

"I think you know what I'm talking about. Did you do something to Camille? That's what I'm asking you, Ralph."

"Do something to Camille, like what?"

"Ralph, don't play dumb with me!"

"Mary, what are you talking about? Did I do something to Camille? I don't know what you're talking about."

"You know damn well what I'm talking about. I want the truth. I'm going to ask you again. Did you do something? I'll rephrase that. What did you do to Camille?"

"I didn't do nothing to her. What? Did she say I did something to her?"

"I'm the one asking the questions. You tell me, Ralph. Something went on, and I want to know what. There's something wrong with her; she's not the same. Why is it she never wants to be alone or

79

around you? You think I haven't noticed how she gets up from the dinner table if you attempt to sit your ass down? You think I haven't noticed she doesn't sleep unless Michael's right there by her side? Ralph, she shakes any time you come near her! She's scared out of her wits of you, Ralph."

"I don't know what you're talking about. I don't know what's wrong with her."

"Michael's even asked, 'Mama, what's wrong with Camille? She acts strange.' He asked me, Ralph, if you did something to her. They were asleep the other night, and you know what Michael said? He said, 'Mama, Camille be talking in her sleep. I heard her say, "Stop, Ralph!"' 'She's never talked in her sleep before."

"Mary, I...I didn't do nothing to her."

"You're lying, Ralph, and you know it! What happened? I want to hear your side of the story."

"Wait, my side of the story! I don't have a side of the story to tell! I know damn well that she didn't tell you I tried to do something to her. If she did, she's a damn liar!" How badly I wanted to come out of that closet and spit on him. "She wanted me to, but I didn't."

"Ralph, cut the crap! What do you mean she wanted you to?"

"She said she wasn't going skating 'cause some boy wanted her to have sex with him. Is that what you're talking 'bout?"

"Finish."

"There's nothing to finish...Oh, she said something about she didn't have her keys and asked me to let her in the house. I told her that I didn't have mine either and that she would have to climb through the window to get in. She said you and Michael were already on the bus."

"And!"

"And what? I don't remember every goddamn thing that was said, Mary. She did ask me if I would show her how to do it 'cause she'd never done it before. I told her she was too young. I told you they be listening by the door."

"I know you don't expect me to believe that. That's bullshit, Ralph!" Mary was mad. I've never heard her cuss the way she was cussing.

"Believe what you want to believe. I didn't touch the girl."

"Well, she told me you raped her."

"Raped her! Please. What I want with her? She's only what, fourteen, fifteen."

"Did you rape her, Ralph?"

"Look, I'm not gon' sit here and get blamed for something I said I didn't do. Where is she? We can get this straight right now."

"You're right! Come on out, Camille!"

Ralph's eyes got big as half-dollars when he saw me come out of the closet. He looked at me, then at Mary, back at me, then back at Mary. I walked over, slowly got behind Mary, and shouted.

"You raped me, Ralph. You know you did! I'm not afraid of you anymore!" I wasn't afraid of him as long as Mary was by my side.

"Girl, you better quit lying on me. You can tell she's lying, look at the faces she's making."

"You said if I told Mary, you were going to get me, and I couldn't come back over here."

"Girl, you better quit yo' damn lying. You know good and well you wanted me to show you how to do it, and I told you that you were too young, told you to go skating. By then the bus had left, and you went to your mama's house where you should be anyway."

"So, is that it, Ralph? You feel because she don't live with her mama it gives you the right to rape her!"

"I didn't rape her!"

"Get out, Ralph! Get the hell out of my house!" Mary shouted, pointing at the door.

"You don't have to put me out," he said, lowering his head while moving in the direction of the door. "'Cause if you gon' believe her, I'ma leave anyway." He turned his slow-foot-walking butt around and walked out.

"It's going to be fine," Mary said, locking the door behind him. She went and sat on the couch and cried into her hands. I sat quietly next to her, knowing things would never be the same. I knew she loved Ralph.

Mary, Michael, and I slowly drifted apart. Mary started having her doubts about what to believe. We very seldom went places anymore. Mary didn't care for me anymore, not because I had been raped, but because it was her boyfriend that did it. The fact that he cheated on her outweighed everything else. I went back home.

Michael called me two weeks later. He cried into the phone. Mary told him what Ralph had done. He begged me to come back even

Camille's Dilemma

though he knew I wouldn't 'cause Ralph and Mary were back together. It was only for a short time though. Someone shot and killed him a couple years later. To this day, I still have a special place in my heart for Mary and Michael. I know there's a special place in their hearts for me, too.

Some people are just mean; they bury their heart
Will go to the extreme to rip yours apart
They prey on the innocent; they prey on the weak
Prone to plots and schemes
With a lack of direction, harm becomes their way
Waiting for an opportunity to ruin a good day
We the victims have to be strong
It's the only way to move on

Camille Jenkins

Chapter 6

What's Going On?

"Two more months and I'm out of here," Camille said, pushing her way through the crowded halls of Theodore High. She was trying desperately not to be late for her fourth-period algebra class.

"Camille, girl, I saw you from way up here flying up them stairs. Calm down, honey. Mr. William's bald-headed butt is not even here today. You got a sub, cuz."

"For real?"

"You know I got baldy third period; like I said, you got a sub. Now, I know you're going to cut his class; we can hang out at the bookstore."

"Leslie, girl, I've had my days of cutting class. I don't care about being late, but I'm not cutting Mr. William's class."

"Camille, you're not going to believe who asked to go to the prom with me," Leslie said blushing, wearing a jet-black, tight miniskirt and a white blouse that revealed two speed bumps. Camille knew it could have been anybody that had asked her. Light skin was in, and Leslie was light-skinned and cute, when she didn't wear her apple red lipstick. She was what Lionel Richie would call a brick house, "just let it all hang out."

"Who, Leslie?"

"Cortez," she answered with a smirk.

"Cortez! I know you're not talking about the sophomore Cortez, the Mexican Cortez."

"He's the only Cortez in the school, Camille. What other Cortez do you know?"

"He a sophomore, Leslie. Robbing the cradle, are we?"

"Girl, I know he's a sophomore. I was just telling you because it freaked me out when he asked if he could go. You know good and well I'm not about to go to the prom with a sophomore," she said, giving Camille a light tap on the hand. If she knew Leslie, she had considered it. The girl loved attention, and it didn't matter who was giving it. "I can't wait for the prom. I already have my dress picked out. It's rose and cream, just waiting for my mama to pick it up," Leslie said, posing. "What color is yours? Did you pick one out yet?"

"No," Camille replied like it was no big deal to her.

"I hope you know it's right around the corner." Leslie interrupted her pose, took a step back, and asked, "You are going to the prom, aren't you?"

"I might go," Camille said as the last bell sounded.

"You might go. Uh-um, uh-um, hold up, I know you're not going to miss the senior prom. What's up?"

"Nothing. Why does something have to be up? I haven't made up my mind."

"Look, this is Leslie you're talking to. Your mind was made up three years ago. Camille, uh-um, something's up, and you're going to tell me what it is. Talk. Come on, talk to me, Camille. What's up?"

"Don't badger me, child. I said there's nothing up. Trust me, if I go, you'll be the first to know. Time's up. See you in the lunchroom."

"Yeah, later."

Leslie just stood there looking puzzled at Camille until she vanished.

As Camille sat ignoring what the substitute teacher was saying, she contemplated going to the lunchroom. She didn't feel like being hounded about why she didn't care to go to the prom. If she didn't want to go, she felt it was her business, and she didn't owe anybody an explanation. Camille's got a whole lot of things on her mind. She's going through some of the trials and tribulations we all stumble across in our lives. She couldn't escape Leslie though; she was waiting for her outside her fourth-period class, after cutting hers.

"Now, what are you talking about you're not going to the prom," she said as she locked arms with Camille and steered her in the direction of the cafeteria.

"You 'bout a nosy wench, always want to know something."

"I'm your friend. I just want to know your business; nobody else's...Camille, you know you live in your own damn world. If I don't ask, I won't know what's going on. Now, quit stalling. Why don't you want to go to the prom?" Leslie asked Camille as she waved at someone she knew.

"I don't know. I just don't feel right. I'm not all excited about going. If I do, I do; if I don't, I don't."

"Camille, girl, this is your last year…well, that's if your ass don't get demoted. I know you're flunking English. Mrs. Whiteside doesn't play. She'll smile in your face and fail your butt at the same time. I'm glad I didn't get her."

"Look who's talking; a C is no better than a D, Leslie. You're not going on no trip."

"Dang, why you got to take everything personal?" Leslie said, rolling her eyes at Camille. "Ugh, your butt done changed in the last couple years."

"It wasn't me. I told you I have a split personality. You should have believed me. I was Sybil a minute ago; this is Camille talking now, and I want to know who you're going to the prom with, while you're all up in my business."

"Oh shit, here you go with your jokes. Then again, you may be telling the truth about being Sybil's ass; you do talk off the wall at times. I was hoping Daniel's fine self would ask me to go."

"Daniel! Earth to Leslie, Earth to Leslie, come on home," Camille said, holding one of her hands sideways to her mouth. "This is not Daniel's prom; boyfriend just works in the lunchroom. Or are we not talking about the Daniel that works in the lunchroom?"

Camille's Dilemma

"You know I'm talking about him. Girl, look at him," Leslie said with a smile. Daniel was behind the counter refilling a tub of mashed potatoes. Camille and Leslie both picked up trays and started down the lunch line.

"Ain't he fine with his chocolate self. I can just eat him up," Leslie commented, turning Camille's head in his direction.

"Here, eat this up," Camille said, tossing a brownie on Leslie's tray.

"You think I should ask him if he wants to go with me? I think he likes me, and if I'm not mistaken, he be checking you out, too. Unless you had planned on asking him to go," she said, tilting her head at Camille.

"He's not the missing piece to my puzzle. You go right ahead."

"You know, Camille, I'm starting to wonder about you," she said, pointing her index finger at Camille.

"Well, wonder, woman."

"Sybil, right."

Leslie was a lot like Camille, said whatever was on her mind without giving a second thought to repercussions. The difference between their directness was that Leslie's comments were intentional. When Leslie hit home, she would end by saying, "Cuts like a knife, don't it?" Her comments were meant to hurt your feelings.

Leslie was what folks called high yellow. She had a short, black Afro and a petite face. Had the whitest teeth. She looked a little old for her age though. Maybe it was the makeup she wore that made her look older.

Now, Daniel, he was a sleek kind of guy. He worked part-time in their school cafeteria. A cinnamon-brown colored young brother who always wore a white apron to protect his well-groomed garb. He did have a crooked smile, but his straight teeth and young mustache seemed to even it out. Just about every girl at that school was trying to get next to him. Camille thought Daniel was okay-looking but nothing to pencil home about. Right about now, no guy was worth writing about in Camille's book. Leslie was seeing something she didn't. And it started to anger Camille that she couldn't see it, too. But you would swear Daniel was trying to avoid Leslie. Every time she walked into the lunchroom, he'd disappear.

Three years ago, Camille couldn't wait to become a senior. Couldn't wait to see what all this prom stuff was about. She already had some boy in mind to go with, Joseph Lee. Joseph Lee and Camille were in the same English class in their freshman year. They were attracted to one another because they both had witty personalities. I guess birds of a feather do flock together because they became a number. Dated all the way through their junior year then broke up. For some unearthly reason, they became bored with one another. Maybe it was because all they did while they dated was joked. While everybody else was being grown, Joseph Lee and Camille would see who could come up with the next joke. They'd bump and grind every now and then, but that's as far as it would go. Joseph Lee never asked Camille to go all the way, and Camille never broached the subject. Now, here she stands a little on the cute side, with a different attitude about life. She could care less about going to

Camille's Dilemma

her senior prom. She didn't see what the big deal was about going, except to find out who was going to sleep with whom afterwards.

Daniel asked Camille if he could escort her to the prom. They would chitchat sometimes when Leslie wasn't around. Camille told Daniel she already had a date for the prom and thanked him for asking. Camille wasn't going to risk throwing away her friendship with Leslie over a prom date.

Camille felt you had to like your prom date as more than a friend, in case you decided to go all the way. She already tried it once with a guy name Bosco. He played on the football team. Flirted all the time with Camille. She was only doing it because of peer pressure. She didn't have any desires for him. She did it to cover herself. She wanted to be prepared to share details with her friends if she started hearing rumors she wasn't ready to deal with. But the strangest thing happened when Camille found herself going all the way: she fainted the minute he touched her with it. I don't know if what Ralph had done played a role in her fainting, but she passed out. The fact that people thought they did it was enough for Camille.

Something was coming over Camille; she had an inkling of what it was but fought herself to keep it in the subconscious state. The last thing on her mind was going to some boring prom. She started to feel like an onion in a basket of fruit. Physical and mental changes were taking place. Physically, her hips and butt were spreading, attracting all kinds of unwanted attention. Mentally, she started feeling people in general to be a pain in the neck, finding it hard to trust them.

She started spending her time at home in the confines of her bedroom. She would play her music for hours at a time. Camille was lost in somebody else's world. Let's let Camille tell you how lost she was.

After about a month of being apart from my friends, in solitude from my family, I started hanging out again. There would be about six of us hanging out together in the playground. I started calling my friends reefer heads because all they wanted to do was get high. Not to say I was an angel or anything, I took a hit every now and then, but to be spaced out all day with Rick James was another story. I grew tired of putting my change on a bag of weed only to have the roller stash a joint or two. Every day had become the same day. The only thing weed was doing for me was giving me a fat butt. As soon as I was high, I'd find myself laughing all the way to the barbecue house and ordering an extra chicken wing with the order I had already placed. Soon as I finished eating, I was burping myself to sleep.

Etta would ask me before I even got fifty feet in front of her, "Whatcha got on a nickel bag, Camille?"

"Damn, Etta, the least you can do is speak first! What I got on a nickel bag," I said with an attitude.

"I know you got some change. You keep a few dollars in yo' pocket. Set it out. Whatcha got give me, two, three dollars on this bag. We a few dollars short, and we want to get a ten-dollar bag. I know you want to get high."

Camille's Dilemma

"That's all y'all think about is getting high. Damn, can't we just shoot the breeze?" They looked at me as if to say, "What damn train just hit you in the head?"

"You all right?" Lil' James asked me.

"She's tripping," Etta said. "Don't be coming around here with a damn attitude. Forget it. You on a bag or not?" she asked me again.

"Not."

"Don't think we gon' let you get a hit either. If you don't put on, yo' ass don't get none."

Lil' James was short for his age of seventeen. He had cute spider eyes with deep, dark eyebrows that almost connected. Every time I looked him in the face, I stared into his eyes looking mean. I didn't want him to get the wrong impression, even though I admired his features. Anyway, the get-high crew decided to walk across on Morgan Street and cop a bag of weed. I sat on the bench in the playground until they got back. The first thing said as they walked up was "If you didn't put on, you don't get none."

"Later," I said and walked away. I didn't want any.

There was always one house in the neighborhood where you could hang out: Dorothy's. It was like the parents didn't care about the company their kids kept. Almost giving them the green light to do whatever they wanted to do. Dorothy had a full house today. We were all in her bedroom talking teenage talk. Dorothy and Paulett were smoking cigarettes. They always thought they were more grown up than everybody else was. Brenda and Linda stared into a mirror that only stared back. They thought they were the finest things that walked

93

the earth. Michelle was sitting in a rocking chair next to Dorothy's bed looking into her compact mirror at herself. Valerie, she was shaving off her eyebrows only to draw them back on with an eyebrow pencil, which I thought was a waste of time. I was no Diane Carroll, but you had to accept the face I was born with if you planned on dating me. Corrine, she was somewhere in outer space; she always appeared to be floating in her own world. She would stand with her hands in her front pockets and check everybody out.

I knew it wouldn't be long before they started to talk about guys. Who was fine and who wasn't. Who was going with who and who was doing it with who. Then Brenda wanted to know why I don't go with anybody. Big-booty Brenda would be the first to trip. The way she charged me you would think she was waiting for this moment.

"Camille, why you don't go with nobody?" she asked, still staring into the mirror.

Being the smart-ass I had become, I asked, "Who is nobody, and where was I supposed to go?"

Linda snapped her compact mirror shut. "Camille always getting smart with somebody," she said.

"Well, if you must know, I don't go with nobody, nosy, because ain't nobody as fine as your man," I said, swaying my head from side to side, rolling my eyes up into my head.

I knew I had just started a verbal war 'cause Linda thought her boyfriend, Roderick, was the finest guy in school.

"Girl, I know you not talking about my man. I'll kick your butt."

"Don't get paranoid, child; I just said he was kind of cute. Didn't say I wanted to date him or get with him, Miss Linda. Though if I wanted to, you know I wouldn't have a problem getting with the brother."

"You let me hear somebody say you were all up in his face, and it's gon' be you and me!"

Shaking her head from side to side, Paulett said, "Girl, Camille just trying to strike a nerve, and you fell for it."

Then Dorothy put her two cents in, "You know she don't want your man, but I'll take him," laughing frantically.

"I'm out of here," Corrine said. She never really said much; she sort of went with the flow. I always perceived her as being secretive. The way she looked at me sometimes confirmed she had a secret she wanted to share.

I thought I'd go back to the playground and see what the get-high crew was up to. Everybody but Lil' James and his radio had vanished. He saw me coming his way and started laughing then took a pull from the cigarette he was smoking. I knew he wasn't laughing at anything; he was just high. That's what reefer made you do, eat and laugh. Lil' James was just a little too funny though, because he was talking and treating me like one of the fellows. Saying things like, "What's up, dude? Hey man, whatcha got on a forty? Oh, that's right, you not getting high today." Lil' James didn't take a lot of things personal; that's what I liked about him. I thought for a moment, then I decided to share my insecurities with Lil' James.

95

"Are you okay, Camille? Why you looking at me like that? If you're going to tell me I'm cute, I already know that."

"You're cute, but I thought boys consider themselves fine."

"Cute, fine, whatever," he said, looking up at me, high as a kite, smiling.

After revealing my secret to Lil' James, his reaction was just as I expected. He was very receptive and sensitive to my secret. He responded by saying he knew. It was my friend Leslie and the outsiders that had a problem with it.

I went to visit Leslie at her house. After hugging like we hadn't seen each other in ages, we went upstairs to the bedroom I envied. She had a full-size bed with a canopy top. Everything from the comforter to the bed skirt, the pillow shams, and the curtains were all of the American flag colors. The inherited oak wood rocking chair sitting in the corner looked as inviting as the small, gold-rimmed vanity set that sat next to it. I would stand at the door and salute her every time I walked into her bedroom, then flop myself down on her bed. There we sat chatting like neighbors, swapping "used to" and "you didn't hear it from me." Then out of nowhere, Leslie struck me with lighting.

"Why you always hanging out with Lil' James, Camille? Girl, you be slapping hands with him like a dude." She got up and walked over to her dresser. "What's up? I know you know what people are starting to say about you."

"No, I don't know," I said, pursing my lips and batting my eyes at her. "What are people starting to say about me?" Leslie stood back looking at me with her hands on her hips as if to say, "you really don't know."

"Camille, this ain't no joke," she said, looking at me as if I should know. "People are saying you're funny."

"Yeah, well, I was the class clown in grammar school, and now I hear I'm being nominated for the class clown in high school; it's to be expected, wouldn't you say?" I said, smiling, still batting my eyes at her, silly.

"You know what I mean! They're saying you're gay! A bull dagger!"

"Did she just say what I think she said? No, she didn't say what I think she said. Wait, she did say what I think she said." I sat there in dead silence. Then I looked around her room and started to hate the colors red, white, and blue. Those colors represented the American flag. In retrospect, it was truly the only thing that was free. It hung above and out of harm's way.

I knew this wasn't going to be easy. Leslie came and sat down at the head of her bed, grabbing her pillow for security. She then squeezed it to her chest with a look of uncertainty on her face. She was waiting patiently for an explanation.

"Tell me it's not true, Camille," she said, looking at me, afraid that I was going to say it was true.

I had no idea *gay* or *bull dagger* would be words to come out of Leslie's mouth. A few minutes ago, we sat talking calm, cool, and collected. Now, I sat gawking into cloudy air, with fire in my eyes, not to mention the feeling of a torch burning inside. Those words penetrated a nerve so deep it cut worse than a knife. I didn't know what to say. I was speechless. I felt as if I had two Adam's apples lodged in my throat. I got up and walked over to her dresser and stared into the mirror.

"Are you, Camille? I need to know."

"You need to know. Why do you feel you need to know? Whatever the answer, would it make a difference?"

"That depends. Look, Camille, I'm not trying to come down on you or anything; I just want to know. You say you don't know if you're going to the prom. You don't have a boyfriend, and, quite frankly, I've seen the way you look at other girls."

"Oh! Now you're watching where I look. I can't believe you. You think you know people, well, at least your so-called friends, and you don't. I'm tired of this shit. I'm tired of trusting people only to be stabbed in my goddamn back! Don't you think this is as difficult for me as it is for you?"

"So, you're saying you are? I knew it! I knew it…they said you were. I was trying not to believe it," she said, throwing her hands up in the air, reaching for a cigarette as if she had had problems all her life.

"You knew it! All this time you had your doubts about me, and you wait for hearsay before you confront me with it; some friend you are. You probably talk about me behind my back." I stood, bucking my eyes at her.

"I don't talk about you behind your back, Camille."

Camille's Dilemma

"Is that why you asked me if I was going to the prom, Leslie? I guess if I had come right out and said yes, your little insecurities would have gone away. Who told you, Leslie? Forget it, I don't even want to know." I walked over to Leslie's bedroom window and peered out.

"Look, Camille, whether you believe it or not, I'm still your friend. I'm not trying to make a big deal out of it, but if you are gay, I think you owe it to me as a friend to tell me."

"Oh, you do. Why? I've never looked at you as more than a friend. Listen to me, this is all new to me, and you're acting as if I've done something wrong. But if you must know, Leslie, I didn't tell you about my own insecurities because I wasn't sure and am still not sure. Besides, telling you would have been giving you an option."

"An option! What do you mean an option?"

"Oh, don't take that the wrong way. What I mean is that you would have had to decide whether or not you could still be my friend. If you had any doubts about being my friend in the first place, this conversation wouldn't have lasted as long as it has."

"What! You're confusing me."

"Look, Leslie, what I'm going through has nothing and probably never will have anything to do with you. I already know that I'm not attracted to you."

Leslie sat back down on the edge of her bed, embracing her pillow. I suddenly felt hot and bothered. I wanted to leave but knew our conversation was unfinished. I walked back over to her dresser.

99

"Leslie, I'm going to be honest with you. I don't know. I might be, okay? Hell, I don't know. I don't know what's happening. Something is happening to me," I said as tears formed, blinding my eyesight. I walked back over to Leslie's dresser. "It's not like I asked to be this way, Leslie. So, I may be attracted to women." Leslie sat there shaking her head back and forth, still embracing her pillow.

"You know, if people think you are, they're going to think I am, too."

"Why, because we hang out together? Leslie, I don't care what people say and think about me, and you of all people know that! Right now I have an issue I need to deal with, and if you don't want to be friends…let me rephrase that, if you can't handle being my friend, then you owe it to yourself to be honest and say so."

Leslie stood up and walked over to where I was, placing her hand on my shoulder, communicating through the mirror at me.

"Why don't you talk to somebody, Camille? Talk to the school counselor, to the principal; maybe it's just something we go through."

"We."

"Don't get me wrong. I mean, I've looked at other girls, but I can't say that I wanted to get with them, you know what I mean," she tried to explain, pushing up her shoulders. "I don't know that I can handle it, Camille. I like boys."

"Move!" I said, pushing her hand off my shoulder. "I don't remember inviting you into my world. I know you like boys. I like boys, too, but I'm also attracted to women. I've got to go. I never

Camille's Dilemma

should have come here." I ran out of her room, down the stairs, and out of her house, slamming the door behind me.

I strolled home leaving a trail of tears as I thought about what Leslie said. Maybe it was just a phase, but for how long? When I reached home, I did what I did best when things didn't seem to go right: I played my music. I played Michael Jackson's "Human Nature" over and over. I grabbed my brown, wooden hairbrush that was wrapped with hair and sang so deep from my soul that it shook me, giving me a chill from inside out. "If they say why, why, tell them that it's human nature; why, why do they do me this way." Then I played one of Smokey Robinson's records called "I Am" over and over. The song brought more tears. I was preparing myself to take the heartaches that were coming my way. Smokey said something like, "I said I am, I am, I am, I am, I am, and you can bet your life I am, and if the world don't like it, I don't give a damn." Cynthia came bursting into my room with a crazed look on her face.

"Is that the only record you got, girl?"

"Get out of my room, Cynthia!" I pushed her out of my bedroom, locking the door behind her.

Leslie and I didn't speak until the next Saturday, partly because I was dodging her between classes. I would rush out of the eighth-period English class we had together. For all I knew, she was dodging me, too. That was my way of seeing if she had told anybody. I figured if she did tell somebody, I was going to hear it through gossip talk. But all was quiet, and through Leslie's initiation, we made up over the telephone.

101

Two weeks later, with my friend Leslie in my corner, I decided to go to my senior prom. I asked Etta's cousin, who was a few years older than I was, if he would escort me. He accepted. I knew him pretty well from hanging out over there, eating those grilled cheese sandwiches.

Thomas was about five nine, the color of coffee with cream. The hair on his face was smooth and soft as a fur coat. I confirmed it when I allowed him to kiss me on the lips before we got out of his car. He could stand to lose about fifteen pounds, but he wore it well. I could tell by all the hungry women drooling at the mouth when we walked in. Thomas was my date, and he captured me for the night. My plans were to go to the prom, show off my date and our matching baby blue and white outfits, then go home.

I smiled cordially as I introduced him to a few friends. Then we took some pictures. I didn't know how to walk in the high-heel shoes I had on, so I suggested that we sit. I chose to sit in the middle of the room where my date and I could be seen. Thomas asked if I wanted to slow dance. I said yes because they were playing a record I liked, and I was enjoying myself.

As we slow danced to the Commodores' "Once, Twice, Three Times a Lady," I observed the room carefully. I saw Leslie a few tables over with her prom date, Cortez (yes, the sophomore), smiling at me. Thomas pulled me in closer. I was nervous but still managed to look around the room to see who was witnessing my behavior with him.

Camille's Dilemma

When I spotted Mrs. Sullivan, a history teacher, a week-old skeleton fell out of my closet. "Is that Mrs. Sullivan over there," I said to myself, gazing in her direction, drawn to her like a bolt of lighting. She was beautiful. Staring at her from the dance floor, I could have sworn there were a hundred stars dancing around her. She was Cinderella. I looked down for the golden slipper. I saw myself slide over to her, landing on a bent knee, asking, "May I have this dance?" The thumping of my heart swelled my eardrums. She was wearing a long, white, silk dress, with V-shape cuts in the front and back. Standing prominent, refined as the glass of untouched wine she held in her right hand, I became thirsty. Her earrings dangled in a motion that hypnotized me, locking my eyes to her. I blinked, and in the same moment, the wineglass met her lips. She sipped with the utmost respect, bringing out the essence only a beautiful, secure woman could possess. I slow danced in my trance as she cradled in her left hand a soft gold and white, Nieman Marcus, double-clutch purse. Not far away, a bold piece of gold caressed her wrist. Her hair was evenly wrapped around her head in a bun style. The S-shaped curls on each side glistened. The guys called her Mrs. thirty-six, twenty-four, thirty-six. You know what, I wanted every thirty-six, twenty-four Mrs. Sullivan had. I had no idea what had just come over me. I saw beauty and indulged myself in it. I didn't wake up yesterday looking for it... but tomorrow I will.

"Are you okay, Camille?" Thomas asked.

I looked at him from across the room, sure that I had left my body. Slipping back into it, I said, "I'm fine. Why?"

"I thought for a minute you forgot where you were. You were about to fall."

I thought, "I did fall. I fell for Mrs. Sullivan." The strong, secure feeling Thomas and I had shared a minute ago had become limp.

"Oh, I'm fine, just lost my step," I said awkwardly as we walked back to our table. I thought that maybe he took my losing my step as a complimentary sign, that he had just swept me off my feet. Thomas smiled at me for the rest of the evening. As he walked me to the side door of my house, I gave him a kiss on the lips and said, "Thanks for taking me to my senior prom."

I was glad I went to the prom. If this was what it felt like to be gay, a bull dagger, a dyke, I would have to walk down life's lonesome road until I found someone going my way.

"Camille Jenkins," the principal called out. I walked across the stage with pride and accepted my diploma...and my certificate for being the class clown.

Chapter 7

Where Do We Go From Here?

(I know it's been a while since you've heard from me, but I'm back. I sleep a lot in case you wonder where Louise done run off to.) Anyway, Camille may have felt good about graduating and going to her senior prom, but the child was still lost. She couldn't decide on what she was gon' do next. She thought about following in Chester's footsteps and joining the military. Deep inside I knew that gal wanted to go to college. But that was a topic that was never discussed in the Jenkins' house. It was probably 'cause the mama couldn't afford to send any of 'em to college.

After two weeks of pondering what she was gon' do, she decided to join the military. She didn't want to find a job, 'cause all it would pay was minimum wage with just a high school diploma. So she took the military's aptitude test and passed. She was going to the army. November 15, she'd be setting out for New Jersey, learning how to embalm dead people. An undertaker, I think that's what they call 'em. She would have that job for the rest of her life. Then somebody would be embalming her. She had five months before she left for New Jersey. She decided to just hang out with her friends until it was time to go on her new adventure.

Camille found herself a part-time job being a waitress at a restaurant. Her first day on the job and Camille had a family laughing at her. After serving them their food, the father of the family asked Camille for a pitcher of iced tea. Camille went and got a big pitcher. She dropped a few tea bags and some sugar in it. Then she filled the pitcher up with ice water and stirred it. She came back with a pleasant smile. That's what her manager say for her to do: keep a smile on her face to make the customer feel good 'bout eating there. Camille sat the pitcher of tea in the middle of the family's table. Then she went to wait on a man that come in alone and took a seat at the counter. All he asked for was a cup of black coffee. Camille was enjoying her first day of work. She was sweeping up tips, excited. Then the manager called her back to the table the tea was at. She asked Camille what was in the pitcher. "They asked for a pitcher of iced tea," Camille said with a smile.

"Well, why did you bring them ice water?"

"Ice water!" Camille looked down into the pitcher she thought was iced tea. "I put tea bags in it," she said. The manager covered her mouth in shame that Camille didn't know how to make iced tea.

"No, no, baby, you use hot water, tea bags, then add the ice."

Camille's Dilemma

Camille covered her mouth. "I'm sorry. I didn't know. I've never made iced tea before." The manager shook her head and led Camille to the kitchen and showed her how to make iced tea. The family still laughed at her when she brought them the new iced tea. The father thought it was cute. He left Camille a ten-dollar tip. After about a month of working, Camille done bought herself one of them big radios all the kids was starting to carry around with them. They called it a boom box. All that noise that thing make oughta be against the law.

A new family moved in on Camille's block. She made friends with one of them. She didn't let her guard down too low, just enough to be cordial. She was a nice person, you know, just a little lonely and a little afraid of life. Started handing the new people she met the short end of the stick. Now every time she left the house, she would carry her little pocketknife with her, and her Chap Stick.

Dwight was the friend of Camille's that moved in the house across the street. He was teddy bear brown with a soft-looking face. About five feet nine, not only tall, he was a big man. I think that's why Camille felt a little secure with him, because he was so big. She knew that if he tried anything, he wouldn't get far. He and Camille would sit on his porch and talk a lot. Mostly he would talk. Camille would listen. He'd be complaining about his wife. Camille sit with him two, three times a week on his porch and hadn't even met his wife or kids. He had been trying to get Camille to come inside his house to meet his family. She would never go in. He said his wife didn't know why Camille didn't want to meet her. Dwight told Camille he had to tell

107

his wife over and over that they were only friends. So, one day, Camille decided go on in and meet his family. (I'm gon' let her tell you what happen after that. Bye.)

While Dwight introduced me to his wife, my attention was drawn to their living room, curious to why they needed so much furniture. The odd thing about the furniture, none of it matched.

"Hi, I'm Sharon...Dwight's wife, excuse his manners," she said, nudging him and extending her hand out to me. Right away I could tell she had a slight speech problem.

"Hi, I'm Camille. I know I've been sort of a stranger to you. Nothing personal. Welcome to the neighborhood." I shook her hand, still utterly distracted by the many things surrounding me. Dwight called out to his son, Lil' Dwight.

"Would you like something to eat?" Sharon asked me.

"No, I'm not hungry. Thanks," I said, following them into a kitchen just big enough for a refrigerator, stove, a table, and maybe four chairs. Somehow they had managed to squeeze a washer, dryer, and freezer in it also. We walked back into the living room, and it looked like the Partridge Family had united with the Brady Bunch. Kids were coming out of the woodwork.

"Camille, this is Lil' Dwight," Dwight said, patting him on top of his nappy, little Afro. "The rest are my nieces and nephews. Y'all, say hi to Camille."

"Hi, Camille!" they all said in unison, sounding like they had rehearsed it for any new company that might arrive. I glanced down at my watch a couple of times as a signal to Dwight I was ready to leave adventure land. I quietly strolled toward the front door. Sharon walked over to me with a short smile. She extended her hand in lieu of saying goodbye. I perceived her to be a bit shy, though she didn't have a problem hinting to me, "You can have him if you want him." It was like she wanted to give Dwight away. Well, I'd hate to disappoint her, but I had no intention of stealing her husband. I didn't like Dwight the way she thought I did. Even if I did, does this little pregnant chick think I had the stamina to come into her house and steal him from under her nose? I left there feeling sorry for her, acting as if she was his slave. Dwight seemed to dictate her every move. Do this! Do that! Did you get this? Did you iron that? Did you feed Lil' Dwight? Nobody in that family looked like they missed a meal to me.

You have to believe me when I tell you this. I was hexed. Hexed out of my mind. Somebody had put the heebie-jeebies on me. After about three months of hanging out with Dwight, I agreed to go to a hotel with him. He acted happier than a kid with a lollypop when I said yes.

On the way to the hotel, Dwight pulled his cranberry and black van over to the curb and said, "I'm going get something to drink," and hopped out of the van. It gave me time to think about his wife and how he treats her. She looked so innocent and deprived. I knew she didn't have any friends because Dwight told me she never goes out of the house unless she's with him. He would never let her sit outside on the porch with us either. I thought with a little makeup and a little confidence, she could be attractive. In my eyesight, Dwight was now a dog, and I decided to dog him out when he got back.

109

"What did you get?" I said, taking the bag from him.

"A six pack of Miller's and some cigarettes."

Calm, cool, and collected, I said, "Now that you have everything you want, I would like some coolers. Oh! And a pack of Doublemint gum." I stared coolly at him. He gave me an "I'm sorry" sort of smile.

"I'll be right back." When he returned and handed me the bag, I looked down in it and asked where my bag of skins was.

"Skins! You didn't ask for any skins."

"I did, Dwight. Weren't you listening? I asked for a bag of barbecue skins," I said loudly, staring adamantly at him.

"I'm sorry, I guess I didn't hear you, skins coming right up." I started cracking up when he went back into the store. For once in my life, I felt in control. People can have as much power over you as you allow them to have. I was feeling good. This was do-what-I-say-do day. I was taking past anger out on Dwight. I knew it wasn't right. But I did it anyway. And it felt good. I wanted to see just how much he was willing to put up with.

As he was driving down the Garfield Boulevard, I shouted over the music on the radio.

"Dwight! Do you love your wife?"

"What?" He reached to lower the music.

"You're not deaf! Do you love your wife?"

"Why are you asking me if I love my wife?"

"Damn! Can't you just answer the question?"

"Yeah! I love my wife...you okay? What's wrong with you, Camille?"

110

Camille's Dilemma

"Ain't nothing wrong with me. I'm fine. Do it look like something's wrong with me?"

"Well, why did you ask me if I love my wife? You know I love my wife. If you feel I'm cheating on her, Camille, we don't have to do this."

I decided to ignore him the rest of the way to see how he would react. A song I liked came on the radio, so I turned up the volume and starting singing with Rose Royce. He glanced at me from the corner of his eyes. He probably thought I was losing it.

As we pulled into the parking lot of the Raleigh's Hotel, Dwight had a big smile on his face. You would have thought it was his first time. I sat in the van while Dwight checked in. All of a sudden, the courage I had started dissipating. Reality checked in on why I was really there. I hadn't a clue. I wasn't physically attracted to him. I wanted to do it, and I didn't want to do it. "Just stay in control, Camille."

Once we entered the room, we both sensed uneasiness in the air. We sat around for a while and talked. Dwight got up to get a beer out of the bag.

"Camille, are you having second thoughts about this?" Dwight asked, kicking his shoes off toward the window.

"Second thoughts? I wasn't quite thrilled with the first one."

"Ha, ha, very funny, you know what I mean. Camille, what's wrong? Why are you giving me such a hard time?" he asked, looking over at me. "Did I do something?"

I raised up from the bed, placing my hands on my hips. "Why is your wife so submissive to you? She acts like she's afraid to do things on her own! Are you abusing her, Dwight?" I asked, staring gravely at him.

"Abusing her, no way. Camille, Sharon's just a little slow at things. She forgets a lot. If she's outside alone, she wanders off. I mean, she's not retarded or anything; she's just a little slow. She lost her mama a few years back and hasn't been right since. I meant it when I said I love Sharon. I wouldn't dream of harming her. I may not be in love anymore, but I still love her. I'm just not happy, Camille. My mama's sick. I'm always running back and forth to the doctor with her. As you've seen, all my nephews and nieces are always there. Now that Sharon's having another baby, she needs to be watched. Camille, I just have to keep a close eye on Sharon." I didn't know what to say after that. So I didn't say anything. It did explain why they had all that furniture. Sharon probably wanted it.

Now, feeling a little uncomfortable and slightly embarrassed at my assumption, I got up and went into the bathroom to undress. I sat on top of the toilet seat for fifteen minutes contemplating if I should go through with it. After being mean to him for the last hour, I figured it wouldn't hurt.

With a towel wrapped around me, I hurried from the bathroom and jumped into the bed, tossing my clothes and the towel into the chair. I pulled the cover up to my chin as if the temperature had just dropped fifty degrees. Dwight was kneeling in front of the TV fumbling with the remote control, probably trying to find some X-

Camille's Dilemma

rated movies. As Dwight stood up to undress, I pretended not to watch but viewed him through the chestnut-brown, oval-shaped mirror attached to the dresser. Dwight was big, and I truly don't mean below the belt. After he had undressed and everything was hanging out, he started to the foot of the bed. Slowly on all fours, he made his way up to where I was. It had to have been the weight of his body, because for a minute I thought we were in a waterbed. And I had specifically said I didn't want a room with a waterbed. He stopped on all fours and smiled down at me. Suddenly, the room spun around. I became faint, losing my breath in his shadow.

"Uh-um, uh-um, I can't do this, Dwight. I'm sorry, but I can't do this." There was no way I was going to let him rest all that baggage on me. I slinkied myself out from under him. I knew I had just hurt his feelings, but had I let him lay on me, every part of my body was going to hurt.

"What's the matter?" he asked, looking disappointed as he sat on the edge of the bed.

"I just can't do it. It will just be for the wrong reason. I like you as a friend, and I hope we can continue to be friends." Dwight was now teary eyed. Now I really felt bad.

"It's because I'm big, isn't it?" he asked, looking away.

"To be honest, yes and no. I'm just not ready for this."

"Hell, my wife says the same thing. 'You too big, Dwight.' Am I really that big?" I didn't say anything. He knew where the mirror was. I guess that's why his wife hinted that I could have him if I wanted him. I didn't want to make him feel any worse than he did, so I picked

113

D.C. Johnson

up my clothes from off the chair and walked quietly into the bathroom.

"We're still cool, right?" he asked, cracking the bathroom door open.

"Of course we are," I said, sitting nude on the cold tub, admiring the toiletries. I felt bad after we left. Not because I had just taken the little soaps, shampoo bottles, and a couple of towels, but because Dwight was a nice person. I really did enjoy his company and liked him as a friend. After that failed mission, I started to chill a bit and not hang out so much with him. I wanted Dwight to know I really wanted to be friends.

Chapter 8

Coming Out

It was mid-September and a Saturday—a clear, lovely day to do just about anything. It was a comfortable eighty degrees. Dwight had gone out of town with his family, which left me a little bored. I went upstairs and peered out of the front window.

"Who you looking at? Girl, you be breaking your neck to look out that window," Cynthia said, creeping down the stairs.

"Nobody with your nosy self. I'm not gon' tell you no more to stop calling me 'girl.'"

"It must be somebody out there the way you be breaking your neck to look out that window." Cynthia went cruising over to the front room window to get her a glimpse. I was glad nobody was out there. I decided to go outside and wait at the corner to see them two mysterious women who recently moved in on the block. That's what I went to that window for in the first place. I was waiting for them to come strutting down the block all hugged up, laughing, and giggling like there was no tomorrow. They fascinated me, and today I wanted their attention. Oh, oh, I just might get it, because here they come, I thought.

"Just be cool," I said. I tried to walk relaxed, which seemed impossible to do. I knew as soon as I got close enough that I was going to freeze up or trip on a crack. Trip on a crack I did as I observed every detail I could about them. One was short, taffy apple brown with finger waves and sort of pimped when she walked. She looked like she had green eyes. The other one was on the sunny side, tall with impressionable dimples. I made it my business to speak to them. "Hi," I said with a smile and nod of the head.

"Hello," they said in harmony. As we passed, we all turned around to catch the other one looking and pleasantly smiling. If that wasn't a stamp of approval, I don't know what is. I walked to the end of the block with a Whoopie Goldberg smile on. Then I went home to entertain my thoughts.

I was becoming obsessed with them. I started clocking them every day I came home from work. I would be standing in my front yard leaning casually on the fence when they left in the mornings and in the same position when they came home in the evening. I worked part-time so I never missed seeing them. They probably thought I was crazy. I didn't care. I knew of no other way to get their attention. The secret Chester and I had shared as kids was coming into practice.

"Camille, your friend is at the door!" Chester shouted from the living room.

116

"Who is it?" I shouted back.

"I don't know. Why don't you come and see."

I opened the door, and Dwight was standing there with a bright smile holding a lilac and purple gift-wrapped box. He handed me the box, and I opened it. It was a Coca-Cola-colored, diamond-shaped bathroom wall plaque with a bell on it that said, "If you have to go, don't stand and yell. Cross your legs and ring this bell."

"Thanks, Dwight," I said with a grateful smile.

"You want to hang out for a while?" he asked.

"Why not?" I galloped downstairs to retrieve my Chap Stick and pocketknife that lay on my dresser.

"Would you believe my sisters live on this block, too?" he said while closing the gate to the fence. "I've been meaning to tell you that."

"Maybe one day I'll get the chance to meet them."

"We can shoot on over there now if you like. I'm sure they're home by now. Camille, I think you should know...never mind," Dwight said, waving his hand down.

"Know what? What should I know, Dwight?"

"Nothing."

As we walked across the street, I noticed we were heading in the direction of the complex those two women came in and out of. My mind rushed to thoughts. "What if one of them happens to come out and see me with Dwight? They'll probably think I'm dating him. What if they are his sisters? Naw, sisters don't hug the way they do." I dismissed my thoughts and just hoped I didn't run into them. But the closer we got to their building, the more nervous I became. I knew sooner or later that I was going to personally introduce myself to them. Now was not the time. Dwight rang the doorbell with the name Davis on it.

"Who is it?" a seductive voice asked.

"Open the door," Dwight said, shaking his head from side to side. "That's Sabrina. She's always trying to sound sexy. She's a trip."

"Hey, Dwight," the seductive voice said. "What's up, come on in."

"Thought I'd drop by and introduce you guys to a friend of mine. Well, she's actually our neighbor, lives right across the street." I was standing behind Dwight. Obviously, I couldn't see whom he was talking to.

As I followed Dwight through the door, I laid eyes on one of my mystery girls. The seductive voice belonged to the tall one, the one on the sunny side. My bottom lip dropped two inches. I just stood there gawking at her. She delicately put her forefinger under my chin, lifting it up lightly to shut my mouth. I shook my head back and fourth, flabbergasted. We both smiled and giggled a little. Dwight turned and said, "Did I just miss something?" He then looked at us suspiciously and said, "Camille, this is Sabrina," pointing at her.

"Your sister?"

"More like sister-in-law." I guess Dwight didn't think I would catch on. "Where's Maxine?" he asked, turning around, looking suspiciously at us.

118

Camille's Dilemma

"You sure you two don't know each other? Y'all acting kind of funny."

"Dwight, what a choice of words," another voice said from the kitchen.

"Oh, that's one of my sisters; we call her Six Pack. You can figure that one out," Dwight said.

"Yuck!" I thought to myself. She was ugly. Couldn't be, couldn't be, couldn't be. Somebody pinch me, pinch me hard because this couldn't be the same person.

"Hi, I'm Sandra."

"Camille."

"Don't pay him no attention," she said, reaching out to shake my hand with her ugly smile. Six Pack looked sixty-two years old in the face. She looked like she was aging for everybody in the family. Her hands were cold and firm. A chill came over my body after I shook her hand. Maxine's got to be the other mystery lady. I hoped my eyes hadn't deceived me. Someone was coming in the door.

"See we have company," a voice said as the door shut.

"Maxine, this is Camille, your...I mean, our neighbor. She lives across the street." Maxine looked a bit bewildered. She knew I had just seen them earlier. Her eyes were really green, well, light green. Eyes I was instantly absorbed into.

Dwight said, "This is my oldest sister. She tries to run everything. But she knows who the man is."

"So, are you guys a couple?" Sabrina asked, addressing the question to me.

119

"No, actually we've been friends a while now," I said, hoping she bought into the idea that we were friends.

"Camille was the first person on the block I met when we moved in."

"I bet she was, Dwight," Maxine said, smiling at me.

"And don't you and Maxine be getting no ideas. You know what I'm talking about," he said, pointing his finger at Sabrina. Playing naive, I asked Dwight what he meant. He shook his head, waving his hand down as if to say, "Forget it."

"Well, I just stopped by to introduce you guys to your neighbor."

"It was nice meeting you, Camille," Maxine said nodding her head up and down.

"Maybe next time you guys can stay a little longer," Sabrina said. I'm sure they knew if I had it my way, I'd hang out with them all night.

Six Pack, smiling that ugly smile, said, "Y'all come back." She looked like she was walking over to shake my hand again and in my mind, I said, "Stay! Stay, boy, stay!" But she went and sat in the love seat.

As soon as we got into Dwight's van, he asked me if I had picked up on Sabrina and Maxine.

"What do you mean? Is something wrong with them?"

"No, I wouldn't say there's something wrong with them...except they're gay."

"So."

"So! You're okay with that?"

Camille's Dilemma

"I don't think you introduced them to me for me to be judgmental, Dwight," I said, rolling my eyes slowly in his direction. "They seem to be cool to me; I like them."

"You sure you don't already know them?"

"What are you implying, Dwight?"

"Nothing. It's just most people get a little paranoid around gay people."

"Sounds like you're the one that's paranoid."

I knew it was definitely going to be hard being his friend. I left him with intentions of going back to see Sabrina and Maxine without him.

(I'm back, and it looks like just in time.) Looks to me like Camille is ready to take on being gay full-time. She knew at an early age that she was different. I don't think she really associated it with being gay though. When they lived in them projects, Camille and one of her friends would follow this lady home when she got off the bus. They both be talking 'bout how pretty she was. Fussing with each other 'bout who the lady was gon' pick. Just when the lady open her door to go in her house, Camille and her friend holler out, "You pretty!" and take off running.

They probably never even heard the word *gay*. How was that child feeling that way when she was just a kid? Who put that in her brain to make her think that way? What makes her see a pretty lady's face and like it so much? Poor child didn't even know she was gay. Didn't know she was doing gay thinking.

Now, that brother of hers, Chester, he gay, too. He knows it's something wrong with it though. That's why he stays to himself. Never did tell his mama how sometimes he'd get called names and chased home from school. Can you imagine being that little and having to deal with them kind of issues? I feel for the both of them. Well, least they got each other. There gon' come a time when they gon' need each other. There's a big ole world out there that's been waiting for them to grow up, just to knock them back down.

I don't know a whole lot 'bout being gay 'cause I ain't never been gay. If I was, I don't remember. But I done seen and heard enough to know that for people who are, it ain't no bed of roses. They always gon' be discriminated against. A lot of folks just ain't gonna like 'em. I don't care if they minding they business or not. Somebody gon' have something to say 'bout it, and it usually ain't good things being said. You know what I think? I think it's a little of it in all of us. That's right. You can get mad at me if you want to, can even stop reading. I'm just telling you what I think. Just like you got your opinion, I got mine. I say you got some of it in you.

Some folks say there ain't no balance in the genes. I can believe that. Some folks say you get that way from being messed with as a child. I can believe that, too. Some say them bad-apple men make you that way. Now, I know I can believe that. See, I knew these two women who were both married with husbands. One of the husbands made a habit of beating on her, going upside her head. Her friend would comfort her, till her husband start going upside her head, too.

Camille's Dilemma

Then her friend comforted her. The next thing you know, they gay. Part-time gay though; they still got they husbands.

That theory of being born gay, now, that's an issue that's gon' be debated forever. I believe you could be born gay. I believe Camille and her brother Chester was born that way.

Being gay when you're real young ain't important, you know. It should be. Look like a good time to nip discrimination in the bud. Most people say, "Give it some time; it'll straighten out." Or say, "Oh, she or he's just confused." Wouldn't that be something to see a parent walk out of her little girl's life when she ten years old 'cause she come home one day and say, "Mama, guess what! You know my teacher, Mrs. Stewart, I love her, Mama! I really do. She sure is pretty, Mama. I'm gon' marry her when I grow up." But they don't get disowned till they grown up or almost grown up. Sho' is a shame.

Now, it was a little windy outside today. I guess Chicago was living up to its name 'bout being the windy city. Dwight wanted to hang out, but Camille said she wanted to be alone. So she sat in her room listening to this new artist in the music industry. He called himself Prince. She sat on her bed staring at the sexy photo that covered the album cover. I have to say he was a sexy-looking man, boy, whatever you want to call him. Camille walked over to her dresser with the album cover in her hand. She held the Prince album cover next to her face and stared at it through the mirror. She put the same expression on her face he had on the album cover. Then she picked up a black eyebrow pencil she took earlier from her sister and carefully drew a mustache on her face that looked like his. She enhanced her eyebrows with the pencil to match his. Then she put a dot right above her left cheek. Camille took her comb and brush and styled her hair just like his. When she was finished, she closed her eyes and then opened them up slowly into the mirror, holding the Prince picture next to her face again. She'd make a good impersonator for Prince. She went over to her stereo and played the latest hit on his album, called "Controversy." In the mirror, she danced. She danced the way she thought he would to that song. She was just a twisting and turning, enjoying herself. Then there was a knock on her bedroom door.

"Girl! Whachu in here doing?"

"If you call me girl one more time, I'm gon' knock you out, Cynthia!"

"Ooh! Look at you! You look like that guy!" Cynthia screamed a little. "What's his name, what's his name? Prince! That's his name. Girl, why you…"

"I told you, Cynthia, to quit calling me girl," Camille said with scrunched up eyes.

"Why did you make your face up like his? Dance, Camille. I know you can dance like him because you like to dance. Too bad you can't sing, you might have something going here. Ooh! I'm going to go get Diane, wait," she said, thrilled.

Cynthia turned to leave and Camille shouted out, "No, Cynthia! I don't want nobody to see me like this."

"You look good. Please, just let Diane see you. Come on, girl…I mean, Camille."

Camille's Dilemma

"Hurry up so I can wipe this stuff off my face." Five minutes later and Cynthia was knocking on Camille's bedroom door again.

"Camille, open the door, hurry up so Diane can see you." Camille opened the door and was startled to see all them people standing outside her door. Cynthia brought Diane's whole family back with her. All Camille heard was:

"Girl, you look just like him."

"Sure do."

"Uh, huh."

"She sure do."

"I'm just in here messing around," Camille said.

"You can make some money if you could dance like him," Diane said.

"She sure can," somebody else said.

"All you have to do is dress up like him and put on a show."

"A show! I'm just in here acting foolish. Get out my room...shoo, shoo, shoo," Camille said in a playful way, shoving them out of her room.

She sat down and thought about what they were saying. Could she really pull something like this off? Then she put that thought on the back burner. She knew she'd be leaving for the army in a few weeks and still had some unfinished business across the street she wanted to take care of.

Most of Camille's neighbors were outside sitting on their porches, chit-chatting. Probably talking about somebody. Why folks do that, sit around and talk negative 'bout folks? Anyway, Camille knew the

125

people next door talked about everybody 'cause sometimes she'd sit with them if Cynthia were over there. Cynthia only let her sit with them when she wanted to wear something new Camille done bought. They would talk about anybody that walked past. Young or old, they had something to say about them. The last time Camille sat with them she ask, "Why do y'all always talk about people?" They looked over at Cynthia. Camille knew then that they didn't want her around anymore. She got up and went in the house.

Tonight she planned on visiting Sabrina and Maxine without Dwight. After showering, she put on a pair of blue jeans and a red sweatshirt, then combed her hair back into a ponytail and put on a new pair of white gym shoes she had bought the other day. She stuffed her Chap Stick down in her front pocket. She then went upstairs and peered out the front room window to see if Dwight's van was parked out in front of his house. It wasn't. Happy, she continued with her plan. Before stepping out of her house, Camille took a deep breath 'cause she didn't know what to expect going over there alone. Didn't know what to say to them. Didn't know how she would conduct herself. "Be you, Camille," she mumbled. Camille walked over to their building and tapped lightly on the door with the name Davis on it.

"Who is it?"

"Camille."

"Who?"

"Camille…from across the street," Camille said, hoping they remembered who she was.

Camille's Dilemma

"Oh, Camille," Sabrina said, opening the door.

"Come on in. Is Dwight with you?"

"No. Just thought I'd drop by," Camille said, biting down on her bottom lip.

"Have a seat," Sabrina said, pointing to the couch.

"So what brings you by…without Dwight?"

"I wasn't doing anything. Thought I'd see what you guys were up to."

"Is that right? Now, why would you be interested in what we're up to? Are you gay, Camille?" Sabrina asked bluntly, turning around to look at Camille, who quickly looked away. She didn't want Sabrina to catch her staring at her rear end. But she knew Camille was watching her. She saw her reflection through the glass on the stereo.

"I guess you can say I am."

"Stud or femme?" Sabrina asked.

Camille looked at her confused. "Stud or fem? I don't understand."

"You would probably pass for fem. But I see a splash of stud in you. Make a cute stud, too. So you're fresh meat."

"Fresh meat? You got me on that one." Camille didn't have a clue as to what Sabrina was talking about.

Sabrina and her dimples smiled all the time while talking to Camille. If there was anything Sabrina enjoyed most, it was probably fresh meat. She was the femme in her relationship with Maxine. She was also a little on the wild side. Probably could have just about anybody she wanted, whether they are a stud or a femme. Maxine, on

127

the other hand, was a stud, acted just like a man. After talking some more, Sabrina finally broke down some things to Camille. Like what a stud, femme, and fresh meat was. Fresh meat is what they call a virgin gay person. A stud was the more dominate one, and a femme was the softer-looking one. In Maxine's book, studs don't date studs. Said they clashed. Camille didn't consider herself either. How could she when she knew she could be attracted to both? She just enjoyed women's company. There was no room for discrimination in Camille's book.

"Is your friend home?" Camille asked Sabrina.

"Maxine? Oh! Got a thing for Maxine? Is that why you sneaking over here, to see Maxine?"

"No. I like both of you, and I didn't sneak over here." Sabrina cut her eyes over at Camille thinking, "Hum, she's straightforward."

"Maxine went to the store to get something to drink. Do you drink? Wait, how old are you, Camille? You look a little young."

"Well, if eighteen is underage, I guess I'm underage. You mind if I ask how old you guys are?" Camille asked, looking at two black statues sitting on a black marble stand. They were statues of two Afro-African women with their hands extended into the air. Sabrina came over and sat next to Camille, which made her nervous.

"We're both twenty-eight. You're cute, Camille," Sabrina said, looking at her. "Yeah, you'll make a fine stud."

Sabrina could tell she was making Camille nervous, so she got up and sat on the loveseat.

Camille's Dilemma

"So, I'll take it you've never been out on the set." Camille lifted her hands up to the air, confused about her question. There was a knock on the door.

"That must be Maxine. Guess who's here?" Sabrina said.

"Who?"

"Camille."

"Camille, the girl from across the street, Dwight's friend. Is Dwight with her?"

Sabrina shook her head no, and they both giggled.

"Hey, what's up! Camille, right?" Maxine said, walking over to shake Camille's hand. "Would you like a beer or something?" she asked, setting the bag on the black-and-gold trimmed cocktail table.

"Sure," Camille said, trying not to stare at Maxine.

"I'm sure Sabrina has already asked you a million questions."

"No, I haven't, Maxine. But she is fresh on the set."

"Wait," said Maxine, slightly smiling, looking over at Camille. "Does Dwight know?"

"He may have his doubts. I've never told him I was gay. I'm still trying to figure it out."

"Maxine, did you get a bag?"

"Look in my coat pocket, Sabrina, and put the rest of these beers in the refrigerator." She shook her head at Sabrina then said, "You smoke weed, Camille?"

"A little."

"Damn, you just get to the point. Ask you a question, and it's a one-word answer." Maxine giggled. Sabrina in her tight jeans and Vcut yellow sweater lit a joint and started prancing around the apartment with it.

"Pass the joint, Sabrina! Damn, always showing off! That's Sabrina for you. Hot ass Sabrina!" Maxine was getting mad at Sabrina for prancing around in front of Camille.

"Wait, I want to give Camille a shotgun."

"How do you know she wants one, Sabrina? Why don't you just sit your ass down somewhere!"

"No, it's cool. I'll take one." Sabrina bent over to give Camille a shotgun, making sure she blinded her with her cleavage. Then she deliberately kissed Camille on her lips. Camille savored it. She couldn't wait to get home to replay it.

"You're going to have to get used to Sabrina. She loves to show off," Maxine said, looking at Sabrina as she changed the record that was playing. She then played a fast record by a group that called themselves "The Average White Band."

Maxine, rolling her eyes at Sabrina again, said, "We don't go out much because of Sabrina."

"I'm not the reason we don't go out. Don't start lying to Camille, Maxine."

"So, you haven't been out on the set yet?" Maxine said, directing her attention to Camille.

"No. That's why I'm here. I'm new at this."

"Are you a stud or a femme?"

"Neither," Sabrina said quickly.

Camille's Dilemma

"I see I'm asking you the same questions Sabrina asked. So what brings you over here without Dwight?" Camille looked at Sabrina, and Sabrina looked at Camille. "Oh, she asked you that, too. Well, what didn't you ask her, Sabrina?" They all laughed.

"Anybody want a cold beer?" Sabrina asked.

"Bring me one, Sabrina."

"I'll take another one, too," Camille said, enjoying herself. Now Maxine wanted to give Camille a shotgun after Sabrina left to get the beers.

"Sure," Camille said, elevated from the first one.

"Sabrina thinks she's slick. I'm going to do what she did without the joint." Maxine kissed Camille lightly on the lips then gave her a shotgun. Camille was flabbergasted that both these women found her attractive enough to cheat on one another. Then she became confused. She was attracted to the both of them. If she had to decide whether or not she was going to be a stud or femme, she would probably lean more toward being a stud because she liked the way Maxine carried herself.

Between working and going over to Maxine and Sabrina's house, Camille was also becoming obsessed with Prince. She would sit in her room and make her face up to look like his. She had even gone and bought one of those ruffled blouses he likes to wear. She couldn't afford to buy the leather pants, so she invested in the pleather ones. She would pantomime a few of his songs. She felt if only she could see him in a video, she could get his moves down pat. She closed her eyes and pictured what he might do.

131

"Camille, somebody's at the door for you," Cynthia shouted downstairs.

"Who?"

"Corrine."

"Who?"

"Corrine. Girl, just come get the door."

"Tell her to wait a minute." Camille wondered what she wanted. She had never visited her before. She used to see Corrine hanging out over Dorothy's. Camille ran into the bathroom to wash the makeup off her face. She didn't want Corrine to see her like that and think that she was crazy. She then ran back into her room and brushed her hair into a ponytail.

Camille stood at the bottom of the stairs to see if it was the Corrine she thought it was. It was.

"Corrine."

"Yeah."

"Come on down." Camille walked over to her record player to take off the Prince album that was still playing and turned on the radio. When she turned around and looked at Corrine, she had a smirk on her face.

"What are you smirking about?" Camille said to her.

"You."

"Me? Why are you smirking at me?"

"Man, you crazy. Look at you! Why you dressed up like Prince?"

"Prince!" Camille looked at what she was wearing. She had forgotten to change clothes.

132

Camille's Dilemma

"Oh this, I just be in here playing around. I'll be back in a minute."

Corrine couldn't stop smirking and shaking her head at Camille, even after she had changed into some khaki pants and a tan sweatshirt. Then she just burst out laughing.

"Now what do you find funny?" Camille asked her. She was getting a little peeved about Corrine laughing at her.

"I like it!" Camille looked mystified at Corrine. "Man, you be doing some bold shit. I've been checking you out a long time. Man, you crazy. I follow you around just so I could laugh. I like you, man; you cool."

"Wait, wait, what's up with this 'man' stuff?"

"Oh! That's just a figure of speech. I got a habit of saying it. I be calling my mama a man; I don't be thinking. You just funny."

"I guess it can't be no worse than being called girl all the time."

"Cynthia's your sister, right?"

"Yeah."

"She's crazy like you. But people getting tired of her always calling them girl or boy."

"So what brings you over here?"

"Nothing, man, I mean, Camille, man. Man, just let me say man." They both started laughing. Camille knew at that moment that she would accept Corrine as a friend. She knew it was nothing like having a buddy to make you laugh. She also knew Corrine was there to find her way out of the closet. I guess Camille was her ticket to common

133

ground. Little did she know Camille was looking out of a cracked door herself.

"Man, if you not gon' put me out, give me a chair so I can sit down," Corrine said as if to ask, "Where's your hospitality?"

"Oh, I'm sorry. I'll be right back."

Camille handed Corrine a chair, and she sat in it backwards.

"But seriously, Camille, man, I just came to see what you were up to. I'm tired of hanging out with Dorothy and them. They get on my nerves, thinking they the finest women that walked the earth. I was glad you busted they asses out that day you came over there."

"And?" Camille said, looking her in her eyes.

"And. And what?"

"And you came over here to find your way out of the closet."

"Man, why you reading me?" Corrine looked away.

"'Cause it's written all over that pimp in your walk. I read you a long time ago. I used to watch how you just sit and stare at everybody at Dorothy's house. You was doing the same thing I was doing, trying to fit in."

"Man, forget that. I'm getting ready to start being me. I don't care what people think and say. My family be tripping on me, too. Do your family know about you?"

"I'm not sure. I haven't come right out and told them. I'll let them come to me."

For the next couple of weeks, Camille hung out over Maxine and Sabrina's. She told them all about her upcoming venture of joining the military to become an undertaker, which was only a week away.

134

Camille's Dilemma

They told her all about the gay life. She also spent a lot of time with Corrine. She would school her on the gay life. They were becoming good friends. Corrine hated the most to see Camille leave. The closer it got for her to leave, the sadder she became. Camille felt like she was the only friend Corrine really had. She asked Corrine if she was okay.

"Do I look like I'm okay? Man, you know I gon' miss you. Why you got to go now? You got plenty of time to go into the white man's army."

"The white man's army, Corrine?"

"Hell yeah, the white man's army. Man, the government don't give a damn 'bout your ass when you come out! I got two older brothers that's living proof. They can't even find a decent job. Man, my brother Johnny so pissed off, he gives away food at the restaurant he works at. That's why my ass is so big. He looks out for me, for real. I ain't joking. Johnny brings frozen hamburgers and shit home with him."

"Well, there's nothing for me to do here. I'm not trying to work in a restaurant and give food away for the rest of my life, nothing personal. Besides, I've already committed myself."

"You've committed yourself all right, to a damn institution. I wish I had been talking to you sooner. You wouldn't be going to no army." Camille just smiled and gave Corrine what they both needed, a hug.

Chapter 9

Hoodwinked

Time was just flying by, and Camille was flying with it. The morning before Camille was to leave for the army was not an ordinary morning. She tossed and turned all night. Something was weighing real heavy on her mind. She'd get up and go into the bathroom. Stay fifteen, twenty minutes at a time, staring at herself in the mirror. Kept getting the feeling that something wasn't right. Didn't feel like she was the same person she was yesterday or the day before that. Felt like her space had been invaded. Like someone was there. All of a sudden, she became nauseated! Camille bent over the sink looking dazed and bewildered. Then she stared at herself in the mirror again. She lifted up her pajama top and looked at her stomach from all angles, as if she was trying to detect some abnormality. After about a minute, she sat down on the cool toilet seat and hugged her stomach gently. She would spend the whole day crying and hating herself for being so careless. For the last five months, Camille was preparing for a trip to nowhere.

When the morning came, all the Jenkinses gathered around the breakfast table. They sat around, talking and laughing about what it was going to be like for Camille in the military.

"Camille, gon' cause trouble for herself, watch," said Cynthia. "The minute they tell her to do something she don't want to do. Watch what I tell you, Mama. That girl ain't gon' be in there long. They gon' kick her butt out."

"You don't know how long I'm going to be in there. I know how to follow orders," Camille said, turning her nose up and rolling her eyes at Cynthia. "It's better than sitting around here doing nothing, hanging out all the time. May as well get paid for doing nothing."

"We'll see. You know you mad at the world, girl."

"It's not hard in the military," Chester said, glancing over at Camille.

"Leave Camille alone. She'll be fine," said Ms. Jenkins. Tears surfaced in Camille's eyes and rolled down into her plate of eggs and bacon. She messed up a good breakfast.

"Girl, what you crying for? You know we just playing with you. We gon' write."

"Write! Who said anything about writing? You don't know what's wrong with me." Camille looked at the breakfast table like she wanted to tip it over. "Sometimes I wonder about you, Cynthia, like which boat you got off of."

138

Camille's Dilemma

"You two cut that out. You'll be just fine, Camille," Ms. Jenkins said.

But everything wasn't fine. Camille wiped the tears away and sat there thinking about how her plans had been ruined by a second of carelessness. Thinking, how could she have been so irresponsible? Even called herself a stupid bitch for what she did. "Why is this happening?" she asked herself. Camille sat there and badgered herself nonstop. Then she looked up, and her mama, Cynthia, Chester, and Clifford were looking at her like she lost her mind. She didn't realize she was babbling out loud.

"Why are y'all staring at me?" Camille asked, bucking her eyes at them.

"Girl, you all right?" Cynthia said, looking distinctly at Camille. "You lost in space, ain't you? We're sitting here talking to you, and you talking to you. Why you call yourself a bitch?"

"All right. I'm not gon' have that type of language in my house," Ms. Jenkins said.

"What did you say?" Camille asked, frowning up at Cynthia. "And when do you plan on calling people by their names? You're not the only one that has one, Cynthia! Call me a girl one more time, and I'm gon' kick your ass!" Everybody at the table became speechless, surprised at Camille's demeanor. She pushed her plate into the middle of the table and turned to go downstairs, leaving Cynthia a nervous wreck, because Cynthia pointed her finger that was shaking uncontrollably at Camille as she was going down the stairs.

139

D.C. Johnson

She said in a low tone, "Mama, there's something wrong with her. You see how she acting."

"Leave her alone. She's probably just a little nervous about leaving."

For the rest of the day, Camille stayed in her room. It was supposed to be the day she said goodbye to all her new friends. But she didn't. She didn't even want to see Corrine. She told her family to tell Corrine she had already left if she came by. Camille took turns looking at TV, listening to her music, and staring at herself and her stomach in the mirror till eleven o'clock that night. She tried to sleep but tossed and turned for three hours. She'd get up, glance out the window, say, "I still have four days before my period comes," use the bathroom, and then hate herself until she fell asleep. She had only been asleep five solid hours when her alarm clock woke her up.

She woke up with the same temperament she went to sleep with. She didn't come out her room until it was almost time for her to leave on her trip to nowhere. After taking her bath and putting on her clothes, she came up from the basement carrying a small, brown suitcase she had bought with her last paycheck from the restaurant. A small, empty, brown suitcase. She didn't even put a clean pair of drawers in it, nothing. All she planned to take with her was her Chap Stick. She sat her empty suitcase down next to her at the breakfast table. Everybody at the table talked but Camille, and most of the time they were talking to her or about her. She just looked at them like they were strangers.

140

Camille's Dilemma

A few minutes later, the doorbell rang. They all looked at Camille and smiled. Camille still had a blank look on her face. She didn't even say hi to the army man that came to pick her up. I guess she was really depressed. Cynthia and the rest of the family said, "Bye, Camille," while walking her and her small, empty suitcase out of the front door.

There was a winter green and white army vehicle waiting for her. Camille turned around before she got in the army car and said, "I'll be back tomorrow." Everybody, even the army man looked baffled at Camille.

The army man asked Camille if she was okay, and she answered with a tiny smile. Camille knew she wasn't going to make it on that plane. While riding to nowhere, all she could do was go over and over in her head everything that happened that day. Etta's cousin had come into the restaurant she was working at. She spent her break talking about how she used to hang out over there and the senior prom he escorted her to. She ended up going by his place after work, and one thing led to another. Camille thought there was no way she could be pregnant from that. Felt she had to have set a world's record. No sooner had the thing went in, it came right out. She tried hard to think positive, telling herself she was just jumping to conclusions.

After a twenty-five-minute ride in silence, they arrived at a hotel packed with military personnel and soldiers-to-be. The soldiers-to-be were all sitting around waiting to take their final physical exam. Then they would be given orders and shipped out that morning. The same would be done for the soldiers coming in today, like Camille. She wouldn't actually be leaving until tomorrow, after her final exam. I guess it was the army's way of making sure they didn't go AWOL.

Camille end up spending the whole day alone in the room assigned to her.

The next morning, the smell of bacon and eggs woke Camille up. A scent that would normally have her racing upstairs for breakfast had her racing to the bathroom to throw up.

After she got dressed, she picked up her empty suitcase and went down to the cafeteria. It would be another hour before she took her final exam. So she nibbled on a piece of bacon, drank her some orange juice, and waited patiently.

She was given an eye exam, hearing exam, and a running-in-place test. Then they gave her a little transparent cup to urinate in. Camille tried to pee negative into the plastic cup. Afterwards, she held the cup up to her face and stared into it, conducting her own examination. It appeared to be a little lighter in color, not as yellow as usual. I guess she was looking for some little, tiny things to be crawling around in it, I don't know. Then she smelled it. It smelled different, not as strong as regular pee. It was real warm to her touch. Somebody was in there. Reluctantly, she placed the cup on the countertop and watched it until the nurse came and took it away. She then sat until her name was called.

One hour later, the nurse confirmed what Camille had feared, that she was going to be a mother. Camille poured down crying. The nurse felt her disappointment and offered words of encouragement. She patted Camille on the back and said, "You have plenty of time."

Camille's Dilemma

Camille turned to walk away, and the nurse called her back. "You need to sign these discharge papers." As Camille signed the papers, her tears smeared her name.

Camille didn't go straight home. She went to a restaurant to think. She sat there in a daze trying to figure out where do she go from here. Camille needed a plan. Before she left that restaurant, she needed to know everything was going to be all right.

"What can I get you?" the waitress asked, standing over Camille, popping her gum like no tomorrow.

"I'll have a cup of tea," Camille said, looking up with a sad smile.

"Will that be all, honey?"

"Yes."

As Camille sipped on her tea, she thought of the simplest plan there was: wait a few years then try again.

Camille rang the doorbell, and Cynthia opened the door with a stunned look on her face.

"Ooh...Mama, Camille's at the door. Girl, what are you doing here? You supposed to be in the army. Ma, Camille's back," Cynthia shouted up the stairs.

"Cynthia, please, you are a trip. Get a life. I told you yesterday that I'd be back. You should have believed me."

"So you was playing all that time? Girl, that wasn't no real army man?"

"What the hell did Mama eat when she was pregnant with you?" Camille said, looking at Cynthia, shaking her head.

143

"What happened?" Ms. Jenkins asked, galloping down the stairs. "Did they get the days mixed up?"

"No. I'm pregnant."

"Pregnant! How did that happen?"

Camille stared at her mother like she would do Cynthia when Cynthia asked something that was self-explanatory.

"I ain't raising no more babies. You and Cynthia on your own," Ms. Jenkins said, after learning Cynthia was five months pregnant. She turned around to go back upstairs. Ms. Jenkins' reaction was just as Camille expected. She didn't think her mama would throw a fit or demand that she'd get higher education before becoming a mother. Everybody in the Jenkins family just looked forward to being kin to the unborn.

Camille waited three months before she told her friends she was pregnant. Boy, Sabrina and Maxine were mad at her when she told them she was going to have a baby. They acted like she had committed a crime. Corrine, she was happy. She knew Camille wasn't going anywhere too soon.

Maxine said, "I don't understand, Camille, how you let him do it. I thought you said you were gay!"

"It just happened, Maxine. I didn't know being gay entailed hating men because I don't!" Camille retorted. "And I did want a kid. My timing might be off, but I did want someday to have a kid."

"Ugh!" Maxine sighed.

"Leave her alone, Maxine. The girl can't help it if she got hot," Sabrina said tartly, looking at Camille from the corner of her eyes.

Camille's Dilemma

"It happened! You two make it seem like it's the worst thing in the world. How the hell do you think you two got here? Damn, give me a break."

"Are you still gay?" Maxine asked, with the *TV Guide* up to her face.

"Am I still gay?" Camille shook her head, not believing the way they were acting. She was being scolded for doing something she chose to do. Camille didn't want to lose them as friends. But if they continued to bash her, she knew she would.

Sabrina read the look on Camille's face and said, "Okay. We just thought you were interested in women."

"I am. Look, I had a reason for doing what I did. And I am not ashamed of what I did. I had to make sure I was making the right choice. If I weren't still interested in women, I wouldn't be here. Should I leave?"

"Naw, naw, we still your friends. You're still cute," Sabrina said, hugging Camille. "Just don't do it again."

"I don't know, Sabrina. She did it once, she might do it again," Maxine expressed, turning up her nose, looking deeper into the *TV Guide*.

"I came over here because I could use a friend." The sensitive side of Camille emerged, and she started to cry. "I am not ready to become a mother," she cried out and left.

Camille went home and called Corrine. She was there in a flat second.

"Pregnant! Damn, man, by who?"

145

D.C. Johnson

"A man could hardly be pregnant, Corrine."

"You know what I'm saying. I'm glad, man! Man, I got my ace boom back," Corrine said, jovial, hugging Camille. "You ain't getting your radio back though."

"I don't want that radio back. I'm mad at myself, Corrine. Damn. Just think, I could have been long gone, preparing for a future. I really wanted to become an undertaker."

"That's right. You did set your goal to be feeling on dead people. Man, that's some freaky stuff. You'll never see me standing over no dead ass, digging in they face," she said chuckling, puffing on her cigarette.

"You don't be digging in nobody's face, silly."

Corrine knew how to cheer Camille up. Camille was almost glad she didn't leave.

"Man, I'm just glad you ain't going away," Corrine said, relieved. "So whose is it?"

Camille just looked at Corrine and said, "That's not important."

"Man, I'm getting ready to run some errands; do you wanna ride with me?"

"Naw. I need to find me a job. I'm not going to end up on welfare. I'm going to see if they'll hire me back at the restaurant, or somewhere."

A few months later and Camille's stomach started to feel as if air was being blown into it daily. She knew she wasn't going to enjoy being pregnant. It was already getting in the way of things. Her itinerary had changed from doing whatever she wanted to do, to what

146

Camille's Dilemma

she needed to do. She walked seven blocks to the store at least twice a week for a hoagie sandwich and a jar of olives. That's what her unborn craved for: olives and hoagie sandwiches.

A couple more months later and Camille got up to use the bathroom. Her rear end was hurting something terrible. She used the bathroom then went upstairs to alert her mama, who was getting ready for work.

"Mama, I don't feel good," Camille said, rubbing her lower back.

"What's wrong with you?" Ms. Jenkins was applying makeup to her face in the bathroom.

"I don't know! I feel like I'm getting ready to have this baby. I keep peeing and won't stop."

"You still have a while to go. You'll be all right."

Ms. Jenkins kept on getting ready for work. Camille went back downstairs to change her underclothes and to pee again. She was a week into her seventh month of pregnancy. She knew something was wrong. She went back upstairs to finish watching her mother get ready for work. She sat on the top step and watched her until she went out the door. Then she got up to go pee some more and to change her underclothes again. The pee was coming faster. She felt a real sharp pain in her bottom. After feeling another sharp pain, Camille called Etta's mother.

"Miss Riley, it's something wrong with me," Camille said, breathing heavy.

"What's wrong, baby?"

"I'm peeing, and it won't stop!"

147

"Where is your mother?"

"She just went to work."

"Get your clothes on 'cause you're getting ready to have a baby. I'm on my way."

Etta's mother worked at the county hospital in the maternity ward. She knew Camille had gone into premature labor. Thirteen hours later, Calvin was born, and Camille was a mother.

For the first two years, Camille pretty much stayed to herself. She would go to work and come straight home. Sometimes, Corrine visited. But she gave all her time and attention to Calvin. Somehow that wasn't enough. Her heart felt empty, like she needed some love in her life. She went back to visiting Maxine and Sabrina.

"What's up, mama? How's the baby?" Sabrina asked, swishing around the house.

"Calvin, he's fine. Are you guys going out tonight?"

"Why? Are you thinking about hanging? Yeah, we going out."

"Where are you guys going?"

"Same place we always go. Maxine, get up!" Sabrina shouted from the living room. "She's been laying around all day," she said, snatching a pillow up from the couch and giving it a few taps to the side.

"Hey, what's up, Camille? Long time no see. Sabrina can't wait to go out so she can shake her ass!" Maxine said, dragging herself in a sheet to the bathroom.

"Nothing. I'm just tired of being in the house."

Camille's Dilemma

"Come on and go out with us. Come on and check out the set," Sabrina said, dancing in front of Camille, rubbing up on her. "You might meet somebody. Just don't tell them you got a two-year-old baby. It's about time you get turned out. Too bad I can't be the one to do it," she said under her breath.

Later that evening, Camille put on a new pair of jeans, a white blouse, and a black leather vest. Summer had turned into fall, and it was a little nippy out. She combed her hair back into a ponytail and slipped on her black dress shoes. She then stuffed her ID into her back pocket. Her Chap Stick and money went into her front pockets. Cynthia was so crazy about being a mother and aunt that she didn't have to worry about a babysitter. By now, the whole neighborhood knew Maxine and Sabrina were gay lovers and that Camille had an interest.

"Going to hang out with your dyke friends?" a voice from the porch next door said as Camille was walking out of the gate.

"She's confused; don't forget, she just had a baby," another one said.

"Dyke!" another shouted.

Camille ignored them and went on her merry gay way. The only reason it bothered her was because Cynthia would sit over there with them and allow them to talk about her.

"It's packed tonight," Sabrina said as soon as they walked in the club, and just as quickly she said, "Maxine, I'll be right back."

149

"That goddamn Sabrina! She makes me sick when we go out! Her ass going right to the bathroom to see who she can see! Let's dance, Camille," Maxine said, pissed at Sabrina.

"Shouldn't we find seats…first," Camille said, being pulled to the dance floor. Michael Jackson's "Billie Jean" was playing. Camille got on the dance floor with Maxine and started dancing away, unaware that every now and then she was throwing in some of Michael Jackson's moves. She turned her back to Maxine and was jamming away. She then looked around, and people were kind of looking at her strange. She turned back around, and Maxine had stopped dancing. She stood gawking at Camille with her hand over her mouth laughing. "Why did you stop dancing?" Camille asked her, still dancing away. Maxine shook her head and started dancing again. Then a slow record came on called "Calling On All Girls" by a group named Switch. Maxine didn't ask; she just grabbed Camille around the waist, and they started slow dancing. There was a message in Maxine's dance. Camille felt it while they were dancing. So, she listened to the words of the song. At this point, Switch said, "Won't you take my heart today?"

Camille couldn't explain what she was feeling. She didn't know whether to take it personal or whether Maxine was just into the song.

Maxine pulled Camille in closer.

"Damn, y'all was mighty close!" Sabrina said, slightly turning up her nose at them.

Maxine, Sabrina, and Camille looked around for some seats. They found some at the bar. As they waited for the bartender to take their orders, Camille glanced around the room. She couldn't believe how many beautiful women were gay. Camille was excited but tried not to let it show. She was looking at all these beautiful women, looking to pick one with a sharp edge, meaning she had to possess a sharp mental keenness. I guess like some straight people, she was expecting to see a lot of women looking like men. There were a few, but even the few that did look like men were nice looking.

The waitress made her way down to where they were sitting and asked for their orders. After Camille ordered a rum and Coke, she sized her up, too. She was short and petite. Her soft brown outfit matched her complexion. She had the look, so it puzzled Camille why she needed to expose her cleavage, not that Camille didn't want to clap. The waitress caught Camille in wonderment about her breasts and gave her a look that said, "Little girl, please." Camille looked away and toward the dance floor, while Maxine and Sabrina ordered beers.

"You see somebody you may be interested in?" Maxine asked Camille.

"I think she's cute," Camille said, nodding her head in the direction of a tall, medium-built woman standing alone.

"She's a stud, Camille," Maxine said, shocked that Camille found the woman attractive.

"I'm not supposed to be attracted to studs?"

"I mean, yeah. It's just you have a little stud in you. I thought you'd be attracted to fems," Maxine stated.

151

"I'm attracted to women," Camille responded, staring back and forth at Maxine and Sabrina.

"What about her, Camille?" Sabrina asked, nodding her head in the direction of a woman who was right up Camille's alley. She instantly reminded Camille of Mrs. Sullivan.

"Sabrina, you probably like her yourself! Take your ass on over there and talk to her. You want to dance again, Camille?" Maxine asked, nearly snatching Camille off the barstool. Rick James' "Super Freak" was playing. "Don't get out here doing no Michael Jackson," Maxine said, giggling and leading Camille to the dance floor. While they were dancing, Camille spotted a woman that nearly blinded her sight.

"Damn, Camille, who you looking at like that?" Maxine turned around to look. She turned back around and said, "Oh, I know who you're looking at. She's real light skinned, isn't she?"

Camille shook her head yes, still looking over at the woman.

"That's Penny. She's got it going on. But you can forget about her."

"Why?" Camille asked, moving in closer to Maxine.

"She don't date nothing but studs."

"I'm a stud," Camille said.

"Studs with money and nice cars." The record was going off. Maxine grabbed Camille's hand, and they went back to the bar.

By the time Maxine and Camille ordered seconds, Sabrina was on her third drink. By the time they left, Maxine and Camille just about had to carry Sabrina to the car. I don't have to tell you where Sabrina

152

Camille's Dilemma

went once they got her inside the house. She went where we've all gone at least once if we had too much to drink: She sat on the bathroom floor and hugged the toilet like it was a special present. Maxine and Camille couldn't do nothing but laugh.

"Who y'all...laughing at? Don't be laughing at me...blurp."

They frowned as Sabrina filled the toilet with sour liquor.

"I told you about drinking so much, Sabrina. You better quit trying to hang with Six Pack. She's used to it."

"Get me a cold towel," Sabrina said, looking dazed into the toilet. After putting Sabrina to bed, Maxine and Camille stayed up and talked. Maxine went to turn on the radio, and Camille headed for the couch.

"You want something to drink or nibble on?" Maxine asked Camille, kicking off her shoes.

"What do you have to nibble on?"

"There's a bag of something back there. Sabrina always buys junk when she goes grocery shopping."

"Yeah, well, I'll have some junk and a cola if you have one."

"Ah, that's my cut playing," Maxine expressed with a smooth groove, handing Camille a can of grape pop, sinking herself into the music.

"Who is that, Maxine?"

"That's Teena Marie, 'Out on a Limb.'" Maxine went to the stereo and turned it up, not too loud. She sure didn't want to wake Sabrina. Then she waltzed to the music. Maxine had a candid look on her face.

153

She motioned for Camille to dance with her by holding out her hand. Teena Marie began singing.

"Tender was the kiss when you held me captive in your sweet embrace."

Camille took the dance and words of the song personal this time.

Maxine and Camille quietly slow danced until the record ended. Maxine then said, sitting in the loveseat, "Camille, I want to ask you something, and I hope you'll be honest in answering."

"What's that?"

"Are you attracted to me?"

"Of course, I am."

"Sabrina? Are you attracted to her?"

"I am. I'm attracted to both of you." Maxine crossed one leg over the other.

"You know you were hot on the set tonight. There's going to be a lot of studs coming your way. One thing's for sure: You won't have a problem getting somebody, whatever it is you're looking for. What are you, Camille? I'm just confused. Sometimes you're fishy, and then you turn around and call the shots."

Camille smiled because she did notice that a lot more studs looked her way. "I never really gave it much thought."

"You know, Camille, sooner or later you're going to have to make a choice. Just about everybody plays a role."

"Why can't I just be me? I'm not into role-playing. If I see something I like, I'm going to go after it. I'm not afraid of rejection." Camille got up and walked over to where Maxine was. She reached out for her hand. Maxine gave it to her, and Camille led her into her spare bedroom.

Lord, would you look at what's going on here. There's some things happening that Ole Louise ain't ever seen before. I almost napped right through this. Well, since it don't include me, I reckon I'd close my eyes till they through.

Now, Camille couldn't look Sabrina in her face knowing she done slept with Maxine. She started feeling guilty 'bout it. So she decided to put her guilt at ease. She watched out her window until Maxine left home. Then Camille went over to they house. She rang the bell with her plan in her hand. I know it was sitting in her hands 'cause she was nervous, and she kept rubbing her hands together till Sabrina answered the door. When she did, Camille put on her smile.

"Hey, Sabrina. I just thought I'd come get on y'all nerves early today."

"We've been up a while. Maxine just left for work a little while ago."

Camille walked over to the couch and sat down. "What do you guys have planned for today?" she asked, looking around, hoping Six Pack wasn't there. She would show up at a drop of a dime.

"Not much. We were invited to a wedding tomorrow, but I doubt if we go. To tell the truth, Maxine don't want to go. You want a cup of coffee, Camille? I was making me a cup when you rang the bell."

"Sure. You know, you guys turned me into a coffee 'holic." Camille watched Sabrina walk into the kitchen. She was wearing her baby blue silk robe with a royal blue towel wrapped around her head.

155

Camille figured she had just gotten out of the shower by the way her robe clung to her, leaving a few damp spots.

Sabrina then shouted from the kitchen, "And when are you going to bring Calvin back over here? I know he's getting big. He's almost three, isn't he?"

"I'll bring him by later on today." Camille rose up from the couch, and a sharp pain struck her in her head. She shook it off and tiptoed into the kitchen. Sabrina turned around, and Camille was standing an inch away from her.

"Girl, you scared me." Camille put her forefinger to Sabrina's mouth, quieting her. She sat the coffee cup on the counter. She then led her into the bedroom she shared with Maxine. She began making love to her the way Maxine made it to her. Camille smiled and closed her eyes to give Sabrina a last kiss when something in her head went POW!

"No!" Camille screamed, opening her eyes that were now staring in shock at Sabrina.

"Camille, what's wrong?" Sabrina said, grabbing her hands.

Camille just stared at Sabrina. "I've got to go." Camille jumped up, put her clothes on, and left.

Camille's Dilemma

Love

It will tell your heart what to say

It will flutter any time of the day

It comes in all colors

Like a rainbow above

Temptations to call you're in love

With every touch your heart measures

Excited by the kindest pleasures

Every day growing closer at heart

Not thinking it could fall apart

If this happens hold on tight

A slip of a finger and it cuts like a knife

Camille Jenkins

158

Chapter 10

To the Bone

Two months had passed, and Camille still hadn't been back to see Maxine and Sabrina. She used the time to look for another job. She was tired of working at that restaurant making minimum wages. She felt she worked too hard for the little tips she would receive. She found herself a full-time job at one of them big companies in downtown Chicago. It was near what folks called the Magnificent Mile.

After a few months, she bought herself a car. Was ready to move out on her own, too. Now, I knew Camille wasn't as happy as she led folks to believe. Even Corrine didn't know Camille was on the brink. Them folks at her job talked about her behind her back. You would think Camille would be able to sweep nonsense under the rug. She couldn't, held it all inside. Sometimes when she left work there'd be a note on her car. It would say, "DYKE," or sometimes it would say

"LESBIAN." Sometimes they wouldn't wait till her back was turned before they talk about her. Do it right in her face. I don't think Camille knew when to be discreet. I don't think she realized that some of the things she did, woman just didn't do for other woman. It was like most things she said and did were in the moment. She felt people should act accordingly. Therefore, she did what was comfortable and felt natural to her. I guess she was about tired of living up to society's standards. She was ready to come out of that closet and stand tall. She wanted to share in the world, too. Figured if she had to put on an act for people, she may as well become an actress and get paid for being somebody she wasn't.

Anyway, she acted accordingly by letting all the women get on the bus before she got on. If one got on after her and didn't have a seat, she'd get up and give her seat to the standing woman. Yes, she would. She opened doors for them, picked something up if they dropped it, even helped old women and some old men, too, carry they bags home from the grocery store. I guess she was just being a gentlewoman. She wasn't trying to get no attention. Attention was just drawn to her 'cause she was different.

She did make friends with one person. Her name was Denise. Denise didn't care what people was whispering 'bout. She thought Camille was a nice person and didn't mind being her friend. Camille kept her laughing. Camille didn't talk and criticize people; it's just the way she said things that made Denise and most people laugh. Denise told Camille she fit right in with people in the country.

Camille's Dilemma

Camille would be waiting on the weekend to come so she could be with people like her. I tell you, the older you get, the more you want to sleep. I'm getting a little sleepy here. Forgive me if I fall asleep in the middle of my sentence. Camille, she went out to the bars with her brother Chester now since she didn't have Maxine and Sabrina to go out with anymore. He always asked Camille to braid his hair in them French braids before they go out. She knew she love Chester; she never told him, but she did. They…went out…to this big club…ZZzzzzzzzzzzzzzzzzzzzzzz…Sorry, I done dozed off. I haven't been feeling well lately. What was I saying? Think I was talking 'bout that club they go to. Where on one side it was all women and the other, all men. Camille never talked to anybody, just sat and stared at folks. She'd go from one side to the other watching people. Smiled when she spotted Chester having his fun. She sipped on the same drink all night as she waited for Chester to finish having his fun. Then they leave. He told Camille she needs to be more sociable. Told her to get up and mingle with people if she expects to find somebody. She said, "I will."

Well, looks like Camille getting ready to have herself some company. Corrine rang her doorbell no sooner than she got home from work every day. She knew she love Camille. I reckon I'll let them talk. Bye.

"Man, why we don't hang out? I know some places we can go. What's going on with them two across the street?" Corrine said to me. "There's rumors going around somebody got shot over there."

"I don't go over there anymore, and they don't live there anymore," I responded.

"What happened? Did Maxine find out about you and Sabrina?"

"There was nothing to find out. It's not like it was a secret! They knew I was attracted to both of them. Maxine shot Sabrina. She didn't hurt her too bad. She shot her in the foot." I sat on my bed to remove my shoes.

"In the foot!" Corrine said, looking like she wanted to laugh. "What the hell she shoot her in the foot for?"

"I don't know why she shot her in the foot. She sure wasn't trying to hurt her if she aimed at her foot. Maybe she did tell her we slept together. I don't see why it would push her to the point to shoot her in the foot. Sabrina had to have done something else. Anyway, we're going to start hanging out."

"Man, I don't believe you kicked them to the curb. I wanted to meet them. They was cooler than a mug."

"How would you know? You hadn't even met them."

"It was like meeting them, hearing you talk about them all the time. I'm depressed now, man." Corrine started wiping her eyes like she was crying. "Can I fire this up?" she said, holding up a joint.

"You're not depressed. You're a reefer head."

"Man, forget you. So when are we going out? I'm tired of always hanging around all these straight people. They get on my nerves, paranoid asses. I hear they opened up a new club out south. Or what about that club you go to with your brother? Let's go there, Camille. You've been taught the ropes. What are we waiting on?"

Camille's Dilemma

Corrine and I started hanging out. Corrine with her Jeri Curls, shirts, ties, dress slacks, and boots looked every bit of a stud until she smiled. Then her feminine side would show. I'd wear jeans, a shirt, and my ponytail. With jeans on, I could pass for stud or fem. Corrine and I didn't really go out to pick up women. If we saw something we liked, we went for it; if not, we'd act like fools.

Corrine and I would sit at opposite ends of the bar. She'd be at one end smoking her cigarettes, sipping her Heinekens, and checking folks out. I'd be sipping on my drink making gestures with Corrine. Just thinking about some of the things we did made me laugh. If Corrine saw somebody she thought was a match for me, she would roll her eyes around to the direction of the person she wanted me to see. Sometimes the woman would be uglier than ugly. When I looked back down the bar at Corrine, she would be laughing. She pissed off many people at that bar, laughing. They didn't know what she was laughing at. One time, we wanted to see just how vulnerable women were. We looked around for someone willing to play our game. Three different women fell for our prank. We asked them if we could kiss them and then they tell us who kissed the best. It ended up being a tie.

If someone sat next to Corrine, and she didn't want them to, she would stare at them until they looked at her. Every time they turned to look at her, Corrine would look away. So all you would see is these two heads at one end of the bar moving back and forth, until the lady get up and leave in disgust, rolling her eyes at Corrine. Corrine also played her games without me knowing. She would sometimes tell folks she thought was interested in me that we were together,

163

obviously turning them away. I would go over to talk to somebody, and they would ask me, "Isn't that your girlfriend over there?"

Baffled, I asked, "Where?"

"Over there." They would point over at Corrine.

"Uh-um, she's a friend of mine."

"Yeah, right." The girl would disappear. I would walk away confused and back over by Corrine.

I'd see somebody else and would approach her. The same thing happened. Then this woman called me over to where she was and said, "I think your partner over there is messing things up for you. She's making people think y'all together. She stares at you and whomever you're talking to, like something's up. Maybe you need to put her ass in check."

I would immediately confront Corrine. "What are you doing?" Corrine would burst out laughing. "Don't be telling people we're together. Why are you doing that?"

"Man, let's get out of here. Ain't nobody in here tonight anyway," she'd say.

I would get excited when I did meet someone. I guess you can say I was a sucker for a pretty face because the next time I saw her, I would have roses for her. It would piss Corrine off. I had met four different women in three months' time. No, I didn't sleep with them. Well, not all of them. After a couple weeks, I always found something I didn't like about them and wouldn't talk to them anymore, which also pissed Corrine off.

"What's going on with Janice?" Corrine asked me.

Camille's Dilemma

"Janice? I didn't tell you? I don't talk to her anymore."

"Man, who the hell you think you is, Elvis?"

"Why do you say that?"

"Shiiit! The way you be dropping they ass...ole picky ass. Man, you wishy washy," Corrine said, shaking her head at me. "You know what?"

"What?" I said as she pierced me with her eyes. I walked over to my closet to look for something to change into.

"What you looking for...you ain't never gon' find it. Camille, you looking for a woman in a magazine. You ain't gon' find her out in no bar. Something ain't right with every last one of us. God didn't make no perfect people, Camille. You better stop being so damn picky. You be passing up some fine chicks, some cutie pies, Camille. Then you kick 'em to the curb 'cause they might have a run in their pantyhose. Man, what kind of shit is that? What's wrong with you?"

"I don't!"

"What! You don't," Corrine proclaimed, sitting backwards in her chair. "What was wrong with Janice, Camille? Tell me, why you kick Janice to the curb?"

"She thought she was cute!"

Corrine looked at me, slowly bobbing her head up and down. "She thought she was cute. Man, you're confused! Where the hell did you come from? She is cute, Camille!"

"So? I don't have time for somebody that's all up in the mirror. You're just looking at folks' looks. I saw selfishness in the woman."

165

"What about Marie? What was wrong with Marie? Shiiit...you could have given her ass to me."

"Marie was seeing somebody. She wanted to have her cake and eat it, too. I'm not trying to be no part-time lover."

"Rashonna, what was wrong with Rashonna?"

"She didn't want to work. She was lazy, and she begged too much. I don't care what she looked like," I said, still looking for something to change into. I couldn't make up my mind because Corrine was coming down on me.

"Man, you're a trip. You gon' keep falling on your face. You ain't perfect. You better learn to take the bitter with the sweet."

"I've been taking the bitter with the sweet all my life. I don't want anything bitter. It's time for a change. I'm in control of me. I don't want just anybody, Corrine. I'm tired of having the rug pulled out from under my feet. If I sense you're not the one, I'm moving on. I want to be loved, not fucked over!"

"Forget it, Camille, 'cause you getting all upset. And where in hell did you get that old-ass, black, granny-looking dress? Man, that look like one of my mama's dresses," she said, cracking up at it.

"This is your mama's dress."

"You three-dollar bill...man, shut up." She threw a beer cap at me then went over to my window, stuck her head out, and smoked her reefer.

I pulled some khaki pants from the hanger. As I changed into my khakis, I thought about our upcoming Christmas party.

166

Camille's Dilemma

"They're going to have a talent show at our Christmas party. I'm thinking about being in it."

"You gon' do Prince? I know you still be playing around with it."

"I'm thinking about it. Just a tad bit nervous. I haven't done it in front of anyone but you."

"I think you should do it. I wish I could be there," Corrine said, putting her half-smoked joint out. She then lit a cigarette.

"I think I can bring somebody. You would go?"

"Hell, yeah, I'll go. You my ace boom! Man, you think I'm gon' pass up a chance to see you act a fool."

"I don't be acting like no fool."

"Yes, you do. You crazy like him…falling all on the floor with his short self. He ain't but three feet tall."

"He's more than three feet tall."

"He's still short."

"You are always tripping, Corrine."

"So. Man, I'm getting ready to get out of here. You still gon' get your own place right?"

"Yeah, I'm waiting for the credit check to go through. I should be out of here in a couple of weeks."

"Yeah, well just make sure there's enough room in there for me to crash."

Camille was skeptical about doing her Prince act at her job. Didn't know how people were going to act toward her afterwards. And especially since there were rumors going around about her. Since it was something she liked doing, she went on and got in the talent show.

Camille and Corrine were sitting at a table with about six other people that come to see the show. Some worked there, some didn't. Anyway, everybody at Camille's table was watching the act already on stage. They were pretending to be Gladys Knight and the Pips. "On that midnight train to Georgia," they sang and danced on the stage. The coordinator of the show walked over to the table Camille was sitting at and whispered in her ear, "You're on in twenty minutes." She knew what act Camille was going to do. Nobody knew except her and Corrine that Camille was even going to be in the talent show. Camille headed to the dressing room.

When she heard her name being announced, Camille walked out on the stage just as Corrine was setting up her microphone and stand. People were startled to see Camille looking like Prince. Started whispering to one another. She had on her black, pleather pants; her white, ruffled blouse; her low-cut, black, leather boots; and her hair was all fixed up like his. That song "Darling Nikki" came on, and Camille started singing and acting. "I knew a girl name Nikki; I guess you can say she was a sex fiend." Camille had one hand wrapped around her head playing in her hair like he did in his movie, *Purple Rain*. People were excited; they were smiling and clapping when she was doing it. When it got near the end of the song, Camille slid across the stage singing, "Come back, Nikki, come back; your darling little Prince wants to grind." She got to grinding on the floor! You should have seen her. She moved the whole audience with Prince moves.

Camille's Dilemma

When she finished, they gave her a standing ovation then started chanting, "More."

Camille had already planned to give them more if they liked the first one. She gave the coordinator a cue to play her other song. It was called "The Beautiful Ones." She started out by cuddling her mike, singing into it. Then she took her microphone on a stroll with her and sang to a man in the audience, giving him the looks Prince gave. She sang to him, saying, "Oh baby, baby, baby, we'll get married, would that be cool," she asked him, backing up.

He, shaking his head, said, "Yes." Mesmerized by Camille.

She had that boy's moves down to the bone. They really enjoyed Camille's act. They talked about it for a week, teasing Camille when they saw her, saying, "Hey, Prince."

Trouble's brewing now because Camille's act has gone to the head of her friend at work, Denise. Denise, she started taking a different kind of liking to Camille. Started taking her home with her in thoughts. You know how people do when you like somebody. They instantly become a piece of your mind. Everywhere you go, they're with you in thought. Camille and Denise never talked on the telephone, only at work. Now Denise wanted to know Camille's phone number. Camille didn't think anything of it, so she gave it to her. Denise held on to it for a week before she called Camille.

"Hello."

"Hey, how you doing?" Denise asked.

"Who is this?" Camille asked, not recognizing the voice.

"Denise."

169

"Oh. Hey, I'm fine. What's going on?"

"Nothing, just thought I'd call and see what you're up to."

"Not much, playing Hot Wheels with Calvin." There was silence for a few seconds.

"Do you have plans for later on today?" Denise asked Camille.

"Actually I do. A friend and I are going out later."

"Well, I'm not going to hold you. You have a nice time. I'll see you Monday."

"All right, see you Monday."

Monday came and went. Tuesday, Camille put the icing on Denise's cake. See they play the lottery at work with this lady. She pays better than the real lottery. Camille had left work early Monday, because Calvin was sick. She gave Denise a few dollars and asked her to play her numbers for her. Denise did and Camille won. Won six hundred dollars. Denise called her at home and told her she won. When Camille went to work the next day, she was excited. The first person she saw was Denise. She was excited, too. Out of their excitement, Camille hugged Denise real tight. When she released her, Denise took a step back and stared at Camille. "What's wrong?" Camille asked Denise.

"Nothing," Denise said, still staring at Camille.

"Lunch is on me," Camille said, still excited about winning as she walked away to punch in for work.

Two weeks later and Denise wanted to know more about Camille's private life. She got real personal, too. Wanted to know

Camille's Dilemma

what two women do together. That question puzzled Camille, so she answered by saying, "I guess you have to get with one and see."

A week later, Denise asked if she could hang out with Camille the next time she goes out. Camille went home and told Corrine about Denise's curiosities.

"You better wake your ass up, Camille! Shiiit, she got a thing for you."

"No, she don't! Why you say that, Corrine?" Camille asked, sifting through her records. "Why can't she just be curious about the life? Don't forget that once upon a time we were. Isn't that what brought you over here in the first place?"

"She's curious all right—about you. And how you know I didn't have a thing for you back then?" Corrine caught Camille off guard. Camille quickly looked over at Corrine. Corrine looked firm at Camille as she took a pull from her cigarette.

"I did. I had a thing for you, straight up. I used to be crazy about you. I didn't tell you because I saw how you cherished friendships. They last a hell of a lot longer than a relationship. So I accepted what you offered, a friendship."

"If you're telling the truth, which I don't believe you are because you lie about everything, I'm glad you did accept a friendship."

"Yep, I did. That's why I trip sometimes when we go out. I used to get jealous. If I sensed somebody wasn't good for you, I run they ass away."

"Shut up lying. You only did that if you weren't talking to anybody. When I'm at the bar sipping alone, you don't be paying me no attention." They laughed.

"But really, I think you better keep your eyes open about Denise. And you say she wants to hang out with us. Man, I don't know. Didn't you say she was married!"

"What does that have to do with it?"

"Man, I don't care what you say, Camille. She's looking for a teacher, and she wants you to do just that, teach her."

"You're a trip. Sometimes I hate telling you things."

"So, it's true."

Instead of taking her to a bar, they took Denise to a house party they was invited to on Saturday. As soon as they walked into the party, Camille laid eyes on somebody. One thing about Camille, if she saw something she wanted, she went after it. "Catch y'all in a few," she said and vanished. Corrine and Denise chitchatted with one another until Corrine's attention was drawn away.

Alone, Denise sat in a chair drinking beer after beer and smoking cigarettes, smiling warmly at people as they passed. I guess she was drinking to keep herself company. Every now and then it looked like she was talking to herself. Camille would come back once in a while to see how her friend was doing, almost wishing she hadn't invited her.

"You okay?" Camille asked Denise, smiling.

"Oh, don't worry about me; I'm fine. Did you meet somebody?"

Camille's Dilemma

"Yeah, but she's giving me a hard time. It might take a while. You sure you're okay?"

"Yeah, it's a nice party. Go on back and talk to your friend; I'm fine." Camille could tell Denise looked a little wasted, but the woman was a lot older than she was. Who was Camille to tell her she thought she had had too much to drink?

"Would you go meet you somebody?" she said and fanned Camille away.

About an hour later, there was some shouting coming from the kitchen. Somebody was in there getting carried away, shouting, "I love her. But I love her. She knows I love her; gon' leave me here by myself." The people standing around were looking at the lady like she was crazy. Wondering what her old ass was doing at a party like that anyway. There wasn't a soul in there in they forties but her. Probably wasn't a soul over thirty in there.

Camille was in another room rapping, so she tuned out the pandemonium coming from the kitchen. By now, the person giving the party was getting tired of all the noise coming from her kitchen. She wanted to know who the lady came with because she didn't invite her. Corrine led her to Camille. She tapped Camille on her shoulder, interrupting her groove. With a cigarette hanging out the side of her mouth, she said, "You need to go in there and get your friend."

"Who?" Camille asked, looking concerned at her.

"That crazy ass drunk broad flipping out in my kitchen, that's who," she responded, pointing toward the kitchen with her thumb, looking intently at Camille.

173

"Denise?"

"Whatever the hell her name is! You need to go get her. She's in there shouting about she loooves somebody. Girlfriend is in there having a hard time. I don't like people disrupting my parties. You gon' have to go shut her up...or I'm gon' have to ask y'all to leave."

"Don't worry about it; I'll take care of it." Camille gave the woman she was talking to a midway smile then headed for the kitchen. She walked in the kitchen and almost didn't recognize Denise. Her wig was all twisted around her head. She was swaying from side to side bumping into people. The woman had wasted beer all down her blouse. And her pantyhose! They had rolled down to the bottom of her ankles! Corrine, standing in a corner, was laughing her head off at her. Denise didn't know it was Corrine laughing at her because she was way under the influence of the alcohol. She just knew somebody was laughing at her. Then, in slurred speech and vision, she said to Camille, "Why you don't love me? You know I love you. Why you think I came to this party with...you?"

Camille, still in shock, just stared at Denise when her drunken words came again.

"Huh, huh, Camille? Why you don't love me?"

"Denise, you just had too much to drink," Camille said, walking over to her.

"I...I...I ain't drunk. I'm looking right at chu."

"Come on, Denise." Camille held her hand out to her. Denise tried to get up from the chair and fell back down in it.

Camille's Dilemma

"No!" Denise said, all slumped over. "I want to know why you don't love me." Camille chuckled at Denise because she felt Denise was drunk and didn't know what she was saying. She grabbed Denise around her waist, lifting her up out of the chair. Denise threw her arms around Camille's neck. Then she tried to kiss Camille on her jaw. Camille let her as she dragged Denise to the door. Camille looked over at Corrine and motioned with her head to help. Corrine hesitated, but went and helped. Once they got her in the backseat of the car, Denise was transported home.

By the time they drove up in front of Denise's house, the alcohol had knocked her out. They had to shake her several times to get her up and out of the backseat. "It's a shame for a woman to drink herself down to the bone," Camille thought then asked Denise for her keys. Denise tried to pull her purse over her head and fell dead on her face. Corrine cracked up laughing and so did Camille. They didn't mean to. But you know that drunk people is silly. They finally got her inside. Camille put her to bed like a little child. Took her shoes off of her feet and rolled the covers up on her. She even put a cold towel on her back before she left.

Camille and Corrine drove the first couple minutes home in silence.

"Man, I can't help it," Corrine said, laughing. "Her pantyhose! Man, tell me this, how did they get rolled around her shoes?" She laughed some more. "Your girl was whacked. And her wig, the front was in the back man…man, how it get back there?" Corrine laughed some more. Camille tried to hold her laugh in while she drove.

175

"Corrine," Camille said, staring out at the road, "I didn't even recognize her when I walked in that kitchen."

"I know you didn't. I saw that look on your face. Man, she embarrassed you in front of that slim you was talking to," she said, shaking her head, still laughing.

"Corrine, stop laughing so I can drive. You're going to make me have an accident."

"Shiiit, Denise was the accident. Man, she drank damn near two six-packs. And that's not counting the carton of cigarettes she smoked."

"Now, you know she didn't smoke a carton of cigarettes."

"And all that crud on her lips. Man, her lipstick was peeling. I just want to know one thing, Camille. I know it's dark. Is it me, or was her house leaning?"

"Shut up, you know good and well her house wasn't leaning."

"Camille, why you run that red light? Don't be trying to crash and burn my ass."

"That light was yellow."

"But you know what?" Corrine said, getting real serious.

"What?"

"She was for real."

"She was drunk, Corrine."

"And she still is. She's in love with you, Camille," Corrine said, bobbing her head up and down with an unlit cigarette hanging out of her mouth. "What the hell did you do to her? She was losing it...I looove her," Corrine said, mocking Denise.

"I didn't do nothing to her."

Corrine then peered suspiciously at Camille. "You turned her out, didn't you?" she said.

"Be for real. And roll your window down before you light that cigarette."

"The hell you didn't turn her out. Why else would she be acting like that? Man, why you do that old drunk?"

"I didn't touch her. Corrine, don't be playing like that. You know good and well I didn't touch her. I would have told you if I did."

"Umf, I wouldn't have told you. I'd been too ashamed. But seriously, what you gon' do? She told me how she felt about you before she got drunk. You need to get her straight…'cause she's out there."

"What do you mean she's out there?" Camille asked, pulling up in front of Corrine's house. "Denise is not gay."

"She is now," Corrine responded and got out of the car with a serious look on her face.

Camille lay in her bed and wondered what she had done or said to Denise to make her act the way she acted. She decided Denise was just drunk. She went to sleep.

Camille and Denise continued to be friends. Denise called Camille the next day and apologized for embarrassing her at the party. Said she only acted crazy when she had too much to drink. So Camille blew off everything else.

Against Corrine's warning to stay away from Denise, they stopped one day after work to have a drink. Camille made sure that all they had was a drink. After the first one, she raised up to leave. Told Denise she was going to meet Corrine somewhere. While driving Denise home, Denise talked Camille into coming inside for a while. Said she and her husband was splitting up, and she needed someone to talk to. Talked about how he abused her. And how she really loved him but was afraid to leave. Camille took everything she said to heart.

When Camille walked in, she looked around and wondered if Denise's husband abused her with their furniture. She couldn't believe how messy it was.

"Excuse the house," Denise said.

Camille stood thinking, "Excuse the house! Excuse your ass! I've never seen a self-cleaning house." The last thing Camille wanted to do was have to use somebody's bathroom and have to scrunch up her face. She knew she was going to end up peeing on the floor or down her leg, trying to avoid touching they toilet.

Everything was fine the first hour. Camille wasn't good at giving advice so she listened as she sat in the orange rocking chair with her feet stretched out on the blue ottoman in front of it, looking at the brown walls. Denise babbled on about how her husband mistreated her. How she wanted to leave. How her teenaged kids only came around when he wasn't there. Then Denise raised up from the couch and headed toward the kitchen. As she passed Camille, she asked if she could get Camille something to drink. Before Camille could reply, Denise was sitting in her lap!

"Denise, what are you doing…get up," Camille said.

"Camille, Camille," she pleaded. "Just hear me out."

Camille's Dilemma

"I can hear you better if you get up, Denise."

"I'm going to get up...I just want to tell you something." In a spilt second, Denise had kissed Camille on the lips, disgusting her.

"No, Denise!" Camille shouted, grabbing both Denise's wrinkled up hands. "Why can't you just accept our friendship?"

"I can't. I tried. I'm in love with you, Camille!"

"No. No, you're not. Why? How?"

"It happened when you hugged me the day you won the lottery."

"What! Get off me! Get up, Denise." Denise went tumbling to the floor as Camille rapidly stood up. She placed her hands on her hips and stared despicably at her.

"One time, Camille, one time. Make love to me just one time." She didn't know it, but she had just sickened Camille to the bone. Camille looked agitated at Denise and grabbed her forehead.

"I'm sorry, Denise, but I am not attracted to you." Camille turned around to leave.

"I'll kill myself." She stopped Camille in her tracks with her words. Camille turned around and looked down at her.

"Nobody's worth taking your life for," she said then turned to leave.

"I swear, Camille! I'll kill myself."

"Do what you have to do." Camille kept on her way. She got in her car and drove several blocks before pulling over and praying that Denise didn't take her life.

Camille didn't go straight in the house when she got home. She sat out on her porch for a while to take in some of the night air and to

179

pray again that Denise was okay. She then noticed that her next-door neighbors kept playing the same record over and over again. It was called "Up On the Roof" by the Drifters. Camille tilted her head to the side to focus on the words of the song. She knew it had to be significant for somebody to play it over and over. They played it so much that by the time they finished, Camille knew the words to the song. She fell in love with it, too. She sat on her porch singing it over and over, gazing at the roof on top of a house across the street, until her neighbors didn't play it anymore. It just seemed to fit in with the night.

Camille went in the house and wrote a poem with Denise in mind.

How Deep Is Your Love
Is love so deep that there's no way out
You would die for me
Is love that strong it makes you weak
But strong enough to die for me
Is all that matters the thumps of your heart
Unbalanced love torn apart
Is love so deep you'll throw it away
Forever lost as you lay
Six feet deep, forever asleep
Unaware that you even died for me
Love can be deep, down to the bone
But never too deep

Camille's Dilemma

Where you'll give up your home
Self destruction, what a price to pay
You think God would accept your chosen way
No matter how deep I fall for you
I'll never submit to die for you too

Camille Jenkins

182

Chapter 11

Giving It the Best That I've Got

At work it was obvious that Denise and my friendship had ended. I would be in the lunchroom at one table eating and Denise at another. We both tried to ignore the people that stared at us from time to time, looking puzzled.

"Do you mind if I sit here?" an unfamiliar voice asked. I slowly looked up from reading my newspaper.

"No, go right ahead." I don't know why, but I quickly glanced over at Denise then back at my paper.

"I'm new here. I've been in training for the last three days. By the way, I'm Ann." She set her tray down then extended her hand to me.

"Camille. Welcome aboard," I replied, shaking her hand. "What department will you be working in?"

"I'll be in Mr. Townsend's department after today."

D.C. Johnson

"Really? I work in his department." I closed my newspaper then scooped up some mashed potatoes.

"How long have you been working here?" Ann asked, taking a seat.

"About a year too long."

"A year too long, how many years is that?"

"A year." We both laughed, attracting attention to the table. "Well, it's time for me to get back. Guess I'll see you tomorrow. Ann, right?" I said, smiling, and walked away. Before I could get back down to the third floor, Denise was at my heels.

"Guess you found a new friend. She's probably more your speed, dyke. I'm going to tell her 'bout your dyke ass," she huffed at me then got off the elevator. Fortunately, we didn't work in the same department, or there was sure to be some conflict. Denise worked on the main floor. She was what they called a Cage Operator. She made sure the work was being distributed to the right departments. That's how she and I became friends in the first place. I had to sign for the work she brought to my department.

The next day, Mr. Townsend introduced Ann to the department. "Everybody, I want you to meet Ann, Ann Joyner." Ann and I sort of smiled at each other when we made eye contact. I guess there's nothing like starting a new job and feeling like you already know somebody.

Ann was slim and hot chocolate brown, bowlegged, and impeccably attractive. I was instantly captivated, nearly melting in her beauty, which spilled out on the table into my plate yesterday.

Camille's Dilemma

"If you're not sure about something, Camille will be more than happy to help you out. Right, Camille?" Mr. Townsend said, looking over at me.

"Of course I will, Mr. Townsend." I was also the go-to person.

"You can take that terminal right next to her," he said pointing at the empty station. It's not like the job was complicated. All we did was transfer orders from the order form to the computer. Typing fifty words a minute was not a requirement. You just had to know the keyboard. We only dealt with a few fields and screens so there was little room for errors.

I saw the agility in Ann right away. I could tell she used good common sense because she worked three hours without having to ask me a question. The last couple of people they hired, well, I won't go there. I was just glad they finally hired somebody that could do the job.

I didn't invite Ann to lunch when I went; I just took off to the lunchroom.

"Girl, I looked up, and you was gone. You must have been hungry." She then said as I bit into a spicy chicken wing, "Look at you, you're already eating."

"I missed dinner last night. You didn't hear my stomach growling in there?"

"Girl, you so crazy. I hope there's something good to eat over there," she said, looking over at the buffet table and back into my plate of food. I don't know why, but Ann made me nervous. I was used to people shrinking away from the likes of me. I thought I'd give

185

her a few more days. I was sure somebody was going to try to corrupt her virgin thoughts. They did it before; they'll do it again.

Ann came back with an inviting meatloaf plate. I almost wished I had gotten the meatloaf plate instead of the chicken.

"At least the prices are reasonable. Two fifty for a meatloaf plate. I might just take one of these plates home," Ann mumbled as she sat down.

"Oh, just come in the door stealing." It took a minute, but she caught on.

"So you say you've been here a year too long. Is it that bad here?" she inquired as if she may have taken the wrong job.

"No, it's not that bad. Sometimes you're just better off minding your own business."

"Oh, it's like that here?" She then sliced into her meatloaf.

"Well, we all know every company has a Peyton Place."

"You can say that again," she said.

"Well, we all know every company has a Peyton Place."

"You're so crazy, Camille, repeating that. Do you have any kids?"

"A little boy, he's four years old." I ripped into another chicken wing.

"Yeah. I have a little boy who's four. His name is Michael. One six, Jermaine, and a daughter—"

"Let me guess, Latoya."

"Camille, you're so crazy. I didn't name my kids after no Jackson Five. You're funny. Her name is Ann, too. Michael was named after his father. What's your little boy's name?"

Camille's Dilemma

"Calvin. Calvin Dion Jenkins," I said, smiling as a picture of him popped into my mind.

"Is that his father's name?"

"Nope, that would be asshole."

She giggled. "You're so silly, Camille. I like you. I got a funny feeling we're going to be real good friends."

I didn't know what to say after that, but Denise did. She must have been over at that other table reading our lips. She brought herself over there, nearly slamming her tray down on the table. Ann and I both looked up bewildered at her. Denise looked unmercifully at Ann. Ann's look changed to "What the hell is wrong with you." Then Denise looked sternly at me. My expression changed to "Bitch has lost her mind."

"Camille, are you going to introduce me to your friend?" Denise said with indignation, looking harshly at me.

"Ann this is Denise, Denise, Ann." Denise picked her tray of food up and shoved it on the rack with the empty trays and stormed out of the lunchroom, leaving the talkers with more to talk about. I shook my head at her storming away.

"What was wrong with her? I'd hate to be her enemy."

"We used to eat lunch together."

"Oh, I didn't mean to come in between you two. I just saw you eating alone. I can eat at another table."

"I said we used to eat lunch together. And that case is closed."

Ann and I were becoming good friends. She introduced me to her three kids and her husband, Michael. I wasn't surprised that he was

187

just as good-looking as she was. I also felt that he leafed through me like a book and appeared to be content with his notions. Their home was warm and placid. A large, beautiful family portrait of them hung above a plant stand in their living room.

It was hard looking past beauty that dominates. Nevertheless, I enjoyed being Ann's friend on the weekends when I didn't go out with Corrine or if her husband had to work. Before Denise and I became friends, I had pretty much tuned the straight world out. I no longer was going to try to fit into a world that discriminated against me. So I pretty much kept to myself. Now that Denise and I were no longer friends, I looked to Ann for balance in staying afloat to what was going on in the straight world.

Ann and I would do things together with our kids. Go to the movies, parks, museums, fairs, carnivals, just hanging out enjoying some of the festivities life has to offer.

One weekend after Ann's husband left home for work, Calvin and Ann's kids went outside to play. Ann and I sat down in front of the couch to play backgammon.

"Camille, it's your turn. Why do you keep getting up, looking out the window? Girl, Calvin's fine. You don't have to worry about him over here."

"I got to keep an eye on my child," I said, sitting back down, rolling the dice.

"Somebody told me you put on a show at the Christmas party. Said you did Prince, and it was a real good impersonation. I wish I could have seen it. You still do it?"

Camille's Dilemma

"No." I moved one of my pieces five spaces and another one two. Ann then rolled the dice.

"I bet you were a trip. Camille, are you seeing somebody?" she asked, capturing one of my pieces and putting it on the bar.

"Damn, now I have to throw doubles," I said.

"Camille, you heard what I asked you. Are you?"

"No, Miss Ann. I haven't found that special someone yet."

"It's just hard to believe you don't have a girlfriend."

"A what?" I felt a rush that went "swoosh!" The six on the dice looked like a twelve.

"Let's talk. Michael already read you like a book to me. I had already put two and two together when Denise went off on you. I want to know why you don't have a girlfriend." I looked at Ann, surprised that she knew what she was talking about.

"'Cause I'm sick of women. I go out with my friend Corrine, just to get out the house. We go out to have fun. It's your roll."

"Are you going to start dating men?" I closed my eyes, tilted my head up, and held out my hands, palms up.

"I don't see that in my future. Now, will you roll the dice?"

"Were you ever going to tell me that you're gay, Camille?"

"It's your turn; roll the dice. You're messing up the flow in the game."

"I want to talk, Camille."

"Well, talk, Miss Ann," I said, batting my eyes and setting my dice cup on the bar in the middle of the backgammon board.

"Seriously, how long have you been gay?"

"As long as I can remember."

"Now, I'm going to really get in your business. Did you and Denise mess around? It's obvious something happened."

I threw one hand in the air as if to say, "Forget Denise." But I said, "Denise and I were good friends until she took our friendship personal. I wasn't attracted to her, and that's all I'm going to say about that, Miss Ann. Now, are you going to take your turn?"

"Are you attracted to me?" Ann asked, finally rolling the dice.

I thought for a moment before I answered her question. "What did Michael say?" I asked her.

"Oh, you're going to answer a question with a question. He said he thinks you're attracted to me, but it will pass because you want to be friends."

"What did you say he does for a living, a fortune teller? I was attracted to you, and yes, it did pass."

"Nothing personal, but if I was gay or even bisexual, I would probably test the water with you."

"You live by the water, you die by the water. You'd drown." I pretended not to be shocked by her admission.

"What do you mean, I'll drown?"

"It just wouldn't go anywhere, that's all. I don't date straight women."

"You don't date straight women. And why not?"

"I just don't."

"What's wrong with straight women?"

Camille's Dilemma

"Nothing, if it's your preference. What, you think just because a woman have desires for another woman that she would sleep with any woman?"

"No. But what's your reason for not wanting to sleep with a straight woman?"

I looked Ann in those lovely eyes of hers and said, "I'll give you my main reason. As far as most straight woman get is being bisexual. That means having to share them with their boyfriend or husband. It becomes complicated. They don't want to be labeled a lesbian, so they secretly love both. Do I look like someone that would live they life in a closet? For me, it's easier to love a born lesbian like myself."

Ann just shrugged her shoulders, I assumed in understanding. She then said, "I'm not trying to confuse you, but could we kiss? I just want to see what it feels like, Camille."

"Have you ever kissed your husband?" I picked up my backgammon cup. "That's what it feels like. Now, will you roll the dice?" Ann made me nervous asking if we could kiss. And as sexy as her lips were.

"Come on, Camille. You know it's not the same," she said, laying her hands on mine.

I shivered.

"I thought you said it passed."

Ann asked for it, and she got it. Only we took it farther than it should have gone. Afterwards, we vowed to never let it happen again. We knew this could possibly destroy her marriage and our friendship.

191

I said, "So, does this mean I can finish kicking your butt in backgammon, Denise?"

"Shit, I'm drained…Denise! Don't be calling me Denise. Whose roll is it?" Ann asked, rolling her eyes at me.

"Whose roll is it? Don't you think we should like…start the game over? Pieces are scattered all over the place." We laughed.

A few months later and Denise still couldn't accept the friendship that sparked between Ann and me and ended up quitting. Actually, I was a little hurt that Denise and my friendship ended.

Ann was now four months pregnant with her fourth child. I spoiled Ann rotten because I was going to be the godmother.

A few months after that and one cloudy morning, I woke up feeling miserable. My stomach, back, head, ass, every part of my body seemed to ache. I went on to work anyway. When I got there, I told Mr. Townsend that I might leave early because I wasn't feeling well. Jokingly he said, "Well, maybe you're feeling Ann's labor pains. Her mother called a little while ago; she's in labor."

On my break, I called Ann's house, and her mother said Ann had just delivered a baby boy. Eight pounds three ounces. It may sound strange, but all my pain went away after I hung up the phone. Ann named him Carlton Dion Joyner. Sounds a little like Calvin Dion Jenkins, doesn't it?

Not having Ann around at work, I started feeling like I needed a change. I was tired of going out. Maybe Corrine was right. I was looking for someone I would never find. I was still up to my old tricks. If I didn't like something, I'd end up leaving her alone.

Camille's Dilemma

"Corrine, I'm going to stop going out for a while," I said, lying in bed on my back, staring up at the ceiling.

"What's wrong with you now? Why you don't want to go out no more?"

"I'm tired of going out. I want to do something different."

"Like what, Camille? What do you want to do now?"

"I hate that goddamn company I work for!"

"What! Camille, who pissed you off?"

"Nobody. I'm just pissed off. I don't know why, so don't ask me why! But I do have something to tell you. I'm going into the military."

"What! Now, how long have you been contemplating on this shit again?" Corrine rose from the chair she was sitting in backwards, placed her hands on her hips, and stared at me. I rose and sat against the headboard and brought my knees up.

"It's not actually confirmed yet. I'm just ready to do something different. I can't sit still in the same place too long. It shouldn't be a total surprise. I told you I was going to re-enlist when Calvin got a little older. I feel now is a good time. Corrine, what have we been doing in the last few years? Nothing, just hanging out. It's time for me to make a move. I still have the desire to go, so I'm going."

"You sure Ann don't have nothing to do with this?" She sat back down shaking her head in incredulity.

"If I'm running from somebody, I'm running from me. I just feel lost, Corrine. I feel out of place."

D.C. Johnson

"Man, you fell in love with Ann, didn't you?" she said, cutting her eyes at me.

"No. Didn't I just say I'm sick of women!"

"Man, don't be hollering at me. Let's just go somewhere different. You probably just need a change of scenery."

"I don't want to stay here anymore! I've got to leave. Something is getting ready to happen, Corrine. I feel like I'm getting ready to crack up. Like my head's going to explode. I feel trapped. And I'm not asking you to understand me, either. Lately, something's been pinching at my nerves. I thought being in a relationship or caring about somebody would ease the tension. It hasn't. Maybe I just haven't found the right person. I probably never will until I find me. I just want to go away. I can't handle what's going to happen."

"What! Man, what are you talking about? You done touched on two, three subjects in one sentence. What are you trying to say? Before what happens, Camille?"

"Nothing."

"Nothing. Then why are you sitting over there talking crazy?"

"You don't understand. Don't nobody understand."

"Understand what!"

"Death! I'm talking about death."

"Death! Hold up, Camille." Corrine rose from the chair she was sitting in. "You're scaring me now. Man, what are you taking about, death? You're talking like you got psychic powers or something. What's up? Tell me something, or you gon' make me think you

194

Camille's Dilemma

cracking up for real." Corrine stood by my bedroom door with her eyes wide. "Tell me now, man, who getting ready to die?" she said.

"I don't know. Girl, don't listen to me. I'm just talking."

"Uh-umm, you're not just talking, 'cause people don't come off like you just did." She narrowed her eyes at me and said, "You probably do be seeing shit." Then she commenced to slowly bob her head up and down, like she was reminiscing about something.

"You knew my brother Bobby was gon' be in that car accident didn't you? That's why you insisted I didn't get in his car. I thought you were just tripping. You knew, didn't you?"

I shook my head confirming I did.

"You probably saved my life, 'cause Bobby damn near lost his." She lowered her eyes at me and said, "You knew Maxine was gon' shoot Sabrina, didn't you? That's why you stopped going over there. You knew, didn't you?"

I shrugged my shoulders.

"Damn, Camille. Man, that's some real heavy shit. I hope it ain't nobody in my family that getting ready to die."

"It's not. It doesn't happen all the time. It comes and it goes. I'm just fickle right now. Forget it, let's go on out tonight."

"Now you're talking," Corrine said, yet still peering at me.

195

196

Chapter 12

Sweetest Taboo

It appeared to be a full house, judging by the lack of parking spaces. Corrine and I circled around the bar three times before we found somewhere to park. It was about a half-foot from being in restriction of the fire hydrant. Lucky for me I had a small car.

It was definitely packed tonight, and time out for jokes because I laid eyes on a prize the minute we walked in. We were lucky to find seats. Corrine went to the bar to get drinks. While waiting, I looked around for the woman that I noticed coming into the place. She was sitting at a table by the dance floor with four other women. I watched for a while to see if she was with one of the women at the table. It was obvious after the next record that two of them at the table were a couple. They slow danced. My prize saw me looking her way, and we locked eyes for a couple seconds. A fast record came on. I hoped that she would look my way again. She did. I pantomimed, "Would you like to dance?" She nodded. Perfect timing; Corrine was just coming back with the drinks, so she could watch my seat while I danced.

Her name was April. After we danced, we stood by the dance floor and talked a while. Then we exchanged numbers. She went to sit back with her friends, and I rejoined Corrine. Occasionally we would look at one another and smile. We got one more dance in, which was a slow dance. There was no doubt which one was the dominant one. She followed my lead as we did some serious grinding and light conversing. I led her off the dance floor back to her table. I smiled and winked my eye at her as I headed back to my table.

"She's the one, Camille. I feel it," Corrine said, looking over at the table April was sitting at. "What's her name?"

"April."

"Camille and April," Corrine said, smiling and shaking her head up and down.

"You might be right, Corrine."

"I know I'm right. Now I'm the one with the psychic powers. Look, look, look over there," Corrine said, knocking knees with me. I looked over at the door to see who Corrine was getting all excited about. "Looks like my ship has just come in," she said, smiling.

Corrine went to the bar and had a drink sent over to the woman, who quickly found a seat. As the bartender took the lady's order, she looked over at our table. I looked away after I got a good look at her. She was ugly! Corrine nodded her head at the lady. The lady smiled. She looked to be in her late thirties if not early forties.

Camille's Dilemma

"I'm going over to talk to her. Pull that chair up just in case she comes over and sits with us," Corrine said, pointing to an empty chair a table over.

Corrine and the lady seemed to be hitting it off. I was glad we had came out tonight. I felt good. I sat and immersed myself in the enchanting music of Earth, Wind and Fire. Then I thought I'd see if April was really interested in me. After looking over at each other's table a couple of more times, I disappeared. I squeezed into a crowd by the entrance and watched for the next time April would look over at the table. I wanted to see her reaction when she looked over and didn't see me sitting there. When she did, a look came upon her face that said, "Where did she go that fast?" She scanned nearly the whole bar and then looked back over at the table. I got the impression that she thought I had left, because she turned her nose up slightly after not spotting me. She turned her attention to the people on the dance floor. I shot back over to the table I was sitting at. She turned to say something to one of her friends and noticed I was back at my table. She looked befuddled as I sat and admired the woman I would soon come to know. I sat and admired her antique brown skin and her dark-brown, shoulder-length, feather-cut hairstyle. I admired her rich, black eyebrows. Each eyebrow appeared to lie quietly beside the other. Her lips were painted a soft plum color. Every time I looked at her lips, mine puckered a little. Each smile was soft and gentle-hearted. April appeared to be about a size ten, which was right up my alley. I never found any comfort in bones. Some of the tricks I had up my sleeve might hurt a bony woman. Trust me, I found it to be true.

199

April looked to be about twenty-five, which would put us around the same age. Because I found April more attractive and intriguing than any other woman I'd met, I decided then that I wouldn't rush my bag of tricks. She was more than sex.

A few minutes later and I noticed that she and her friends were gathering up their belongings to leave. Before she could stand all the way up, I was standing behind her, holding her jacket up for her to put on. One of her friends smiled an "all right now" smile at me.

"You know you be moving," April said, blushing. "I didn't even see you walk over here."

I smiled, winked my eye, and said, "Have a nice night."

For the next couple of weeks, Corrine and I were busy getting acquainted with our new love interests. I thought about Ann and gave her a call.

"Hey, how you doing? How's Carlton? And when do you plan on coming back to work? It's been a year."

"Hey, Camille. It hasn't been a year, but I might not come back."

"Run that by me again."

"You heard me; I said I might not come back. Michael wants me to quit. Plus, my mother won't be able to watch the kids anymore. She's going back to work. I still have two more weeks of maternity leave left. We're just going to weigh it out, see if we can make it off his income until the baby gets a little older. It will be both our decisions for me to quit. I'll let you know. And what have you been up to? You've only been by here twice to see the baby. Some godmother you are."

200

Camille's Dilemma

"I went to take a blood test to make sure Carlton wasn't mine."

"You so crazy."

I then said jovially, "I met somebody, Ann."

"Did you, Camille? What's her name? I'm so happy for you."

I told Ann all about April.

"Sounds like you hit the jackpot. The next time you visit Carlton, your godson," she stated with emphasis, "bring your friend with you. I want to meet her. I have to make sure she's all you said she is, or I might have to dismiss Miss Thing."

"Miss Thing. Where did you pick that up at? Miss Thing," I said, tickled at her language.

"Don't worry about it. She just better not be full of shit."

"Shucky, shucky now, go on with your bad self. Well, kiss Carlton for me. If you're not busy next weekend, give me a call. I'll come by. I have something for him. Talk to you later."

I guess you can say Corrine and I had really come out of the closet, because six months later and April had moved in with me, and Corrine had moved in with Elma. April had taken to Calvin like he was hers, and Calvin was crazy about April. She spoiled him rotten. Her family was crazy about him, too. Me, that was another story. Her mama wasn't fond of the lifestyle April had chosen to live. Especially after April had decided to move in with me. I got the impression she thought I played a role in her decision making.

I was glad April asked to move in with me, even though I wasn't sure if she did it because we had grown to love each other, or because she wanted to leave the nest to feel more independent. I would get mixed signals. After six months together, April still partied with her friends on the weekend, every weekend. I went sometimes. I was starting to grow out of partying all the time. So most of the time, April would go alone. I trusted her, so it didn't bother me that she went out without me.

After about a year, April made a habit of coming in the house at all times of the nights and mornings. She swore that she wasn't out messing around. I would believe her until I saw with my own eyes she might be lying.

Anyway, Corrine and Elma invited us over to play cards on a Friday night. It was the first time I had seen Corrine and Elma together since the night they met. Corrine and I would meet up sometimes and talk about our relationships. Corrine had fallen in love with Elma. Every time she spoke her name, she'd smile and glow. Corrine felt like she was the man because she had run Elma's husband away. Said her husband got so tired of her coming around, he told her and Elma while they were sitting around in the living room watching TV that the house was theirs. Said he walked right out the front door with a little, gray and black pinstripe suitcase. Said all Elma and her husband did was fight.

After introducing ourselves, we all sat at the dining room table. Corrine and I were card partners, and April and Elma were partners. April didn't know how to play bid whist, so we played spades. While Corrine dealt the cards, I got up to fix April and myself a drink.

202

Camille's Dilemma

As I dropped ice cubes in our glasses, I thought to myself, "Elma don't look that bad at all." I couldn't figure out what the bubble was on her neck, but she looked okay.

I returned with our drinks and sat April's down in front of her, giving her a quick smack on the neck. We all sat laughing and enjoying ourselves as we played spades. When it was Elma's turn to deal the cards, she took off her rosewood-colored jacket that was part of the two-piece skirt set she was wearing. Her rosewood jacket exposed a white, short-sleeved blouse. As she was dealing the cards, I noticed a lot of marks and scars on her arms. They weren't just scratches, nor simple bumps and bruises; they were of the keloid form. When all the cards were dealt, I put my hand in front of my face, shuffling the cards around into their respective suits. When I finally made eye contact with Corrine, I looked down over at Elma's arms and bucked my eyes a little. April shouted out, "Y'all cheating."

"We're not cheating," I said. "I was just getting ready to ask Corrine how many books she thinks she can make. How many books do you see, Corrine?" I said, rolling my eyes at April. I was not about to let April spoil this for me. It was payback time for Corrine. She had embarrassed me after I had introduced her to a woman that I met, and whom she apparently found unattractive. Corrine looked at me with the sad expression on her face that said, why. She then burst out laughing.

"Yeah, you got to watch them closely," Elma said, looking at me and then at Corrine. "I know Corrine cheats. She cheats when it's just us two playing."

203

D.C. Johnson

"Man, we not cheating," Corrine said, lighting a cigarette. "Camille, man, how many books you see?" she said, looking at me, about to sip from her drink.

I quickly looked over at Elma's arms and back at Corrine and shouted, "They dead, man."

Corrine spit her drink out across the table. She slowly moved back from the table then burst out laughing. She almost fell over trying to stand up. She laughed herself into the kitchen, bumping into the counter, into the refrigerator, and back into the dining room. I sat looking crazy at her like everybody else, trying hard to keep from laughing.

"What's wrong with Corrine, Camille?" April asked, laughing a little, tickled at the way Corrine was carrying on.

I knew all eyes were on Corrine, and Corrine was now looking at me. I couldn't help it. I quickly glanced back at Elma's arms and frowned up.

"Man, stop!" Corrine said, still laughing.

"What the fuck's going on?" Elma snapped, demanding to know. She then looked at me and turned up her nose. I assumed she knew it was a private joke. She got upset and said, "Corrine, I'll see you after your little silly ass friends leave. I don't have time for this shit, sure don't have time for y'all side shows." She went upstairs.

"Man, why you do that shit?" Corrine said, still laughing a little. "Look what you did."

204

"I didn't do nothing," I said as a chuckle escaped. "I guess this party is over." I rose from my seat, trying hard not to burst out laughing.

"Would somebody please tell me what's going on?" April said, still confused.

"Come on, baby, let's go. All I can say is, there's a whole lot of truth to 'what goes around, comes around.'"

"Man, you're not right," Corrine said, shaking her head at me. "How am I going to explain this shit to her?"

"What?" April said, stamping her feet.

I patted Corrine on the back. "You'll be all right."

I explained to April what the act was all about on the way home, and she just shook her head at our silliness.

Six months later and I was bitterly tired of April wanting to party all the time. I was giving this relationship the best that I had, and April was acting as if she was single. I couldn't understand her passion for wanting to go out every weekend. Everything seemed to be going good until Saturday came, then she wanted to run the street with her friends. I can't remember even having an argument with April with the exception of her staying out all the time. I didn't feel the sex was boring her, because most of the time when she'd come home from her late night out, she would initiate it. Her hanging out was beginning to wreck my nerves. The last person I should have talked to about my insecurities was Ann.

Deep down inside, I knew I loved Ann, too. But I couldn't have her unless it was a package deal. She spoke candidly to me about having a threesome with her husband. That was one boat I couldn't float in. Besides, I wanted to be with April. But nature has its way of making us temporarily forget about the ones we love. After Ann and I made love, I went home.

I stayed up until April came home, which was a little after three. I talked about her hanging out, and she talked about my attitude, which she said had stunk for the last month and how she didn't appreciate me walking around the house, ignoring her, the morning after she stayed out. She also said that lately I'd been calling out Chester's name in my sleep. She wanted to know what that was all about. Talking about our problems and succeeding with resolutions lasted all of three weeks. April was back hanging out, and I was still fighting the demons to come. I thought about just letting the relationship go. I even thought about taking Ann up on her offer. But it wasn't me. I knew what I was doing with Ann wasn't right, but April had left the door open for it to happen. Whether she was messing around or not, I decided to stop seeing Ann to recollect my thoughts about what I was going to do with April.

It was Labor Day. We had just come home from a barbecue at my mother's house. The smell of barbecue and music followed us home. Calvin was so worn out that by the time his head hit the pillow, he was knocked out. I took his clothes off and put him to bed funky. Then I ran some water in the tub for me to take a bath. I pulled my red and purple checkered pajamas out of the drawer and laid them on top of the toilet seat. I sat on the edge of the tub and squeezed a few drops of bubble bath into the water, swishing my finger around in it to increase the bubbles. April peeped into the bathroom and asked if she could join me. I told her I wanted to be alone. She knew things weren't well. As I soaked, I thought to myself, "This will be the night to tell her."

"April, we need to talk," I said as I lay across the bed with my crossword puzzle book.

"About what?"

"I'm leaving." I felt her eyes on me as she stopped shuffling through the drawer.

"You're leaving? What do you mean you're leaving? Where are you going?"

"Into the military."

"The military. Why do you want to go into the military? What about us?" she said, shutting the drawer with her baby blue, silk nightie in hand. The one she knew sends me up the wall when she puts it on.

"You can't be worrying about us? That's a laugh. Three letter word for a metered vehicle," I mumbled.

"You getting ready to start this again?" She came and sat down on the edge of the bed. "Look, is this about me hanging out? I got a right to hang out with my friends, Camille."

"It's not about you hanging out anymore. Cab." I wrote the letters C-A-B in then said, "It's about what I want. April, I told you what I was looking for when you decided to move in. If I wanted to sleep alone, I would be living alone. I know what you're going to say. You're not out there messing around. Regardless of what you're

207

doing out there, it's disrespectful. Plus, going into the military is a decision I made long before I met you. Since I have the free time on the weekends, I figured I'd get paid for my time. What we need is some time apart. I'm going in as a reservist. I'll be gone six months. You can stay here if you like. If not, I'll ask my brother Clifford to watch the place for me. It's about time he got out on his own anyway. Calvin is going to stay with Cynthia. I've already been to court; she has temporary custody of him now. Another word for untamed."

"That's what you went to court for the other day? I thought you went to pay a ticket. Damn, you had it all planned. I don't believe you, Camille. You just gon' up and leave, to hell with our relationship. Why can't you believe that I'm not out messing around? I love you, Camille. I'm in love with you." April walked over and lifted my chin up with her finger. I looked at her, and the word I was looking for quickly came to mind. "I would never mess around on you. I just like hanging out with my friends."

I penciled in the word *wild* then said, "April, I understand that you like hanging out with your friends. It's just not right. It's not like it's once or twice a month. It's every weekend. I don't like feeling lonely when I have somebody in my life. You don't understand how it makes me feel. Put your feet in my shoes. Would you want to sleep alone and you live with someone? You leave enough space in our bed for intruders. And believe me, they are out there waiting to fill the void."

"You would mess around on me, Camille? Have you messed around on me, Camille?"

Camille's Dilemma

I ignored her question. I wanted to leave her with something to think about.

She shook her head and disappointedly said, "Sounds like you really have your mind made up about this. I'm going to wait for you, Camille. And I'll keep Calvin if you want me to," she said, sitting down on the bed. "If I stop hanging out, will you stay? I don't want to lose you. I love you, Camille; I really do."

"It's too late; I leave in a month." Tears fell into my puzzle book and in her lap.

210

Chapter 13

Private Jenkins

"Left, left, your left, right, left," soldiers dressed in camouflage sang as they marched toward a sign that said "Mess Hall." They were all looking sharp, snappy, and distinct. "So this is Ft. Jackson. Didn't think I'd make it here." I knew for sure that the plane I came in on was going to fall right out of the lovely blue skies at any minute. I sat in that seat scared stiff the whole flight. Just terrified, afraid to move. It was my first time flying. I felt that if I looked left, the weight of the look would take the plane down left. If I looked right, the weight of the look would take the plane down right. It surely wasn't the plane I saw in the video. This was a red and white, dingy-looking, three-seat plane! I sat right behind the pilots, vowing to never fly again unless I grew wings.

"Reception Center," a sign read. I then thought, "It'll all be over in no time. Do my duty and collect my dues, which were college funds from Uncle Sam, and back to the Windy City I go."

"Wonder what's going on over there," I said as I watched a soldier do pushups in the middle of the street while a drill sergeant huffed and puffed over him.

"What are you looking at, Private?" someone shouted in my ear. "Aren't you supposed to be emptying your pockets, Private!" I wasn't even in uniform yet, and already I was being screamed at. I wondered where the hell he came from so quickly.

"You won't be needing that," he said as I pulled from my pocket a pack of Doublemint gum. "You may as well get used to bad breath!" I tossed my pack of gum into a barrel, thinking, "And you're living proof I'm going to have bad breath." I then glanced down into the barrel, and it was loaded with enough gum and candy to plaster a wall. I was then searched from head to toe and told to go wait on the bus sitting out in front of the building.

While waiting for others, I looked out of the window, wondering what was going on back home. I had never been apart from my child before. I was missing Calvin already. It was probably the distance between us that caused me to miss him. I wondered what he would think after a day or two when I wasn't there. I hoped he didn't think I had abandoned him. I knew what that felt like. Then I thought about Chester, hoping he was okay. My gut feelings kept telling me he wasn't. To keep from thinking about my family, I took some

Camille's Dilemma

satisfaction in admiring the colorful scenery of green, black, and brown—colors I would grow accustom to seeing.

The bus pulled up to what looked like a giant warehouse. Inside housed uniforms and army equipment that were stacked from the floor to the ceiling. I've never seen so many shoeboxes in all my life. I exited with a ninety-pound sack on my back. I was issued six pairs of socks, five golden brown T-shirts, four sets of fatigues, three pairs of gloves, two pairs of boots, a canteen, a flashlight, and a laundry bag. Did I mention a raincoat and a belt? That was just the half of it. I still had to be fitted for this uniform called dressed greens. That would be the garment to wear on special occasions, like when someone prominent visits the base. I would also wear it on graduation day.

Once we arrived at our living quarters, the barracks, we were told, "You have two minutes to put away your sacks and be standing outside in formation. Fall out!"

"Fall out! Fall out of what?" I was thinking. All the soldiers who arrived with me scattered into the building throwing their sacks into the first empty room they saw. I threw mine in one, too, and ran back outside. Most of us spontaneously stood around waiting for the drill sergeant to return. Some soldiers sat on stoops. Some conversed with one another. I don't think anyone knew what formation was. But it didn't take long before we found out. The drill sergeant appeared from nowhere and took a stand on the podium. He crossed his arms and looked at us look at him. Looking composed, the drill sergeant said, "Delta Company, I want all of you privates to look to your left and tell me what's wrong with the picture you're in!" We looked to

213

the left and saw Alpha Company standing in straight lines with their feet spread about a foot apart. Their hands were entwined behind their backs, and they were looking straight ahead, presumably at their drill sergeant, as they babbled out in unison. We figured that was the position he wanted us in.

"Delta Company, you've got five seconds to assume the position." We weren't totally stupid.

"Delta Company, leffft face. The next time I say formation, you'll know what the hell a formation is, won't you, soldiers!"

"Yes, Drill Sergeant," we all said in unison.

"I didn't hear you, Delta Company!"

"Yes, Drill Sergeant!"

"Delta Compannny, right face! Left face! Commannnd, march!"

"Left, your left, your left, right, left," we all sang simultaneously.

After marching a half-mile to the mess hall, which I learned later lived up to its name, it would be twenty minutes before we got in to eat. We just stood there at parade rest, waiting patiently for our turn to chow. I got a little tired of standing with my hands entwined behind my back and sort of dropped them to my sides.

"Do you have a problem, Private?" The drill sergeant shouted some fifty feet away. It looked as if he was speaking to the soldier next to me. I just stood looking at him, unaware he was speaking to me. "I asked if you have a problem, Private!" I knew then that he was talking to me because he was one inch away from my face.

"No."

"No what, Private?"

Camille's Dilemma

"No, I don't have a problem."

"No, I don't have a problem what, Private?"

"No, I don't have a problem at all." A few soldiers giggled. I wondered why.

"Are you being funny, Private? Do I look like a joke to you, Private?"

"No," I shouted.

"Oh, I think you're being funny. Drop and give me five." I dropped down and did five pushups.

"I'll ask you one more time. Do you have a problem, Private!"

"No!" I said as loud as I could.

By then, I guess he knew I didn't have a clue as to what he wanted me to say. I just stood there looking him straight in the eyes.

"I think this private needs training! There's no doubt she's a dunderhead!" he bellowed into the face of the soldier standing next to me.

"What do you think, Private Her-na-dez! Do you think Private Jen-kins needs training!"

"Yes, Drill Sergeannnt! I think Private Jenkins needs training, Drill Sergeannnt," Private Hernandez said, spitting the name "Drill Sergeant" out at me. Then it hit me. I'm supposed to end everything I say with "Drill Sergeant."

"This is the last time I'm going to ask you. Do you have a problem, Private Jenkins!"

"No, Drill Sergeannnt!"

"I can't hear you!"

215

"No, Drill Sergeannnt!"

"Private, any time I or any other drill sergeant addresses you, you will end by saying what, Private?"

"Drill Sergeant, Drill Sergeannnnt." Asshole, I added in thought.

After my confrontation with Drill Sergeant Greenleaf, I didn't feel I was military material. To hell with Uncle Sam's funds. I was not getting ready to have somebody all up in my face. This was not like the video I saw. From that day forward, I wanted out of the military. Things were not going to go well for me. I didn't see the logic of him being an inch away from my face, screaming at me to get his point across. I was not hard of hearing and a long way from being dense. I thanked God I had only enlisted as a reservist. Once again, my timing was off. I didn't need added pressure from the military life, too. I thought joining the military would lessen some of the pressure that had been disturbing me for the last few years. Give me peace of mind, you know. I decided if I was going to survive in the military, I would have to keep my mouth shut and do what I was told to do, regardless of how stupid the task may seem. But I would learn the hard way.

When I did find time to wonder, which was at night in my bunk, I thought about my family. I wondered if April and Calvin missed me. I wondered if Chester was okay; he was weighing heavy on my mind. I would get headaches thinking about him. He was the reason I couldn't stay focused on my training. I wondered if my mother had noticed the difference in Chester, and I had a talk with her the day before I left.

"Mama, have you noticed any changes in Chester?"

Camille's Dilemma

"No, is something wrong with him? I saw him yesterday; he looked fine to me." She had that look on her face as if she knew I knew something she didn't.

"There's something wrong with your son. Have you taken a real good look at him lately?" I asked, standing at the foot of her bed.

"What do you think is wrong with him?" She tried to focus on the TV and me at the same time.

"Mama, I think Chester has AIDS!"

"What makes you think that?"

"I don't think it, I see it. He doesn't look right, Mama. He's changing; go look at him. I always see him looking at himself in the mirror, like he's searching for something."

"Okay," she said, raising up to go check on Chester. A few minutes later, she returned and said, "He looks okay to me."

After only a week in the military and I got an emergency phone call from Mama. She told me Chester was just diagnosed with AIDS and that his immune system had broken down, and he was admitted into the hospital. I wanted nothing more than to go home and be with Chester. I didn't know anything about AIDS, but the word scared me. The way my mother described Chester to me, I didn't think he would be around too much longer. I lay in my bunk that night and started immediately reminiscing. Thinking about the times we would go out partying together. How we made each other laugh doing something stupid on the bus and train. How we'd played cards until one of us was broke. How he would say once we entered a bar, "What you looking for is on the other side." He'd point in that direction, and

217

when I turned around, he would be somewhere laughing, enjoying his friends. I reminisced on how he would beg me to braid his hair in French braids. It's odd how we bury people that aren't dead yet.

I became impossible to deal with. Unintentionally, I refused to follow orders. Every time I tried to concentrate on the task at hand, my mind would roam back home, wondering what Chester was doing, if he was okay. I even had the drill sergeant thinking I went AWOL. After talking with her about what was bothering me, she refused to grant me a leave of absence. She told me the only way I would be able to take a leave of absence was if there was a death in the family. I told her a family member on the brink of death is death.

I returned to the barracks where most of the soldiers were off somewhere enjoying their pass time. They could be seen or heard in the pool hall, the TV room, the weight room, or alone writing overdue letters to loved ones. I chose to be alone, nothing unusual for me. So where's a better place to be alone than in the broom closet? It wasn't like I could just take a stroll on Myrtle Beach to clear my mind. I went into the broom closet because it was quiet. I sat on the floor in my green and brown army clothing between a mop and a broom. I wanted to have a talk with Chester, pray, let him know that everything was going to be all right. I wanted to talk to my son. I just wanted some peace of mind for a change. I had no plans to fall asleep, but off to dreamland I went. I woke up and all I heard was my name being spoken, over and over. "Private Jenkins," "Private Jenkins is missing," "All the drill sergeants are looking for Private Jenkins,"

Camille's Dilemma

"Nobody's seen Private Jenkins in hours." Then I heard two privates conversing.

"Private Jones, have you seen Private Jenkins?"

"No. The drill sergeants say they think she went AWOL."

"I don't know why they won't let her out. They see she don't want to be here. You can tell by the way she acts."

"Frankly, she scares me. You see how she be looking at people?"

"Yeah, she just be staring."

"You check out the way she be eating. She eats like a madman. Just be pushing food in her mouth."

"If I was them, I'd let her ass out. She acts like she's crazy. That's why she sits all by herself in the mess hall. I wonder what she does with all that hot chocolate she takes from the mess hall. I see her put it in her cargo pocket every day. I hope they don't find her crazy ass. I hope she did go AWOL. I'm glad she ain't my buddy."

"Uh-um, wait, you see what she wrote on her iron and on her shoes? She wrote 'Touch and you burn.' On her shoes she wrote, 'Steal and be killed.' Soldier girl is crazy."

"I think she wrote that stuff on there 'cause Private Riley be stealing everybody's stuff. I know Private Riley was the one that stole my shoe wax. She's just a common thief from New York."

I started to bust out of that closet and scare the hell out of them. Who did they think I was? I wasn't crazy. I just wanted to go home. Then I looked at where I was, sitting between a mop and broom enclosed in a closet. I would think something's wrong with me, too. I must have been a tired soldier. I pushed the light button on my watch

219

to see what time it was, and it read twenty-one hundred hours. I had been asleep for four hours. I missed roll call. I wanted to come out of the closet, but because I had been in there for so long I was scared to. I didn't know what was going to happen to me. So I stayed in the closet until all the soldiers went to sleep, and the drill sergeants went into their living quarters. There were always two guards on duty in the barracks, so I waited until their backs were turned to dash out of the closet. I swiftly hopped into my bunk. No one had seen or heard me. It was now midnight. I knew the guards would be changing shifts soon. I hoped they wouldn't notice me in my bunk. They didn't. I wasn't sleepy, so I just lay there thinking about what was going to happen once the drill sergeant discovered me.

I heard the flick of the switch and on came the lights. "All right, girlies, rise and shine...Well, I'll be damn!" Drill Sergeant Williams said, looking at me. "Take your 'brellas 'cause it looks like rain. Private Jenkins, dressed and in my office in twenty."

A second after the drill sergeant left, Private Riley rushed me. "Private Jenkins, where have you been? They had the whole base out looking for you."

"I want to know how you got back in here without anybody seeing you," Private Hernandez said.

"I walked!" I retorted.

"You're a creepy ass soldier, Private Jenkins, but I'm on your side. I don't want you to say poof, and my ass disappear," Private Riley said.

Camille's Dilemma

I went and took a shower, put on my uniform, and reported to Drill Sergeant William's office.

"Drill Sergeant, Private Jenkins reporting," I said, standing in her doorway at parade rest.

"Come in, Private. At ease," she commanded.

Everybody in the room was of different but superior rank. Even the private standing in my shadow was of higher rank than I was. She was a private first class. There's a rule that says no soldier is allowed in the drill sergeant's office without the presence of another soldier, preferably your buddy. They serve as a witness to whatever is said and done in there.

Drill Sergeant Williams, sitting with one cheek on the edge of her desk, said to me, "Private Jenkins, you want to tell me and everybody else in here where you've been for the last twenty-four hours and how you managed to appear without a single soul seeing you?"

For some reason, I was getting the impression that they were amused. They all stood quietly and waited patiently for my explanation. Like someone had finally sneaked something past the military. I had this strange feeling that I had them at my command. I thought how rare that was, a private in charge. So I remained quiet.

After a couple of minutes, what appeared to be a captain said, "We understand you're having some personal problems, but you have to understand that you are now a soldier in the United States Army, and we are not going to tolerate this kind of behavior." He then raised his voice rigorously. "Now, your commanding sergeant asked you a question, and with due respect, you answer it!"

221

I stared impassively toward the floor. To be honest, I didn't know what to tell them. The truth wasn't believable.

"Private, are you aware that at this moment you are considered AWOL?" someone with authority said.

"How is that when I'm standing right here?"

"You better address me, soldier, when you're talking to me. I am a lieutenant, and I will not be disrespected!" he said, cutting his eyes at me. "I suggest you start talking or start packing, because where you're headed is nowhere close to home. You can bet on that."

"And you can jump off a bridge," I thought, then said, "I fell asleep in the broom closet, Drill Sergeant."

"You want to repeat that, soldier!" the captain said, looking surprised with his hand cupped to his ear.

"I fell asleep in the broom closet…Drill Sergeant!"

The captain's eyes expanded to its fullest. "You fell asleep in the broom closet! You fell asleep in the broom closet! Well, wake me up. Twenty years in the military, I have never heard such a tale; this is the first."

"There's a first time for everything, Drill Sergeant," I said.

"Do you have a problem recognizing rank! Do I look like a damn drill sergeant to you, Private! Look at me when I'm talking to you!" I locked my eyes on the rim of his hat. "Oh, we got a live one here," he said, walking back and forth past me, huffing.

"Private, do you realize you have just disrespected a superior officer?" Drill Sergeant Williams said.

Camille's Dilemma

I stared coolly at him thinking, "Superior officer, Officer Friendly, who gives a damn." I was getting mad. I heard myself breathe from my nose, and my chest was rising rapidly. I didn't even know why I was getting mad. I was just pissed. Everybody in there started to get on my nerves, and I'm sure my expressions told them that because my nose turned up, and it wouldn't go back down. From the outside looking in, I was losing it.

"You know what I think? I think you just got a chip on your goddamn shoulder, Private," the captain said.

I said, looking toward the floor, "Look, all I want to do is go home and see my brother. I don't know how much time he has left, and I don't want to be here if something happens to him."

"Sergeant Williams, you want to talk to this private? I really don't believe she knows how serious this is."

"Private Jenkins, where were you at eighteen hundred hours yesterday?"

"Drill Sergeant, I wanted to be alone yesterday. I wanted to be somewhere quiet where I could sort things out. So I decided to sit in the broom closet on my free time, but I fell asleep. When I woke up, I heard Private Jones and Private Patterson and, I believe, Private Riley whispering about the army and how they were thinking I went AWOL. Private Jones said she was scared of me. I was scared somebody might think I was crazy coming out of the closet, so I decided to stay in there until everybody went to sleep. When it was quiet, I came out and got in my bunk. That's where I was, Drill Sergeant Williams. If you don't believe me, I can tell you who was on

223

guard duty and what time you left the barracks. I was scared to come out, Drill Sergeant." A tear fell from my eye.

"Well, you're just as nutty as they come, Private," a commanding officer said.

"Who asked you to put your two cents in? Shouldn't you be retired?" I thought.

"Wait right here, Private Jenkins." Drill Sergeant Williams left her office and a minute later returned with Private Jones and Private Patterson.

"Private Jones," Drill Sergeant Williams said, taking a seat on the edge of her desk.

"Yes, Drill Sergeant."

"Did you and Private Patterson have a discussion yesterday evening after Private Jenkins disappeared?"

"I don't understand what you're asking, Drill Sergeant."

"Did you and Private Patterson discuss Private Jenkins in the latrine?"

"All we said was that we heard she went AWOL, Drill Sergeant."

"Are you sure that's all that was said?"

"Well, we did say she be staring a lot and she scares us."

"That will be all. You're dismissed," Drill Sergeant Williams said.

"I want a report in one hour," the captain said and marched out of the office.

Drill Sergeant Williams became a little more sympathetic to my situation, even though she made it clear to me that the army was not

Camille's Dilemma

going to give me a leave of absence, and if I pulled another stunt like that, I would suffer.

I was given permission to call home and check on Chester. A little favor from Drill Sergeant Williams. Chester was doing better. The hospital had released him. But he was bedridden. The fact that he had been released gave me enough strength to focus back on the tasks at hand.

Sound off, one two, three four, break it on down, one, two, three, four, one, two, three, four. Everywhere we marched, we sang cadence. We were marching to the obstacle course. Personally, I was beginning to like it. Didn't make any new friends. They were all still afraid to talk to me, except for Private Riley with her gay self. I knew she was gay because she was always checking out Private Hernandez, this Spanish chick. She didn't know I was watching her. I watched her, frugally, waiting for her to steal something of mine so I could beat her down. She knew not to touch anything that belonged to my weak ass buddy or me. I would leave my locker wide open at night and dare her to touch anything. I told her I would cut her head off and throw up down her neck if anything came up missing. She believed I would do such a horrible thing because I was from Chicago.

Chicagoans are stereotyped in the military. They're known as bad asses, as were the soldiers from New York. Riley also thought I drank hot water because I filled my canteen up with it. Little did she, or the rest of them soldier girls, know I was adding flavor to my drinking water. That hot chocolate I would put into my cargo pocket in the mess hall went into the canteen. It was thirty degrees outside. I sipped on sweet warmth.

I made it through the obstacle course. I even beat up a soldier with this big Q-Tip-looking thing. What I was afraid of was parachuting off the wall. Once I got up there, it took a captain to get me to jump. He kept saying positive things to me like, "You'll make it. You're a good soldier. You will get through this." It sounded good, but I knew he couldn't wait for me to get down so he could chew my ass out. This one drill sergeant I didn't particularly care for, and who sure as hell didn't care about me, waited patiently for me to jump. It was like he had it all planned: you'll never make it down. I didn't trust the way he strapped me up either. I just didn't feel right. Then I thought, "I'll show him," and parachuted off the wall. I don't know what happened, but a second later I was dangling ninety feet from above. He looked down at me with a smile. I held on to that rope for dear life. My hands had swollen up to grapefruit size by the time they got me down.

It was now me against that drill sergeant. I stared him down each time our unit marched to the mess hall, which was three times a day. Okay, sometimes I didn't feel like I was playing with a full deck. I wouldn't take my eyes off of him. At times I would do things with my free hand, as I ate my food with the other, like I knew witchcraft. I would blow air off my hand in his direction. Heavens forbid if he just so happened to get up and stumble. It made it look like I put a hex on him. He asked me to fall out of formation after about a week of my wicked staring. He pulled me over to the side and said, "You got something on your mind, soldier girl?"

Camille's Dilemma

"I have a lot on my mind, Drill Sergeant."

"You want to tell me why you stare at me?"

"Is this on or off the record, Drill Sergeant?"

"Off the record, soldier. What do you have to say?"

"I don't have a damn thing to say, Drill Sergeant."

"Are you playing games with me, soldier girl?"

"Only if you're playing games with me…Drill Sergeant."

"Get back into formation, Private. Let's start new."

Bivouac was next week. That's where you go and live out in the woods for a week. We would each sleep in a three-foot, plastic, green tent. There was a wooden house in the back of the woods where you showered. A disgusting-looking outhouse was back there, too. I went the whole week of bivouac washing up out of my canteen inside my tent. There was no way in the world I was going to use either of them disgusting-looking fart houses. I would pee behind my tent and, when no one was around, would do number two.

Things were going smooth until Drill Sergeant Merrill decided to give me midnight till two in the morning guard duty time. I was not about to cruise through the woods and guard over fifty green, three-foot tents in the dark. If somebody wasn't willing to change shifts with me, then they were out of luck. When it was time for me to go on duty, I stayed right there in my tiny tent.

"Come on out, Private Jenkins. I'm ready to hit the sack," Private Hernandez said, already on guard duty.

"I'm not standing over no tents! You're working overtime."

"Here comes the drill sergeant."

"So."

"Private Jenkins, I believe you're scheduled for duty at this time," Drill Sergeant Merrill said.

"I don't feel good, Drill Sergeant."

"Private, you come out of that tent right now and relieve this soldier."

"My stomach hurts."

"You know what I think, Private Jenkins? I think you're fine, and if I were you, I would come out and let this soldier get her proper sleep. You're not the only soldier scheduled for night duty! You report to your post at once."

"I told you, I don't feel good."

"Okay, soldier, you stay right on in there!"

When day broke, someone let me know it by kicking at my tent. It was Drill Sergeant Merrill again.

"Come out of there right now, Private."

"Why you kick me in my head?" I said, peeking out of my tent.

"That was an accident, Private. I was kicking at the tent to wake you."

"Well, I'm woke."

"I don't know what your problem is, Private, but you have broken the rules." I stood with a frown on my face, looking her up and down. Until now I hadn't noticed how cute Drill Sergeant Merrill was, and I laughed a bit.

"What is your problem? What are you laughing at, Private?" she said, a half-inch away from my face.

"You're cute, Drill Sergeant Merrill! I'm not fraternizing. I'm just paying you a compliment." She stood back with her hands on her hips looking puzzled at me. Then she shook her head and looked down to the ground.

"Private Jenkins, Private Jenkins," she said, looking back at me. "What is the army going do with you?" She walked away. When we got back to the barracks, I paid the price for skipping out on guard duty. I had to paint the same wall over ten times in different colors, ending in white.

You know what the funny thing was? When it came time to train with our M-16 rifles on the range, after I was issued mine, none of the drill sergeants wanted to be responsible for training me with it. They practically left me on the range alone. "You train her. No, you train her. I'm not going to train her. She's in your unit; you train her. I don't want to be nowhere near that private; you train her." Maybe they thought I was going to do something demented. I wasn't the one losing it. I witnessed a soldier nearly commit suicide at my post while I was on guard duty one day. He slit both of his wrists with a razor. He was what they called a weak soldier. Just couldn't do anything right. Failed every test they gave him.

By the time I graduated from basic training, advance training had gotten the word I was a problem child. They wasted no time finding out which of the sixty-two soldiers sent to AIT was Private Jenkins.

"Dump your bag, Private!" That's all he said. I dumped my bag, and everything in it hit the floor. He told me to put everything back into it. I did. Then he said it again. "Dump your bag, Private!" I looked at him for a second and dumped my bag again. "Pick it all up and put it back in your bag!" I did. "Dump your bag, soldier." Again I dumped my bag. "Pick it all up and put in back in your bag, soldier girl." Again I picked everything up and put it back in my bag. He screamed, "Can you follow orders, soldier? I said to dump your bag." I looked at Drill Sergeant Bernstein like the rebel I was. He knew what I was thinking. "Fuck you, you dump it." After about the fifth time of dumping and re-packing my bag, he decided to give me a break.

I lay in my bunk that night contemplating going AWOL for real. Then I wondered what AWOL actually stood for. I came up with "A Way Out, Leave." But the thought of spending the next ten years confined in the walls of the military made me dismiss the thought. I tried to convince myself that everything was going to be all right. Just do what you're told to do, and you'll be fine. Don't blow it, Camille. You made it through basic training; you'll make it through AIT.

They didn't lie when they said we do more by 6 AM than most people do all day. We were up at the crack of dawn every morning, running. I was never a runner and had a hard time passing the PT (physical training) test in basic training. I knew it wasn't going to be any easier in AIT. The only difference between being in basic training and advance training was after school you pretty much did what you wanted to do.

One morning, my heart decided it had enough. Alpha Company was out in stride, running the two and a half miles we ran every morning. I stopped running, grabbing my chest trying to catch my

Camille's Dilemma

breath. My buddy ran back to where I was. Drill Sergeant Bernstein shuffled back to where I was, too.

"Come on, Private, another mile," he said, still shuffling his feet.

"I can't...I can't run anymore." I was slumped over out of breath. Before I knew it, the drill sergeant was all in my face screaming.

"Private! Did I tell you to stop? You better get yourself up and catch up with your unit! You don't stop until I tell you to stop! You hear me; get up, Private!"

"I can't run no more." I looked up at him, panting, hoping he understood.

"Can't!" he said, out of breath himself. "That word is not in the army's vocabulary. Get yourself up now, Private, and catch up with your unit!"

"Drill Sergeant, my heart hurts; I can't run no more."

He snatched off his Smokey the Bear hat and slammed it into the ground.

"Yes, you are going to run some more, Private. You better believe you're going to run some more! Oh, you're going to run some more."

I stood up and yelled at him, "Look, it said, 'Be all that you can be.' I done been all that I can be, and I can't run no more!"

"You've done it now, Private! Oh, you've done it now," he said, picking his hat back up and brushing it off.

At that point, I didn't care what they did to me. Confine me, send me to the moon, cut my damn feet off—I didn't care. I wasn't running anymore. I knew my body and what it was capable of doing.

"I'll see you back at the barracks, soldier!"

D.C. Johnson

My buddy and I walked back to the barracks in silence. For the next three months, I spent most of my time kissing the ground. There were times when I saw a drill sergeant coming my way, and I would start doing pushups. Some would just look at me and shake their heads; others would tell me to get up. The strangest thing happened the week of graduation. A few drill sergeants, a colonel, commanding sergeant, whatever, walked over to me and said they were glad I made it. I got the feeling they were sad to see me go. Hello, Chi-town.

Chapter 14
Everything Must Change

Camille's mission was finally accomplished. It may not have been the best six months of her life, but she made it. She done been all she could be in that army. I knew she would make it. Them drill sergeants and everybody else with they high ranks knew she was gonna make it, too. They gave her a hard time 'cause it's part of they jobs to do so. They don't want you to forget that you were there, so they try to put something on your mind for you to remember them by. I bet they ain't gon' never forget Camille either.

Camille looked at the front of the apartment building she lived in from ground up. Then she took a deep breath and stuck her key into the lock, unlocking the door.

She walked into the house. Everything looked the same as before she left, clean. After locking the door, she dropped her duffel bag down by the dining room table and strolled into Calvin's room. She inhaled deeply to calm the excitement of being back home. "It sure smells stale in here," she thought then looked at Calvin's bed. It looked as if someone had slept on top of the covers. She peered into his closet. The clothes that were left behind, which were only a few, were pushed to one side of the closet. She then glanced out of his bedroom window and noticed an ashtray on the windowsill; it had a cigarette butt in it. The cigarette butt had raspberry lip imprints on it, which explained the stale smell in the room.

Camille strolled on toward the kitchen, stopping at the tall wooden table the telephone sat on to scan through the mail stacked next to the phone. Only one overdue bill in the whole pile. Camille wondered why the telephone bill would be overdue when she sent money home to April.

Camille walked into her bedroom. She stood by the door with her hands stashed deep into her front pants' pockets and scanned everything in it. Her king-size bed, the deep chocolate brown dresser, the brass lamp, the nightstand, the clock radio, the tiny lamp with the six little white cotton balls hanging from the shade, the other nightstand, the cream-colored walls that she painted without permission, the bare hardwood floor. She pulled the top drawer of the dresser out and glanced inside. Junk as usual. She shut the dresser drawer back then ran her finger along the top of the TV. She then laid down on her bed, noticing the dull blue sheets on it and changed them to her favorite purple and lilac striped ones. She then smiled to herself and stretched out on the sheets, closing her eyes for a brief second. She then kissed her purple and lilac sheets, grabbed the matching

Camille's Dilemma

pillows, and kissed them, too. "Home at last," she said in a whisper. Camille felt happy and she felt sad. So she smiled and cried on her purple and lilac sheets.

Camille wiped at her eyes then looked over at the clock radio. It displayed in big, red, digital numbers 3:00, and at the same time the telephone rang. She reached to answer it, but didn't; no need in spoiling the fun, she thought. She had planned on surprising April. April wasn't expecting her home until Friday. Camille was two days early, just the way she had planned it. Out of curiosity, Camille wondered who had just called. She put in her memory bank to buy an answering machine.

Camille went back into the living room and picked up her duffel bag. She stuffed it into Calvin's closet, smothering most of his toys. She then went back to enjoy the comfort of her own bed again, when she noticed she had fitted the sheets on the bed the same way the military had trained her to do. She immediately unfolded all corners and let them hang. Felt they were as free as she was. She then plopped back down on her bed and wondered how April would react when she saw her. Wondered if she had got partying all the time out her system. "I love you, April," Camille said aloud, "but I'm not going to finish where we left off." She then wondered how Calvin would react when he saw her. Wondered what he thought of her leaving him behind. She then wondered what Chester and the rest of her family was doing. (That child is doing too much wondering for me. I gon' let her talk. Bye.)

235

I wondered if I should change my clothes. No, wait, I wanted to burn my clothes, but that would be like burning the American flag. I rose up to take a quick shower. I had gained between ten and fifteen pounds, though most of it was muscle. After showering, I tried to squeeze into a pair of my Levi's denim blue jeans and laughed to myself. I knew there was no way I was going to squeeze into them. Lucky for me, April was a couple of sizes bigger than I was, so I pulled a pair of her jeans from a hanger and pow wow, a perfect fit. I also slipped into one of her button-in-the-front sweaters, a red one. I wanted to spray on a little Estee Lauder Cinnabar, her favorite, but I knew the scent of the perfume would linger in the air—a sure indication that someone was or had been here.

It was now three forty-five. April would be home any minute, if she had planned to come straight home. As I patiently waited, I fantasized about being with April again. My body began to swell from the thought. Just as I shook the thought away, I heard someone at the door. It was April. I jumped up from the bed and ran into the closet to surprise the woman that stole my heart two years ago. I stood in the closet with a smile on my face, shaking a bit from my own excitement of wanting to surprise her. I heard her say, "Y'all come on in."

"Y'all," I uttered under my breath. I scanned through my memory to see whom she could have brought home with her.

"Anybody want a beer? There's only two in here," April said.

"April, when are you going to buy some food? Look at this empty refrigerator. Didn't you say Camille was coming back home Friday? What the hell she going to eat? She should put your butt out when she gets back. Move; I got to use the bathroom." There was no doubt that was Tracee. Tracee was April's best friend. I thought sometimes she envied April's and my relationship. Tracee was soft yellow, petite, and cute. Always running off at the mouth. Just sitting around listening to some of their conversations, I knew if the right woman came along, Tracee would make a good companion for her. She loved to huff and bluff, but she knew she wasn't the type to blow the house down. I saw a little of myself in Tracee. She didn't wait until the shit hit the fan before she blew you off and said, "Next." Tracee was a sweet person. She was just in search of genuine love. You can fool yourself into thinking that it's not out there, but it is.

April walked into the bedroom and pulled out one of the dresser drawers. I decided to wait until her friends left before I came out. At least I wouldn't be considered AWOL when I came out this time.

"Trina, come here for a minute. I want you to see what I got Camille." Trina. Figures; you usually wouldn't see Tracee if you didn't see Trina. Trina was a nice person. She was on the stud side, tall, slim with smooth chocolate skin, thick eyebrows and lashes. I thought she was mildly attractive. It's amazing what dimples can do for a person. Anyway, she would give her mate the world whether they deserved it or not. I guess she felt just having somebody was good enough. She drove a red hot Camero and wore nice jewelry, which made her look more attractive.

"Damn, this is nice, April. When are you going to give it to her?" Trina asked April.

"I'm not. I'm going to put it under her pillow and let her find it."

I spoiled that surprise, I thought. But then again, I didn't. I still didn't know what it was.

"What's nice? Let me see," Tracee said. "Damn, how much you pay for this, April? This is nice. She should still put your ass out until you learn how to come home. I know what it is. You're on a guilt trip."

"I ain't on no guilt trip. That's my baby, I love Cam…"

"We know, April; we don't need to hear it again. Your butt just got a strange way of showing it. See, I would have put your ass out a long time ago," Tracee said, laughing.

"You wouldn't have done nothing, Tracee. You're saying that because you don't have nobody to go home to," Trina said harshly.

"I don't have nobody to come home to by choice. Let's just get that straight, okay. There are too many high-maintenance women out here for me. They see you with a little money, and they want it. They want you to take care of they ass. I'm not taking care of anybody but me. You got that? Me, me, me, nobody else. April's butt just got lucky. Camille damn near take care of her."

"It wasn't luck, and Camille don't take care of me. We're in this together."

"Whatever. I'm not ready to be tied down. I'm too young for that. There are too many cutie pies out here to be tied down. And do Camille still think you're…wait, let me get this right, you was nineteen when you met her, y'all been together about two years and a couple months, that makes you twenty-one, with your fake I.D. ass. Now, you told her you was twenty-four so that would make you

238

twenty-six, am I right? You lucky you look older than you really are," Tracee concluded.

"Hit her, April, she always got something to say."

I almost stuffed a sweater down my throat to keep from making a sound. Twenty-one? She's only twenty-one years old? Lying wench.

"You going to pick her up from the airport, April?" Trina asked.

"I don't know. She said she'll call me if she needs a ride."

"She gon' call you," Tracee interjected. "April, tell me this. How are you going to know if she call! You don't stay put long enough for the phone to ring. While I'm talking about a phone ringing, I'm out of here. I got a cutie pie waiting on my call now."

"Tracee, you wish. Tracee know she's lying," April said as they all laughed.

"We'll see you at work tomorrow."

Finally, all was calm. As April went to let her friends out, I crept out of the closet and laid on the bed with my hands entwined behind my head. I laid there with a little smirk on my face.

"Camille!" April shouted, obviously shocked by my presence. "Where did you come from? You were hiding? You back! My baby's back! My baby's back!" she said, jumping up and down, clapping her hands, spinning around, then diving on top of me. "When did you get in? You've been here all that time? You back!" I calmed and quieted April with a succulent kiss. I rolled her over and started to undress her, peeling away at the royal blue three-piece skirt outfit she was wearing. Excited, she started to undress me.

"Twenty-one, huh?" I said, still a little bugged that she lied to me, but more excited to be back home.

"Oh, you heard that. Are you mad at me?" she asked then began undressing me.

"It hasn't soaked in yet. Did you miss me?" I asked, passionately kissing every inch of her rich, dark, caramel-colored neck.

"Ooh, did I," she replied, caressing my back and buttocks.

"Tell me how much you missed me," I said, smoothing out her eyebrow with the tips of my thumbs.

"I miss—" I covered her lips with mine. I didn't want to hear the answer. I wanted to feel it. I cruised through the feathers in her hair with my fingertips. Then I slowly slipped both of my arms under hers, holding on to her shoulders. I massaged her body with every inch of mine until they both became moist.

"Damn, I missed you," April whispered. I rolled her over and began twirling her golden brown nipples around the walls of my lips, restraining her with our locked fingers and the passion in my body. She moaned as I slipped my fingers inside of her, massaging the walls that her love would soon be flowing down. As her body began to hoola hoop, I filled my other hand with one of her breasts, squeezing the nipple around for her pleasure.

"Ooh!" she expressed as I dazzled her jungle of love with the warm confines of my lips, keeping it in sync with the notes I played on the walls inside of her. Seconds later and the sounds of lady Tarzan followed.

Camille's Dilemma

Disturbed, the upstairs neighbor stomped on the floor several times—a stomp we were all too familiar with.

I woke up singing the next morning, "No left, no left, no left, right, left." Then I said to April, "I know my breath is funky, but I feel the need to kiss you, and ask you why you lied to me about how old you were." I gave her a quick smack on the lips and waited for her answer.

"I don't know, Camille. I probably didn't because I had to lie to get into the club. I guess I just started believing my own lie and never thought about it again. Would you have dated me if I told you I was only nineteen?"

"Maybe. It explains why you still like to hang out. I'm at the point where I'm looking for stability, and you're just getting your feet wet."

"I ain't no baby," she retorted then said, "So does it change anything?"

"Six years apart is not that bad. But I'm going to tell you point blank. I had as much time as you had to think about our past situation. We both know what the problem was. I'm giving it one more shot. If it doesn't work…I'm moving on."

"That's fair," April replied, nodding her head.

"But you know what? I had no idea of the challenge that was waiting for me in that damn army. I nearly lost my mind. I don't know how I made it. It seemed like two years instead of six months." I rolled over on my back and stared up at the ceiling with my hands clasped behind my head.

241

"Well, whoever said you don't miss your water till your well runs dry ain't never lied," April confessed, rolling over on top of me. "I missed you, Camille. You just don't know. I missed you so much." I slipped my hands under her pajama top and caressed her back.

"I missed you too, April."

"I also wore my friends out with one of Anita Baker's songs. I thought about you every time I heard it."

"Yeah, which one was that?" I gazed into her dark brown eyes. Eyes that I pretended didn't exist while I was away.

"'Been So Long.' Tracee got so tired of it she took the tape from me."

"What a coincidence," I said, reminiscing. "One of the drill sergeants sang that same song to us. Drill Sergeant Mason. She sounded good, too."

"Is that the one you said kicked you in your head while you was in your tent?"

"You remember me telling you that? No, it wasn't her. That was Drill Sergeant Merrill." It surprised me that she remembered. I had only called April twice while I was away, mainly to make sure the bills were being paid. I told her I wouldn't write and not to write me.

April said, rising from atop me, "You know what, I'm going to take the day off. I'm going to spend it with my baby."

"Don't forget I have to pick Calvin up today."

"That's right. I'll tell you what, let's go have breakfast, come back home, have breakfast again, then pick Calvin up."

"Sounds like a plan."

242

Camille's Dilemma

"Oh, I need to run by my mother's. Come with me, Camille. She hasn't seen you since you left."

"You're right; she did write and call a few times. April, you know your mama couldn't care less about seeing me."

"I know, just come with me, please," she said with praying hands. "I'll cook you a special dinner today. By the way, I've got something for you." April pulled out the bottom dresser drawer; she reached in and pulled out a small white box. I was actually surprised; I had forgotten she even had something for me. She sat on the edge of the bed and handed it to me. I raised up to open it.

"It's beautiful, April, thanks," I said, delighted. It was a fourteen-carat gold ring with five small diamonds sparkling across it. I gave her a kiss on the lips.

After showering, we slipped into blue jeans and sweatshirts. As planned, we headed out for breakfast. We decided to eat at the IHOP. The one we would normally go to was overwhelmingly crowded. So we drove to the one out in the suburbs. We were both in cavorting moods, so we decided to have a little fun when we got to IHOP. I ordered the blueberry pancakes and a cup of coffee. April ordered the grand slam and a large orange juice. A couple minutes later and the waitress returned with the coffee and orange juice. That's when April and I began flirting with one another using a British accent.

"You look enchanting this morning," I said.

April, in a couple notches above her normal tone, said, "Well, thank you, darling, and you're just breathtaking."

"You know, my sweet tambourine, you dance me right off my feet."

"And you, love, dance the little bubbles up in my bath," she said, flashing her eyelids.

"You know, every time you blink, the world shines a little brighter, darling. What you say we diddle on down to the waterfront, take in some fresh air." I sipped from my coffee cup with my pinky finger extended.

"Only if you promise to let me get my feet wet." April began to admire her fingernails.

"For you, baby, I will swim the ocean," I said.

"And for you, love, I will climb the highest mountain, just to hear the echoes of your name."

"Well, I never," someone mouthed.

"Isn't that just sickening," someone else added.

The waitress, a blond-haired woman with a polite smile, brought our food. Slightly giggling, she asked, "Can I get you two anything else?"

I looked at April. "Darling, do you have everything you need to make your breakfast complete?"

"From the looks of it, I do."

"Well then, I'll have another cup of that divine coffee you're serving to complete mine. That will be all." I focused my attention back to April. "These blueberry pancakes are as satisfying as the kiss you left upon my lips, tulip," I said, lifting the tiny silver tin can of syrup up into the air, letting it rain down on my pancakes. "Here, taste

Camille's Dilemma

the beauty in these cakes." April leaned over, and I fed her some pancakes off my fork. "Here, allow me," I said, wiping a dab of syrup off of her top lip with my napkin. We sat feeding and complimenting each other until we were finished eating. Then we both stood up and looked around. If you could have seen some of the expressions on people's faces. They were confused and amused.

"You've been a splendid waitress," I said, paying for our food. I handed her a five-dollar tip. I held my arm out, and April and I galloped out of the restaurant.

We laughed laboriously in the car. We hadn't had fun like that in a long time. We drove on over to Cynthia's house.

As we were walking up to Cynthia's house, one of her neighbors shouted across the street to me. "Hey, Camille, you back, huh? How was it?" she asked, sweeping off her porch.

"Long and hard," I shouted back at her, waving.

"You got yourself a sweet little boy. He don't cause no trouble." I smiled at her as I rung Cynthia's doorbell.

Cynthia looked out of the window. "Calvin, your mama's home," I heard her shout. She opened the door smiling then hitting me on the arm. "Girl, look at you. You done got big. I bet it's all muscle. Hey, April; y'all come on in."

"Mama!" Calvin said. Thrilled to see me, he jumped up into my arms, and I immediately shed some tears.

"My baby! Ooh, I missed you. I missed you," I said, hugging him real tight.

"Dang, Mama, you squeezing me."

245

D.C. Johnson

"I'm sorry. Mama just missed you." I released him. "Step back so Mama can see you."

"I'm still Calvin, 'cept I got a new bike. Come see it," he said, grabbing my hand and pulling me with him. "See," he said, pointing at it. "See what Auntie Cynthia bought me." I guess Auntie Cynthia didn't tell him I sent the money home for his new bike.

"Ooh, can I ride it?" I said, rubbing my hands together.

"Mama, you know you too big to ride my bike," he said then sat on it like he was going to ride it. I kissed and hugged Calvin again before following Cynthia and April into the kitchen.

"Y'all want some coffee or something?" Cynthia asked.

"I'll take a cup, knickknack lady." I looked around at all the new little things Cynthia had bought while I was gone. Cynthia was obsessed with little objects. She loved to collect things.

"Where did you get these?" I asked, removing from her refrigerator a miniature magnet telephone. There were several of them, all different types. The artificial food stuck to it looked quite inviting. "And these?" I said as I observed a little copper iron windmill sitting on the stove. I took a seat at the kitchen table.

"Cynthia, don't forget, Monday we have to go back to court, unless you planned on keeping Calvin forever. I know him and James just about wrecked your nerves."

"They sure did. Girl, you lucky this was for only six months. You would have been out of luck."

"Where is James at anyway?"

246

Camille's Dilemma

"His father came and picked him up for clean-up week." Cynthia set my cup of coffee down in front of me.

"Cynthia, can I use your phone? I need to call my mother," April said, about to pick the cordless up off the kitchen wall.

"April, you know you don't have to ask me to use the phone…just leave your quarter on the table," Cynthia said playfully.

"How's Mama, Chester, and Clifford doing?" I asked Cynthia, pouring some liquid creamer into my coffee.

"Mama and Clifford is fine. Chester…he's not doing too well, Camille. He don't look nothing like the Chester we knew." I felt tears welling up in my eyes but managed to retain them. "I'm for real. April seen him." April turned her back to us to avoid agreeing with Cynthia. She then walked out of the kitchen with the cordless.

"But he's okay?" I inquired. Cynthia looked away.

"He's sick, Camille." She sipped from her cup.

"It's that bad, huh?"

"You haven't been over there yet? When did you get in, and how did you get home?"

"Yesterday. I took a cab from the airport." I tried to picture what Chester might look like.

Cynthia, distorting the picture, said, "And you're just now coming over here to pick Calvin up?"

"Cynthia, I needed some time to unwind," I said, stretching and then yawning.

"Are you going to stop by Mama's when you leave here? You know Chester is looking forward to seeing you. That's all he talks about, when he can talk, is when you coming home. He just sits and mumbles your name. 'When is Camille coming home; when is Camille coming home?' It's like you're the only person he wants to see." Her words forced me into a burst of tears. I sat crying in my hands. Cynthia walked over and started rubbing my back.

"Camille, you about ready?" April asked, walking back into the kitchen. I wiped at my eyes. "I'm going to go on by my mother's, so I can get back. Are you okay?" she asked me.

"Yeah. Thanks, Cynthia, for keeping Calvin...and don't forget about Monday." I sniffled then called out to Calvin. "Cynthia, I'll be back tomorrow to pick Calvin's stuff up. I don't feel like lugging it all now." Thinking about Chester had drained me.

"Okay. Just make sure you come tomorrow," Cynthia said then shouted at Calvin as he brushed past her heading for the door. "Boy, you better come give your auntie a hug goodbye."

We pulled up in front of April's mother's house. I truly didn't want to go in. It made me think about the time when that old wretch had the nerve to pretend like she didn't know who I was. I saw her in the grocery store one day. I spoke to her, and she looked at me like it was her first time seeing me and said, "Do I know you?" I had been coming to this lady's house with her daughter for six months. I said, "Oh! I'm sorry," putting my hand to my chest. "You look exactly like my wife's mother." I turned my nose up, leaving her stunned and wordless.

After speaking to her mother, the air in the room was the same as before I left, turbulent. I almost hated myself for coming. I knew

Camille's Dilemma

nothing had changed. I called April over to where I was, standing by the front door.

"Why don't you drop me off by my mother's. I'll call you when I'm ready. If you're not here, I'll walk home; it's only a few blocks. Or I'll have my mother drop me off."

"You want Calvin to stay here with me? Let him stay, Camille. He's upstairs playing with Ramey," April said.

While riding over to my mother's, I told April not to ever ask me again to visit her mother. I was not going to talk to someone who despised me.

My nerves fluttered as I rang my mother's doorbell.

"Who is it?"

"It's me, Ma." Mama opened the door the same way Cynthia opened it, with a smile.

"You're back! I thought you wasn't coming back until Friday," she said, surprised to see me. "Give me a hug." I hugged her and then took a seat at the dining room table. "How did you get home from the airport?"

"I took a cab."

Mama quickly inhaled, covering her mouth with her hand. "I know it cost you an arm and a leg, didn't it?"

"It wasn't too bad."

I looked my mother hard in the face. I wondered where all her black hair had gone. She had aged rapidly in the last six months. There she sat, barely fifty years old, almost completely gray, with stress and hardship written all over her face.

249

"So, what was it like? Talk to me," she said, patting me on the knee.

I looked around the dining room and then into the living room and noticed a ceiling fan.

"I see you got a ceiling fan," I said, pointing up at it.

"Yeah, Chester put it up for me a couple months ago." She looked over at it.

"How's he doing?"

"Well, it's just day to day. Sometimes he feels well and will get up...then other times he just stays in the bed. He's tired a lot. He's been in and out of the hospital. He's really sick, Camille. Go on down and say hi to him," she said, pointing to the basement. "He's down there, been asking when you was coming home. He wants you to braid his hair for him."

I got up and rushed out of the house. I wasn't ready to see Chester. I was afraid of what he might look like. I walked a few blocks, crying. A part of me was dying, and there was nothing I could do about it. I sat down on a stoop in front of an abandoned church. I put my head down on my knees. I kept seeing this pale face, with gray eyes and a callous smile. A face I had only seen once before. It belonged to a friend of Chester's.

A couple of years ago, Chester introduced us to him. When I shook his hand, I felt something that instantly jerked my hand away from his. He stared at me with a deadened smile. He knew that I knew all was not well with him. We stared into each other's eyes. Mine told him to leave, which he did shortly after. I asked Chester who he was and where he met him. He said he met him out sometime ago. Said he was just a friend of his. I told Chester that his friend was sick. I didn't know from what. I just knew he was sick. Now Chester is sick.

I put my fear aside and walked back to my mother's house. I trembled going down the steps to what used to be my bedroom but what was now Chester's.

He was sitting straight up against the backboard of his bed, with the support of three pillows, watching television. He turned to look at me, and I instantly covered my mouth in reverence of his condition. His right eye was covered with a white patch, and he was wearing dark sunglasses. The shades were all drawn. His face had sunken in, and his hair was very thin in patches. His skeleton-like arms lay at his sides. A brown wooden cane with black tape wrapped around it lay on his bed beside him, along with a silver, oval-shaped pan. It looked like Chester had only one leg underneath his covers. He had lost an enormous amount of weight. I couldn't believe what I was seeing. Chester had gone from being my brother to being a complete stranger to me. He called out to me with a smile, reaching for his cane. "What is he doing with a cane?" I asked myself. I began to shake. My throat began to swell. My breathing wheezed as if I had asthma.

"No, noooo, you're not Chester. Mamaaa!" I cried out, running upstairs. "Who is that? That's not Chester. Mama who is that down there? Where is Chester? Where's Chester at?" Mama grabbed at me, and I resisted. I couldn't shake the present image of Chester now imbedded in my eyes. I couldn't stop the trembling of my body. I couldn't stop crying. My head and heart began to pound like a drum. I ran out of my mother's house and down the block. I stopped and rested on my knees to catch my breath. I strolled home, thinking about Chester.

I was afraid of him. I was afraid of the way he looked. Chester was reaching out to me, and I ran away. I couldn't think straight. My thoughts clashed with the image of the new Chester. I was not strong enough to deal with his sickness. I stopped and leaned on a fence and cried some more. Thinking about the pain and suffering Chester had to be going through. If you can see it, you could feel it. Where did this disease come from? AIDS. It's such a small but deadly word. Why had Chester been stricken with it? Who gave it to him? I instantly began to hate all gay men. I blamed his disease on every last one of them. The only thing I knew about the disease was that only gay men contracted it. It was a gay disease. It was punishment to all homosexuals. Chester was chose to be punished.

I knew I had to face Chester; he was my brother. I loved him. I never told him, but I knew he knew I did.

The next time I visited Mama, which was two days later, she gave me some materials to read. She didn't want me to be ignorant about the disease like so many people were. Thinking you could get it by just touching someone infected. Or, you could contract it by being in the same room with them. AIDS was not airborne.

After reading the pamphlets, the fear that it wasn't just a homosexual disease was exposed. Knowing that the homosexual community would not be the only community affected by it gave me a sense of consolation. Not that I wanted to see other people inflicted with AIDS, but homosexuals are already outnumbered, and that would be all that's needed to kill us off one by one. What it meant was that the disease was running rampant. It was a plague with no brakes. There was no cure for it. This sick love disease could strike anyone anytime. I also learned that there was a difference between HIV and AIDS, which to me didn't make much sense, because sooner or later they both will kill you. It was like saying cancer and cancer in remission was different. It's still there. A bear hibernating is still alive, isn't it? AIDS is actually a bullet; it has no name on it. Chester was shot, and now had full-blown AIDS and was sitting on the edge of death.

I still couldn't shake my fear of Chester and would only go down into the basement when I knew Chester was asleep. He slept a lot. I would stand in his doorway and watch him sleep. I would watch him suffer in his sleep. Every now and then he would moan. I prayed that Chester would die in his sleep. For the next few months, I would watch, pray, and communicate to Chester while he slept.

One day after visiting Chester, Mama telephoned me. She said Chester had just been admitted into the hospital, and he wanted us there with him. Mama was standing in his doorway when I got there, a nurse by her side. I looked and Clifford, Cynthia, and Aunt Cathy were standing at his bedside. Mama said, before I stepped into the room, "Chester told me to tell you not to be afraid of him. He said he wants to look nice when he goes to heaven. He wants to know if you would braid his hair for him so he'll look nice when he go."

D.C. Johnson

"I can't, Mama," I said, holding my hand over my mouth, and a waterfall of tears ran from my eyes.

"Try, just try, Camille."

I stepped in, and the nurse handed me a pair of clear, plastic gloves and a little, black comb. A voice whispered out of my ears as I took the gloves and comb from the nurse. The voice said, "He won't go until you look him in his eyes." I slowly walked over to Chester's bed. I took a deep breath then looked him in the eyes. He tried to smile, and I could tell it pained him just to smile. I began to cry, and he slowly shook his head. Looking deeper into Chester's eyes, I saw his courage. I could see the fight he fought was not against his disease. His fight was against his fear of dying. A battle he won. He was no longer afraid to die. Sometimes we wonder why a person suffers before they die. Could it be that God is just giving you time to accept Him into your life? He doesn't care about the lifestyle you led, because He's willing to forgive. God understands. He was just holding out a helping hand. He just prefers you to be ready when He comes for you.

I smiled down at Chester and began braiding his thinning hair. I put three little braids in Chester's head. Afterwards, he smiled a smile that didn't seem to pain him at all. He whispered to me, "It's time to go. I'm going to die tonight."

I smiled at Chester. "I know. See you when I get there." I gave him a wink, and he closed his eyes. The next day, we made preparations to bury Chester.

A poem for Chester:

Camille's Dilemma

No Ordinary Bird

Of a feather we flock together

Birds of the sky

Careful where we land our wings

We fly untimely by

Sharp, snappy, and distinct

You stand wondering

Was that a bird I saw

Or did heaven open the sky

We congregate, sing in harmony

It echoes, pleasing to the ear

Jubilant across the world

Pure as the mighty sea

As we land our wings on shore

Our whereabouts unknown

The scent we leave in the sand

Brings people to our land

Camille Jenkins

Chapter 15

Closer Than Friends

Camille's been home for a while now from the army. She's been going out looking for work. They taught her how to work on cars in the army, so she looks for work in that field. She put a few applications in at some auto repair shops, but no one's called her for a job. They all say they don't need any help. Most places she put her application in don't have woman mechanics. That's probably the way they want to keep it. The man she working with now, JW, he pay her a little something for helping him out. She does small things for him like change the oil, put on some new brakes, tune people cars up, maybe put on a new alternator or put in a new battery. He always says he going to get his own company and want Camille to work for him. Camille's tired of waiting because she's got a mouth to feed.

Camille applies for a job at an automotive store. The manager wants to hire her as a cashier. She tells him that the sign said they're looking for somebody with mechanical experience. Told him she had some and told him where she got her mechanical experience. He's skeptical, but he gives her the test anyway. She passed. So he gives her the job.

Camille knows she's not going to have that job long. For one thing it doesn't pay much money and there isn't any benefits. It pays just enough to keep a roof over her head. She doesn't count the income April brings in because it isn't hers. She wants to know she can always make it on her own.

A few months later and she finds her a job at an advertising agency. They had a job opening for a Receptionist/Typist. The benefits are a lot better and so is the pay.

April, Calvin, and Camille had taken a trip to Wisconsin Dells. That's where April wanted to go for her birthday. They also went to Great America twice. They took April's little brother along with them to Great America. Most of the time, Camille would watch April and the kids as they swung and spun. Camille found out when she was in the army that she had vertigo. So, all them fast rides were out. She would stand in line for the bumper cars or play some games while they riding rides, hoping to win one of them cute little stuffed animals for April, which she did shooting basketball. Then they visited the zoo. Like a lot of people, they all made fun of the animals, just enjoying themselves. Camille's favorite was horseback riding. April's brother, Ramey, loved to horseback ride, so he tagged along. April and Calvin weren't too fond of horseback riding, but they rode anyway.

Camille's Dilemma

Then they went go-cart riding. Calvin and Camille would race. Camille always zoomed up on Calvin like she was going to run him off the track. He would be cracking up laughing.

It was mid-November and a Saturday. Winter was setting in. So that meant a lot of folks were getting ready to hibernate. Not April— she started hanging out on the weekends again. Camille didn't say a word. She'd let her have her fun.

April had gone to visit her mother, and Calvin was outside playing. Camille then thought about Corrine, wonder what she might be doing. She hadn't talked to her in almost a year. Hadn't talked to Ann either. But that's just the way it is sometimes. We don't think about a lot of people until there's no one there.

Anyway, Camille decided to call Corrine, but before she did, she took two aspirins. She all of a sudden came down with a headache.

"Hello," someone snapped into the phone.

"Corrine?"

"Who is this?"

"Why are you answering the phone all on the defense?" Camille asked her.

"Camille, man, what's up! Why you leave without telling me? I thought I was your ace boom. Why you do me like that out of all people? So how was it?"

"Corrine, it was definitely something to write home about. I had a hard time. But I brought it all on myself. You heard about my brother, right?"

259

"Yeah, I'm sorry. Why you didn't call me when he died? You know I would have come to the funeral."

"We had a private funeral. You know Chester didn't hang around the hood. So how have you been?"

"Camille, I'm about to pick up your old habit. I'm getting ready to kick Elma to the curb. Man, you just don't know. I furnished her whole crib and co-signed for her a brand-new car. She had the nerve to bring this other woman she met out to the crib. She says they're just friends. But I'm not stupid, Camille. That's the same way she introduced me to her husband. People don't change, especially when they get as old as her ass is. Man we gon' have to hook up. What's been going on with you?"

"I don't know, Corrine. For one thing, April's only twenty-two."

"Twenty-two! Man how she gon' be twenty-two when she was twenty-four when y'all met? It's been damn near three years. Her ass ain't getting no older?" They laughed.

"Corrine, she lied."

"Well, why she lie?"

"That's not important. What's important is that she doesn't know how to come home. Every weekend she's hanging out with her friends. I really can't complain because she's been doing it ever since we've been together."

"Man, what do you expect at twenty-two? Where was you at twenty-two?"

"I know, Corrine. But my feelings are involved. I love April. And I know me. April's getting ready to get kicked to the curb."

Camille's Dilemma

"Man, check this out. I need to make a run. Why don't we hook up this weekend? Give me your phone number again." Camille told Corrine her number. "Maybe we can get together and play some cards, you and your two kids."

"Bye," Camille said then hung up.

Camille decided to go sit on the porch and watch Calvin play. She grabbed her jacket and went outside. It was nice and breezy, not too cool. It was almost the perfect pre-winter day. She sat on the step with her arms resting back on the step above. She then tilted her head back and inhaled the cool breeze. Camille's heart began to ache a bit because she knew she would soon be leaving April. She tried not to think about it because she already had a headache. She heard someone coming out of her upstairs neighbor's house and looked up at her door. She knew her neighbor wasn't going to speak first, so she spoke to irk her. She gave Camille a nasty hi and turned up her nose. Camille knew she was angered at her because she and April were forcing her to wear the heel out on her shoes, stomping on the floor all the time. "Have a nice day," Camille said as her neighbor got into her car, slightly rolling her eyes at Camille.

Camille decided to pay Ann an unexpected visit.

"Camille! Girl, how you doing?" Ann said after opening the door. "I thought you fell off the face of the earth. Where have you been, that you're just now getting in touch with me? Hey, Calvin. You've gotten a little taller. You can go on back there with Jermaine and them," she said to him.

"I went into the army," Camille said as Calvin jovially hurried away. "I've been back a while though. How's the baby?"

"Carlton, he's doing fine. He'll be three next week, not that you're keeping up, Miss Godmother. Come on," she said, walking into the living room. Everything was just the way Camille remembered it. Ann's white, three-piece, Italian leather sectional was still glowing. Her glass cocktail table didn't have a speck of dust on it. Neither did the matching end tables or cream, vase-style lamps sitting on them. "I wasn't doing anything, just lounging around the house. Michael just went to work. He had asked about you."

Camille observed Ann, thinking, "Damn." Ann had dropped all that baby fat and picked up some baby doll weight. She quickly forgot about April. They sat around talking. Camille laid her blues on Ann. Ann told Camille it was time for her to go shopping again. Camille told her it wasn't that easy because she still loved April. But she knew Ann was right. It was time for her relationship with April to end. And from what Ann said, nothing was going right for her either. Her husband had become abusive to her. Camille commented that it must be the change in the seasons. They were both vulnerable and knew it. Ann went to check on the kids. When she came back, Camille was led to her bedroom.

Afterwards, Camille and Calvin went home. Camille will tell you what happened after that.

April came home about two hours after I got in from Ann's. It was an early night for her. It was one o'clock in the morning. I found it odd because she'd usually come in way after three. She was in one of

262

Camille's Dilemma

her kinky moods. It didn't faze me because I had started losing feelings for her. You know, you can cry all night long, but sooner or later, that last teardrop will fall. It fell for me.

"What's wrong with you, Camille? Why'd you throw my hand off you?" April said, raising up a bit.

"'Cause I don't want you to touch me."

"Oh, we getting ready to go through this shit again about me hanging out."

"You're getting ready to go through this shit again. I'm going back to sleep."

"Naw, we're going to talk. I know you got your ass on your shoulder. I want to talk, Camille."

"About what, April? What did I tell you when I came back from the army? I'm through talking. You should have been keeping a diary so you wouldn't forget the important things I say to you. What I did forget to tell you is one day you're going to come home and find somebody else here. So if I were you, I'd write that shit down. I don't have nothing else to say about it."

"Are you threatening to cheat on me, Camille? I'm not out messing around. I'm just hanging out with my friends. I like being with my friends. Damn. Why can't you believe me?"

"You still don't get it, do you?" I said over my shoulder. "You really don't get it. April, you can be with your friends. I've never said you couldn't hang out with your friends. Nonetheless, I don't expect you to hang out every weekend either. It's a matter of respect. So you decided to come home early tonight. What happened? Did the bar

263

shut down early tonight? Do what you want to do, April. I'm going back to sleep."

"Camille, I don't want to lose you. I really don't."

She went into the bathroom crying, and I went to sleep.

For the next three months, Ann and I found comfort in each other. I compared my relationship to Ann's. I could probably put up with April's long nights out a lot longer than Ann could put up with her husband's abuse. She said everything changed after Carlton was born. Said Michael started complaining he had too much weight on his shoulders, even after Ann went back to work and picked up a part-time job on the weekends. Then he began hanging out with some of his co-workers. She suspected he was doing drugs because she found little white packs in his pants' pockets along with women's phone numbers. Said they don't go out anymore because Michael accuses her of flirting with every man that walks past. He told her that he knows she's cheating on him. She said she hasn't really been out of the house since she had the baby. Said it was like he changed overnight. It was hard for me to believe that Michael would take that route. He always appeared to be level headed. But everything that glitters ain't gold. I learned that from being with April. I would tell Ann that she should leave him if he hits her again, and she would tell me I should put April out the next time she comes in after two in the morning. She really didn't want to leave Michael, and I really didn't want to leave April. I guess that's why they were still around.

But enough was enough. Michael had jumped on Ann again and took the kids to his mother's house. He left Jermaine, who was the

264

Camille's Dilemma

oldest boy, because he wasn't his paternal son. Ann called me and asked if I could watch Jermaine for her while she went to work.

I cried when I laid eyes on Ann. Michael beat Ann up so bad she could barely walk. She said she confronted Michael about a pack of cocaine she found on their dresser. After that, all hell broke loose. He began degrading her, saying it was her fault that he was hooked on drugs. He even accused her of getting pregnant on purpose. Said she knew they couldn't afford another kid when she got pregnant. Said she did it to trap him. They were married, for crying out loud. I'll be damned if drugs don't make you hallucinate.

Jermaine was ten. Two years older than Calvin was. Calvin was glad Jermaine had come over because he loved to play. Jermaine would sometimes get irritated about Calvin's constant frolicking.

Well, one weekend of babysitting turned into a month of weekend babysitting. I guess that's when April started to take notice.

"Who is this boy? The nephew I never met. He's here every weekend," April said, closing the front door. She handed me the grocery bag. I had noticed a change in April. She was becoming more and more aggressive. Wearing more pants and pant suits, and less and less dresses and skirts. She almost began to walk with a little pimp.

"Jermaine. I told you three weeks ago who he was. I used to work with his mama. She needed a babysitter, so here I am. He gets along with Calvin, so it's not a problem."

"You sure you don't have a thing for his mama?" April said then looked for a pot in the cabinet under the sink.

265

D.C. Johnson

"If I develop some feelings for his mama, I'll make sure you be the first to know." She looked repugnant at me then asked if I wanted anything else with the steak and potatoes. I told her to throw in some veggies as I sliced up a green pepper.

"You don't want to go outside? What did you say his name was?"

"Jermaine." I smiled at him.

"Huh, Jermaine. You don't want to go outside?"

"Nope. What y'all getting ready to cook?"

"Some steak and potatoes. Are you hungry, Jermaine?" April asked him.

"A little."

"I'll tell you what. You go on outside and play with Calvin, and we'll call you when the food is ready," she said, smiling at him. Jermaine grabbed his jacket and headed for the door.

"Cute little boy. Is his mama cute?" April asked, walking up behind me and sliding her hands into my front pocket. I took a deep breath.

"She'll be here in a little while." I removed April's hands from my front pocket and turned around to her. It had been a long time since her touch had turned me on. She backed me up to the stove, turning off the pilots. I grabbed April by the back of her hair and kissed her. First the sound of little soft kisses, then sounds from deep, long, tongue kissing. April grabbed my ass, and I forced pumps into her. I walked April back to the kitchen table and ran my hand between her legs, which made her chest rise up and down. "Mmmm," April chuckled. "You think we got time?"

266

Camille's Dilemma

"Time waits for no one." I lifted April off the table onto the floor.

We started to melt into the floor when April said, "Camille, the door. Jermaine may not have locked the door." I shuffled to lock the door. April undressed herself while on the way to the bedroom. Our clothes went in every direction. We knew we didn't have a lot of time and began making up for lost time. Our exchanges of desire grew into something lusty. It was like we were on a race to ecstasy. Enjoying what we had while we had it. April's breasts swelled and her chest tightened as I fingered her with healthy pushes. The exquisite feeling of the walls of her tunnel tightening around my fingers, I moaned.

"Camille, Camille, baby, I want it now. Give it to me, give the combo, give me the combo, baby." April's request was at my command. I gave her the combo. I pumped my fingers and kept my lips glued, twirling her clitoris until we came. The fire between us wasn't completely out because the neighbor banged with her shoe. We cleaned up and resumed cooking.

The phone rang, and at the same time, somebody knocked on the door. April went to the phone, and I went to get the door.

"Hey, Ann, how was work? You look beat." "But still ravishing," I added in thought as I went back to the kitchen to finish cooking.

"Y'all cooking up a storm in here," Ann said from the front room.

"So, how was work?" I asked, looking at the steak in the oven.

"Camille, girl, I'm a tired sister. I can't keep working like this. He…" I assumed she saw April come out of the bedroom and ended her conversation. She was probably going to say something about

Michael. I stashed the tail end of the towel into the back of April's jeans as we walked into the front room.

"Ann, I don't believe you've met April. This is April. April, Ann." I felt a little uncomfortable. I felt like I was introducing my wife, April, to my girlfriend, Ann. April spoke, and all of a sudden, the extreme feminine side of her emerged. A side I hadn't seen in a long time, unless we were in bed. She walked over to Ann and extended her hand. I could tell she was taken in by Ann's natural beauty. I read it in her face. It said, "Damn, she's fine." She backed away, almost unable to keep her eyes off of Ann. I was sure Ann could tell April was drawn to her.

Ann sighed. "Well, let me get my butt on out of here. Lord knows I don't feel like driving halfway cross town home," she said, shaking her head.

"Why don't you and Jermaine stay and have dinner with us. I'm sure Jermaine is looking forward to it." All of a sudden, a sharp pain penetrated near my right temple. I massaged it. It lasted about ten seconds.

"Are you okay, Camille?" April asked me, putting her arm around my shoulder. Ann looked away and out of the window.

"I'm fine. Let me go check on the food before I burn it up." As I turned to walk away, the pain struck again, this time a little sharper than before. I grimaced, and April went to reach for me again. "I'm okay," I said then went into the kitchen. I rested my arms on the countertop and massaged both my temples.

April and Ann started making small talk, which was probably what it was to Ann, small talk. She thought April was too young for me. Regardless of the fact, we all looked around the same age. I took the steak out of the oven and called out to April.

"I don't feel too well. Why don't you set the table."

"You sure you're okay, Camille?"

"Just a little dizzy, I'll be fine. Don't forget to clean the table off. You know your funky booty was just on it." She threw the towel at me as I walked out of the kitchen back into the front room. I turned the radio to a new station that recently came on the air called V103. I liked the station because it played a lot of dusties. I couldn't get with the so-called house music they were starting to play on other stations. It was too loud. I took a seat on the opposite end of the couch Ann was sitting on.

"Camille, I don't want to impose on you and April, but I really don't feel like driving."

"Don't worry about it. It's not a problem."

"Where is Jermaine, anyway?" she said, admiring a picture on the wall.

"He's down the street with Calvin, playing." I got up to call Calvin and Jermaine in the house. I scrunched up my face so I wouldn't attract attention to the present pain in my head as I walked over to the door.

"Where did you get that picture?" she asked, pointing at it.

"Swap-O-Rama. So I don't have to tell you what I paid for it." I called out to Calvin and Jermaine.

"It's a nice picture. I like those kinds of pictures. They're so in-depth. Makes you feel like you're actually standing near the waterfall. Calgon...take me away," she said. Jermaine and Calvin came flying into the house. Calvin had to be hungry because normally I would have to call him two or three times before he came in the house.

"Hey, Ma," Jermaine said, waving at Ann. "Auntie Camille said we can stay for dinner. Can we stay, please? Please, Mama, can we stay," he pleaded, unaware that the invitation had already been extended to his mama.

"Well, if Auntie Camille don't mind, I guess we can stay."

"Yippee!" he said, following the scent coming from the kitchen. We looked at him and each other and smiled. He came back into the front room and took a seat by his mama. "My mama was probably going to stop at Biggie Burgers. I'm tired of eating hamburgers. Mama, why you don't cook no more like Auntie Camille and her friend...what's her name again?" he asked, looking at me.

"April."

"April cook. They always have home-cooked food. Calvin be eating good."

"Mama's going to start back cooking soon," Ann responded, patting him on the head. April called out to us, and we all went into the kitchen for dinner.

A little while later, we all walked out of the kitchen with our bellies stuffed. The telephone rang. April went to answer it in the bedroom. Calvin and Jermaine went into his room, and Ann and I headed for the living room. I turned on the TV then took a seat in the recliner. I looked over at Ann on the sofa. I sensed Ann really didn't want to go home by the way that she sat and gazed out of the living room window. Michael would come back home every now and then just to have sex with Ann. Then he would leave and go back to his mother's house. She appeared to be at peace staring out of the window. She was probably looking at nothing. Probably didn't notice how orange sherbet the sun looked while it was setting. Probably didn't hear the birds chirp as they congregated to fly home to their nests. Probably didn't notice how on one side of the street all the houses' lawns appeared to be freshly mowed. For a second, she closed her eyes and leaned her head back into the cushion of the sofa. Michael's violence had driven her all the way across town for a minute of inhaling, exhaling peace. She looked so serene that I didn't disturb her with chitchat. I knew her blues were a lot bluer than mine was. Then I wished that I were with her instead of April. As I watched her in peace, she looked to be the spitting image of the woman I was told you only find in magazines. My heart ached from my finding as my eyes filled with tears. She was picture perfect. I've always been a firm believer that you can have anything you want if you believe. I believed that that woman in the magazine was out there. And here she was, sitting across from me. I hoped that Michael didn't scar her too deeply, killing the joy she probably once felt being a black and beautiful woman.

Ann opened her eyes and glanced over her right shoulder. She shook her head and said, "Camille, I was in another world."

"I know. Was it peaceful?" She nodded as Calvin and Jermaine came flying out of his room toward the front door.

"Where do you think you're going?" I asked, stopping Calvin and his water blaster in their tracks. April then called out to me from the bedroom.

"I'm going back out to play with my friends," he said, with his water blaster pointing down at the floor.

"Not if you don't ask. I told you about leaving here and not telling me where you're going. You just wait right there, Calvin. I mean it." I rose to see what April wanted, looking at him as if he had lost his mind.

"I'm just going out in the front, Mama."

"I don't care if you're going to the moon; I said wait."

April, standing by the dresser, said, "I'm going to run by my mother's for a little while. Then I'm going to go by Tracee's house for a while. You want something while I'm out?"

I waved my hand at April. "Go do what you have to do; we both know what day it is. You know and I know you're going out." I left the room. Frankly, I didn't care where she went.

"Ma, now can I go back outside?" Calvin asked, his water blaster now pointed at the TV.

"Don't go off the block, Calvin," I said, pointing a finger at him. He grunted as he went out the door, with Jermaine following.

"And where do you think you're going, young man?" Ann asked Jermaine.

"I was going back out with Calvin."

Camille's Dilemma

"You can tell Calvin goodbye because we're getting ready to leave."

Calvin gave Jermaine a look that said, "See you when I see you." He disappeared.

"We got to leave?" Jermaine grumbled with his arms across his chest. "Mama, you know you don't want to go home 'cause Dad—"

"All right, Jermaine. Watch your mouth. I told you about talking so much."

"Can we stay just one more half an hour?"

"You've been over here all day, Jermaine. Auntie Camille is probably tired of you. She's probably tired of us." Jermaine looked over at me and started pleading his case with a sad smile.

"I don't mind, Jermaine. It's up to your mama." He turned around and looked at his mama with a silly smile.

"A half an hour, Jermaine, and we're leaving." Jermaine went flying out of the house, calling Calvin's name as he shut the door. Then April walked out of the bedroom into the living room. She walked over to where I was and bent down to kiss me. I turned my head sideways, and she kissed me on the jaw.

"She's not coming back, is she?" Ann asked as we watched her get into her car and pull off.

"She'll be back...in the morning." We chuckled. "It's okay because time has run out. I told her one day she's going to come home and find somebody else here."

Ann tapped me on the knee. "You told her that?"

D.C. Johnson

"I'm not playing her game anymore. It's just a matter of time. I'm about ready to start going out myself. Her ass should have thought about how much fun she wasn't going to have before she moved in. Anyway, how are you doing? Has Michael gotten any better?"

"You mean has he started hitting me with his left hand yet?" We laughed then Ann started crying uncontrollably in her hands. "Jermaine is right. I don't want to go home. I know he's there. All he's going to want to do is fight and fuck me. I'm tired! I'm so tired, Camille. I wish he would just stay away. I don't know what to do. It's not easy when you have kids involved. Especially four kids—three I only see when he feels like bringing them by. And he follows me sometimes." I looked out of the window, just by instinct. "I'm scared of him, Camille. Every time I try to leave, he threatens me. The sad part is I still love him."

I sigh. "I know that feeling."

"What am I going to do, Camille? I can't keep throwing Jermaine off on you every weekend."

"Jermaine is not the problem. Why don't you see if you can get Michael to commit to drug rehab."

"Camille, every time I bring that up, he gets to screaming and yelling he don't have a drug problem." Ann wiped at her eyes.

"They say the hard part is accepting that you do have a problem. I don't know, Ann. I know I care a lot about you and hate to see you going through this. But something will give." The front door opened. We both looked over at it. Then the pinching at my temples started again. I closed my eyes a second to ease the pain.

274

Camille's Dilemma

"I'm just coming in to use the bathroom," Jermaine explained. I guess he wanted us to know his half an hour wasn't quite up. Then he looked over at his mama.

"What's wrong with you, Ma? What's wrong with my mama? I know," he said, unbuckling his belt, slowly walking backwards to the bathroom. "It's my daddy. She talking about my daddy, ain't she, Auntie Camille? He the only one that makes her cry." He went into the bathroom.

"Yep, something's going to have to give. Jermaine surely don't need to see you like this," I said.

Ann tried to straighten herself up while Jermaine was in the bathroom.

Jermaine walked back out fixing his belt. "I gon' beat his ass when I get big, messing with my mama." He shocked Ann and me with his blunt comment.

"Jermaine, don't you ever let me hear you say that again! Do you hear me?"

He came and sat next to Ann, sitting on the edge of the sofa. He lifted one of his mama's hands and put it in his lap. He lowered his head in shame of what he just said. I told Jermaine to go back outside and play. Told him his mama was going to be fine.

"If we stay here, she gon' be okay," he said, his eyebrows raised. "Not if we go home." He quickly covered his mouth with one hand. "Oops, I'm talking too much. Bye, Ma. Bye, Auntie Camille." Jermaine walked back to the front door with his hand over his mouth. There was silence. I thought about asking Ann to stay the night. Then

275

D.C. Johnson

I thought about April and how she would feel about Ann spending the night.

"Ann, it's Saturday, and you're off tomorrow. Why don't you and Jermaine stay here tonight? Jermaine can sleep in Calvin's room, and you can make a cot right here," I said, patting on the sofa.

"Are you sure, Camille? What about April? I don't want you guys getting into it because of me."

"This is my house. I run this show. I have no control over what she does in the street. Besides, I'm helping a friend. I'm sure you would do the same for me."

Ann got up and went into the bathroom. When she came out, she walked over to me and kissed me lightly on the lips. "I love you, Camille," she said. She sat back on the sofa and gazed out of the window. Maybe this time she actually watched the sun set.

I went to the door and called Calvin and Jermaine in the house. They were both excited about Jermaine spending the night. "Good," Jermaine said, smiling, making goo-goo eyes at Calvin.

Calvin found something for Jermaine to sleep in. He removed his sleeping bag from his closet, laying it on the floor next to his bed. After they were all washed up and ready for bed, we told them they had one hour to look at TV. After that, it was lights out for them.

I went into my room to find something for Ann to sleep in. I returned with an orange, oversized T-shirt. After Ann was settled in, I took a long bath. While I sat in the tub, I tried to force myself to see exactly what was going to happen. The picture that came into focus was of the sky. I knew this was different. It was not like other premonitions. I shook the sky away then thought about April again and how she would react when she saw that Ann was spending the night. Then I berated Ann's husband for abusing her and hoped that their situation would improve. That he would get help and they would become a loving family again. I knew I really didn't have enough space to put them up for more than one night if she decided to leave Michael for good.

As I was putting on my pajamas, the phone rang.

"You in bed?" April asked.

"You still in the streets?" I answered.

"Why do you got to get smart, Camille? I was just calling. Is your friend still there?"

"Why don't you come see for yourself?"

"Forget it, Camille." She hung up. I watched TV until the TV started watching me. A couple hours later, I got up to use the bathroom and turn the TV off when I climbed over who I thought was April.

"If you want me to, I'll go back and sleep on the sofa. It's too little, Camille. If I hear your friend come in, I'll go back on the sofa."

"Don't worry about it. I didn't hear you come in here. Half the time I don't hear April come in," I said, heading to the bathroom. I stayed in the bathroom a few extra minutes wondering if it was a good idea, Ann sleeping in my bed. Then I thought, "It serves April right. Love would have had her ass home tonight." All of a sudden, I hungered for Ann's love. I needed her warm embrace. I needed to feel wanted. I didn't want sex. I just wanted to cuddle. I hoped that she

277

would initiate a cuddle. I didn't want her to think I was taking advantage of the situation.

I walked around to the other side of the bed to get in. I lay with my back against Ann's.

After a few minutes, I wondered if it felt odd to her, too. I wondered if she was thinking the same as me and wanted me to reach over and cuddle her. I then wondered if she had fallen on asleep in the midst of my wondering. Ann was just too close and too bare for me to ignore. I turned over and held her from behind. I closed my eyes to drift off to sleep, but my bottom had other plans. It wanted to pump. I started out slowly with my pumps. Then my hand found its way under her top and began to caress her sleeping breasts. As Ann turned over to face me, the little love I had left for April went out of the opened window. I said something in the midst of our lovemaking to Ann that I've never said before. I told Ann that I love her. She said ditto, and we went to sleep.

April came in about two thirty in the morning. No sooner had she clicked the light on, she clicked it right off. Because it was only a few minutes after our lovemaking, we both heard her come in so we separated ourselves. Ann was on one side of the bed, and I was on the other with our backs against one another. She took Ann's place on the sofa.

After Ann and Jermaine left, resentment hit the fan. I told April to wait until Calvin went outside before we discussed why Ann was in our bed. I didn't want her accusing me of sleeping with another

Camille's Dilemma

woman in front of Calvin or while he was in the house. She couldn't wait.

"What the fuck was she doing in our bed, Camille?" She snatched the sheets off the bed.

"What did it look like she was doing? Sleeping." The phone rang.

"Who is it?" April snapped into the phone. "It's for you," she said, tossing the receiver on the bed. She took a seat on the edge of the bed, staring at me.

"Hello," I said, looking stoic at April.

"What's up, man? I've been trying to get in touch with you. You know I'm back at home with my mother."

"Corrine, let me call you back. This is not a good time."

"So, whose idea was it that she sleep in our bed?"

I crossed my arms under my armpits and said, "Don't come in here harassing me, trying to interrogate me. If you'd been here, you would have known."

"Did you sleep with her, Camille?"

"Did she look like she was sleeping when you turned the light on?"

"Oh, now you trying to be smart. You know what I'm talking about. Did you fuck her, Camille?" she asked, snatching a pillow from the bed and throwing it across the room near me.

"What do you think?" I reached for the remote and turned on the TV to block out some of the shouting that was going on between us.

"Don't fuck with me, Camille!"

279

D.C. Johnson

"You know, we're not in this apartment alone. I do have a child here. I would appreciate it if you'd watch your mouth."

"I want to know if you slept with her," April said, walking over to pick the pillow up. She tossed it back on the bed.

"I'm not going to answer that question. The next time you go out, leave one of your eyeballs at home." I turned to open the door, and April nudged me with her elbow.

"Tell me if you slept with her," she said.

I narrowed my eyes at her and said, "April, I have never had to defend myself to a woman. If you put your hands on me again, you might see a side of me you don't want to see." I walked out of the room into the kitchen to make a pot of coffee.

"Yeah, you fucked the bitch," April said, walking behind me. "You let me catch her ass in our bed again."

"You better watch your mouth, April, before Calvin hears you. You need to chill out. You sound insecure. You don't have a reason to be insecure, do you?" I began filling the coffeepot with water.

"I didn't make the threat, you did," April reminded me. "You're the one talking about me having a new home and somebody else being here."

"And you think Ann's here to fill your shoes?"

"I wouldn't doubt it. She looks like your type."

"And what is that?"

April rolled her eyes at me and sighed. "Forget it, Camille, just forget it!" She went back into the bedroom and slammed the door behind her.

280

Chapter 16
It Ain't Over Till It's Over

(I know I been gone a while, but Ol' Louise haven't been feeling well.) Now, Camille knew she didn't have any room for Ann and Jermaine. But she made some. Sho' did. See, while she and Ann was doing that lovemaking thing the other night, Camille told Ann she could stay with them as long as she needed to. Said her door was always open for them. Ann accepted the invitation 'cause she didn't want to go back home to Michael in the state he was in. But she stayed with her husband three more days before she left him. Just like with April, the little love she had for her husband went out the window, too. That's how I know it was real love that sparkled between Ann and Camille. Neither one of them left they other half to be together. I like Ann. She a pretty woman. Her legs sho' look cute in them Farragamo shoes she wear and her off-black pantyhose. She reminds me of that woman, what's her name…uh, Pam Grier. That's her. That's who she reminds me of. April's a mighty fine young lady too, she just too young for Camille. And you know what, she really wasn't out there messing 'round. I know 'cause I see some things myself. Camille's not the type to snoop. Says it's a waste of time. Says what happens in the dark comes to light sooner or later. She trusted April. She just wanted April to be home at night to cuddle her, to say goodnight, too. To hold her and tell her everything's gon' be all right when it wasn't. She wanted her there to warm her when she was cold. Excuse me a minute. I need to take my medicine. I said before I haven't been feeling well. Maybe I'm just getting too old, or maybe it's time for ole Louise to go. I know I haven't talked that long, but I'm gon' go take me a nap. It seems to be all I want to do now. And I like sleeping. Feels like I'm sleeping on one of them clouds up there. Like they say, see you when I see you. And if I don't, it was nice knowing you all. Plus, April ready to fuss about Ann coming to stay with them. My eardrums can't take all that fussing no more. That child doesn't do nothing but give me a headache.

"Don't she have family she can stay with?" April shouted, leaning back against the kitchen counter.

"Why are you making a big deal of this? Ann is my friend, and she needs somewhere to stay. It's not like it's forever. I don't think it's forever."

"I'm just not comfortable with it. Where is she going to sleep…in the bed with us?"

"Well, I guess that's up to you," I said, adding cream and sugar to my coffee. "If you're here, I doubt that she would get in the bed with us. I don't know what she's going to do when you're out partying and the sofa becomes a little too much to bear." I looked out of the corner of my eye at April.

"You know what, Camille. I don't even care anymore. I'm getting sick of this shit. It sounds like you set it up to be this way. I just think it's your way of trying to keep me at home."

"If I wanted to sleep alone, I would be living alone."

"What the hell is that supposed to mean?"

I didn't respond. I took my cup of coffee to our bedroom.

Two weeks after Ann had moved in, April had made some minor adjustments, like picking me up from work a few times and cooking more. She even started calling me while she was out partying. She would say she was coming home at a certain time then would come home about two hours earlier. I guess she was trying to catch Ann and me together.

The next Saturday afternoon, Calvin and I were home alone. Calvin was in his room glued to the television. I had no idea where April was. She had gotten up early and left the house. Ann and Jermaine left about an hour earlier to visit her mother. I decided to pay Corrine a visit.

On the way over there, I had to pull the car over. I had become dizzy and started seeing the road in dimensions.

"What's wrong with you, Mama? You okay?" Calvin asked, as I lay slumped over on the steering wheel with my eyelids flickering.

"I don't know, Calvin. Mama don't feel good."

"Well, let's drive to the doctor. Even though he can't help you. There's something wrong with you, Mama. It's gon' pass though, because it's really not you that something's wrong with."

I slowly looked over baffled at Calvin and asked him to repeat what he said.

"You heard me, Mama. I said you gon' be fine."

I peered at him, tried to make sense of what he said: "Because it really ain't you something's wrong with." And he said it without a trace of doubt. It was the assurance in his voice. Like he knew more about the headaches than I did. But what did he mean? Where had his words come from? How did he know? I wondered if Calvin had ESP because he was definitely reading my mind. I wondered if he had inherited it from me. I felt extremely weak as I tried to resume driving.

Calvin wanted to go by grandma's house instead of over Corrine's, so I took him over there. I told him not to mention to Grandma that my head was hurting. He said okay. I then drove to Corrine's house.

"Man, look at you. Are you seeing shit again? You look lost," Corrine said, stepping onto the porch, closing the door behind her.

"Uh-un. Calvin just said something that startled me. Corrine, why don't you go see if y'all have any aspirins." While Corrine went to look, I sat on the top step and observed my old stomping grounds. It had been a long time since I had been back around this way hanging out. If I wasn't coming to visit my mother, I didn't see a reason for coming back. Corrine's house was on the corner across from the

284

playground. A comfortable spot to just sit and watch everyday activity.

"Here you go," Corrine said, handing me two Tylenol and a Dixie cup full of water. She then took a seat in a chair that was on the porch. "Man, I had to get away from Elma. She tried to play me for a fool," Corrine said. She then reached into her shirt pocket and pulled out her cigarettes. "Yep, but I wasn't going out like that," she said after lighting her cigarette. By this time, I was hardly listening. My headache had turned into a migraine.

"You know what, Corrine," I said, barely able to lift my head up. It felt like a ton on bricks was sitting atop it. "I need to go lay down."

"You look like you need to see a doctor. Man, what's up? You all right?"

"I'll be okay," I said then went slowly down Corrine's steps. Though I was moving forward, I felt like I was being pulled backwards.

I walked into the house totally exhausted. I staggered all the way to my bedroom.

"I don't know what's wrong with her. Do something, Ann!" April said.

"Where did she get that ugly black dress from?" Ann said, frowning at it. "Camille, Camille, wake up, Camille." She shook Camille over and over, and Camille wouldn't budge.

April, crying, said, "She was like this when I came home. And why is she laying there with her hands crossed like she's in a casket?

What's wrong with her? Is she dead? Wake up, Camille! Camille, please wake up!"

"Where is Calvin?" Ann asked, trying to hold in her emotions. She didn't want April to know how much she cared about Camille.

"I don't know. I just came in minutes before you did. We got to get her some help, Ann. We got to call somebody." April went for the telephone. Ann put her hand over her mouth and cried softly.

"What's wrong with Auntie Camille, Mama?" Jermaine asked, creeping into the room, staring at Camille as she lay there.

"Get back, Jermaine," Ann said then led Jermaine to Calvin's room.

"Ma, is Auntie Camille dead?"

"We don't know, baby. Just stay in here until I come get you."

"The ambulance is on the way," April said when Ann walked back into the room. Ann stood next to April then placed her arm around her.

"It probably has something to do with those headaches she was getting. Please, Camille, wake up," Ann said as April rested her head on Ann's shoulder.

"She's dead, isn't she, Ann?" April lifted her head and looked in Ann's eyes.

"I don't know, April." They heard the ambulance out front, and both hurried to the front door.

"We received a call that someone is ill."

"She's back here," April said. Ann and the paramedics followed April to Camille's bedroom.

Camille's Dilemma

Roy, one of the paramedics, checked for a heartbeat. He then took Camille's blood pressure. He opened Camille's eyes and examined her pupils with a pen-sized tool. "She has a heartbeat," he said, "but it's beating at a very slow rate—a very, very slow rate. Her blood pressure is extremely low, too. She's not dead. But I can't say what's keeping her alive, either. It's like she's dead and alive, or half-dead." He shook his head as he looked over at the other paramedic, who looked as confused as he did. Roy then said, "We're going to take her to the hospital. Are you family members?" he asked, looking at April.

"Yes," they said in unison.

Ann said, "You ride with them, and I'll drive my car." They hugged and then followed the ambulance to the hospital.

Camille, lying on a gurney, was rolled into a well-lit room. On the count of three, Camille was lifted up and onto a bed. A doctor and a nurse was working fast, checking for a heartbeat and taking Camille's blood pressure, looking her over for signs of trauma. After hooking Camille's arm to an IV machine, the doctor came up with the same conclusion the paramedics had. They didn't know how to treat her because they weren't sure what was wrong with her. April, Ann, and Jermaine sat in the waiting area. April would get up and pace the floor every ten minutes. Jermaine started getting restless from sitting, and Ann tried to calm them both. The doctor finally came out of the room to talk with whom he thought was Camille's relatives. He knew April looked far too young to be Camille's mother, so he addressed Ann.

"Well, right now there's not a whole lot I can say or do for her. She just appears to be out of it."

287

"Out of it? What do you mean, out of it?" April said.

"I don't want to alarm you, but we can't find anything wrong with her. We ran several tests, and they've all come back negative."

"Well, why won't she wake up?" April asked, stomping her feet.

"We're going to run some additional tests on her. We're going to keep her overnight for observation. She appears to be fine." He shrugged his shoulder and said, "This is the first patient I've received like this." He shook his head, boggled by Camille's unexplained condition. "Has she been acting strange or given either of you the indication that something was wrong? Is she taking any kind of medication?" he asked, looking at both of them.

"She has been getting headaches," April said with her arms crossed.

"Headaches. How often did she get them?" the doctor asked.

"Lately, two, three times a day," Ann said.

"Has she been under any kind of stress lately?"

"A little," April said discreetly.

The doctor turned to Ann. "We're going to run some more tests. As of now, she's fine. I don't think you really have anything to be worried about. She's not in a coma, just appears to be unconscious. If her condition changes, we will contact you immediately." Ann nodded her head at the doctor, and she, Jermaine, and April left.

There was silence for the first few minutes of their drive home. Ann broke the silence.

"April, we're going to get through this. I believe in my heart that Camille is going to be fine. What we need to do now is find out where

Calvin is. I've never been to Camille's mother's house, but we need to check with her to see if he's there."

"Ann, I understand you're worried about Camille because she's your friend. But just how close of friends are you two?" She looked over at Ann for an honest answer. "I need to know. I need to know if I've lost Camille." Ann took one hand off the steering wheel and placed it on top of April's hands that lay in her lap.

"April, I'm going to be honest with you. But you have to promise me you'll listen to the whole story before you say anything."

"Okay. I'll listen."

Ann pulled the car into a park she saw to talk to April. She told Jermaine to go play for a minute. She turned toward April to look her in the face. She didn't want her to think she was hiding anything.

"I'm going to start from the beginning so you will understand how things came to be the way they are. I met Camille a few months before you did. We met at work. I didn't have a gay bone in my body. I was happily married to a wonderful man. What brought us closer together were our kids. They enjoyed playing with one another. Then somehow we ended up in bed. We decided afterwards to be friends, and that's what we were. Then she met you. April, Camille was crazy about you—"

"Was!"

Ann put one finger up as if to say, "You said you would hear me out first." April let her continue. "I was happy for Camille that she had met someone. I was still crazy about my husband. Then things started to change for the both of us. My marriage was falling apart at

289

the same time Camille started having problems with you being gone all the time." April sort of rolled her eyes. "We would talk about our problems to each other. Again, we ended up in bed. We found what we were missing at home in each other. April, you can believe me if you want, but Camille loved you. I know. I had to sit and listen to her sob about you not being there." Tears slowly began to fall from April's eyes making a puddle in her lap. "Then things just got too unbearable for me at home. I didn't try to impose on you and Camille; I just didn't have anyone else to turn to. We both wanted the relationships we were in, me with my husband and you with her. April, it's impossible to work things out if you're not there. Camille wanted and needed you there. I won't say that Camille and I are in a relationship, because we're not. But I would be lying to you if I said I didn't love Camille and Camille didn't love me." April cried silently, peering out of the side window.

"So, where does this leave me? I still love her, Ann. Why didn't Camille just tell me she had fallen in love with you?"

"I don't know, April. Maybe she thought you would have felt that it was all planned, and it wasn't. Especially after I came to stay with you guys for a while. I don't make it a habit of falling in love with my friends. Life's unpredictable. And Camille's an easy person to love. I don't dislike you, April, and I hope you're not harboring bad feelings for me."

April leaned over and kissed Ann on the jaw. "Ann, if I lost Camille, she couldn't have fallen for a more honest and beautiful woman," she said and managed a smile. "Now, let's go find Calvin,

Camille's Dilemma

our son." Ann called out to Jermaine, who in the last ten minutes had made new friends.

The first thing they did when they got home was call over to Camille's mother's house.

"Hello."

"Hi, Miss Jenkins, this is April."

"Hi. How you doing, April?"

"I'm fine. I was calling to see if you knew where Calvin was." April bit down on her bottom lip waiting for an answer.

"Of course I know where my grandbaby is. He's right here with me. Well, he's here, down in the basement with his uncle Clifford. Is everything okay?" There was a brief pause. "April," Miss Jenkins called into the phone.

"Not really."

"Well, what is it, April? Is Camille all right?"

"I'm not sure, Miss Jenkins. Camille has been admitted into the hospital," she replied, still biting down on her lip.

"The hospital! What is she doing in the hospital? I just saw her a few hours ago. Is everything okay?"

"The doctor said she's fine. They just don't know what's wrong with her. When I came home, me and another one of Camille's friends found her laying in the bed with a black dress on like she was in a casket."

"What? A black dress! Camille doesn't like dresses. April, what's going on?"

D.C. Johnson

"We think she's okay. Miss Jenkins, is it okay if we come by there? Maybe Calvin knows something."

"Of course it is." Ann and April made their way over to Camille's mother's house. In the interim, Miss Jenkins had called Calvin upstairs to question him about his mama.

"Calvin, do you know where your mama is?" Miss Jenkins asked, pointing at a chair for him to sit into.

"She said she was going to visit Corrine."

"She didn't say she was going anywhere else after that?"

"No. Not to me."

Miss Jenkins got up and looked out of the front window. She saw April getting out of the passenger side of a car. "They're here," she said.

"Who's here, Grandma? Auntie Cynthia?" Calvin said, racing over to the window to see.

"No, it's not Auntie Cynthia. It's April and another one of your mama's friends," Miss Jenkins said, walking over to the door.

"Ooh, it's Ann. Is Jermaine with her?"

"Jermaine. Who's Jermaine?" she asked, opening the side door.

"He's my play brother," Calvin said, looking around her to see if Jermaine was with her.

"Y'all come on in and have a seat," Miss Jenkins said, pulling chairs out from the dining room table. "You must be Jermaine," Miss Jenkins said, smiling at him. "Now, what you say happened? Oh, I'm sorry; I'm Camille's mother, and you are?" she said, extending her hand across the table to Ann.

292

Camille's Dilemma

"Ann."

"Hi, Ann." Miss Jenkins quickly turned her attention back to April and asked, "Now, what's going on?"

"Miss Jenkins, we just found Camille laying unconscious in her bed dressed in a black dress." Miss Jenkins looked down to the floor baffled, shaking her head. She then looked at Calvin, who was standing next to her.

"Calvin, how was your mama acting before she dropped you off over your grandma's?" Ann asked him.

"Dang, why everybody worried about my mama. She's fine," Calvin said with his head leaning to one side.

"She's fine. How do you know that, Calvin? How do you know your mama's okay?"

"'Cause I told her she was gon' be fine."

Ann got up and whispered into Miss Jenkins' ear. She asked her if she had told Calvin that his mama was in the hospital. Ms. Jenkins shook her head no. She then looked at Calvin and said, "Do you know where your mother is, Calvin?"

"Nope. But I know she's doing fine. Grandma, what we gon' eat? You don't have any food in your refrigerator. I already checked. Can April take me to get something to eat?"

"Calvin, your mama's in the hospital," April said, kneeling in front of him, putting both hands on his shoulders.

"She's still fine. Why y'all worried about my mama? Grandma, I'm hungry," he said, looking over at her.

D.C. Johnson

"We're going to get you something to eat, baby. We're just trying to find out what's wrong with your mama." Calvin took in a deep breath and sighed.

"Miss Jenkins," Ann said, "I think it may have something to do with the headaches she's been having." That remark caught Calvin's attention. He quickly looked over at Ann.

"Calvin, do you know something and you're just not telling us?" He put a look on his face assuring them he knew something.

"My mama told me not to tell," he said, folding his arms across his chest.

"Calvin, this is Grandma. You know your grandma loves you. You have to tell me what's wrong with your mama if you know." She looked over at Ann and April and said, "I'm almost certain he knows something.

"I need you to tell Grandma everything that you know, Calvin, so we can help your mama," she said, pulling him into her lap. "Don't be afraid; we need to know so we can help her."

"She told me not to tell, Grandma," he said, looking into her face with a crooked smile.

"Calvin, we're all worried about her." He looked at everybody, even Jermaine, then told what he knew.

"When we were driving to your house, Grandma, my mama said she didn't feel good and pulled the car over. So I told her it was gon' pass because it wasn't her that something was wrong with. Then she told me not to tell you her head was hurting. Now can we get something to eat? I'm hungry, Grandma."

294

Camille's Dilemma

"One more question, Calvin. What did you mean when you said it wasn't your mama that something was wrong with?" his grandma asked him.

"It's her friend, Grandma. Her friend Louise is the one that don't feel good."

"Louise," everybody said under their breaths, looking confused at one another.

Calvin knew they still didn't understand and knew the only way he was gon' get something to eat was if they understood. So he said, "My mama's friend Louise lives with her. Everywhere that mama go, Louise go, too. But Louise is old, and it's time for her to go away. 'Cause she was my mama's best friend, she went to her funeral. That's why I said she gon' be fine. She be back."

"How do you know all this, Calvin?" Ann asked him.

"I just know." Calvin got up and hollered downstairs, "Uncle Clifford, can you take me to get something to eat?"

"Miss Jenkins, is it okay if we take him?" April asked, smiling at Calvin.

The next morning, April and Ann went to visit Camille in the hospital. They spoke with the doctor before going into her room. The doctor told them they still weren't sure what the problem was. He told them that at intervals Camille would start to cry. Said tears would flow from the corner of her eyes. Said every now and then she would smile, and then she would look sad. He told them that it wouldn't surprise him if Camille were having an out-of-body experience. He then escorted them into the room.

They stood around Camille's bed watching her cry off and on. April and Ann took turns wiping her tears away. Camille, while April was wiping away her tears, opened her eyes. April gasped and grabbed at her chest. Ann and the doctor looked shocked. Camille then looked bewildered at April. She glanced around to see where she was. She then attempted to rise, and the doctor told her to lay back down.

"Do you know where you are?" he asked her.

"It looks like I'm in a hospital. Where is my son? Where is Calvin?" Camille asked frantically. She tried to rise again, and the doctor stopped her.

Ann then smiled, which started everybody else to smiling. She said, "He's fine, Camille. He's at your mother's."

"Well, if you guys don't mind, I'd like to go home. Why am I here, anyway? Can somebody tell me that?" Camille said, looking back and forth at them.

"Can you tell us where you were a little while ago?" the doctor asked Camille, feeling her pulse.

"No, I can't tell you where I was. I don't even know what I'm doing here. But I feel like I've been to a funeral from the way everybody's standing around me." Ann and April both put their hands over their mouths. They both thought of Calvin and what he had said. The doctor took Camille's response as a joke.

"You passed out," the doctor said, coming up with the only explanation he knew. "Just relax. In a couple of hours, if everything is

Camille's Dilemma

well, you'll be released," he said, patting Camille on the arm. "This is definitely one for the books," he uttered then left the room.

When Camille got home, she took a deep breath then grabbed the remote from on top of the stereo. She then sat down in the recliner and clicked the stereo on. April and Ann plopped down on the couch, looking exhausted. A word hadn't been said since leaving the hospital.

"It's been a long day," Ann said, initiating conversation while removing her shoes.

"You can say that again," April said, glancing over at Camille.

"It's been a long day," Ann repeated. "I got that from Camille, repeating when someone used the phrase 'You can say that again.'" Camille chuckled; she tilted her head back and pushed the recliner back with her back to extend it. She then closed her eyes, bobbing her head as she immersed herself in a Lenny Kravitz tune spilling out of the stereo. Ann said, looking over at April, "Maybe I'll go by my mother's for a little while to give you and Camille some time alone."

"You don't have to leave, Ann," April said, smiling at her.

Camille began crooning with Lenny Kravitz singing "It Aint Over till It's Over.

"Here we are, still together, we are one." Camille was obviously deep into the song; Ann and April were now staring at her. Tears broke free from Camille's eyes. Ann, after listening to the lyrics Camille crooned, covered her mouth. A few tears trickled down her

297

face. She wiped them away with the joint of her thumb. Camille crooned on.

As the song was ending, Camille looked peaceful over at April. "It's over," she said. She rose from the loveseat and kneeled down in front of April. She took April's hand in hers. "I have to say this," Camille said. "I can't explain what has happened in the last day or two, but whatever took place left me with a sense of serenity. For some reason, I feel as if I've weathered a storm, like a weight has been lifted, like I'm feeling my own spirit for the first time. Not to say that the one that was here before was a burden. Please don't ask me to explain what I just said," Camille said, shaking her head a little. "It's time for Camille to start looking out for Camille. I don't have any regrets. I just need to start a new life, and to do that, I need time to myself. April, I would like to stay friends with you, but the only way that that can happen is we have to go our separate ways."

Camille then looked over at Ann, scooted over on her knees, and held Ann's hand the same way she did April's. "Ann, I've been blessed to have someone like you come into my life. You've been a true friend, and I thank you for being here for me, but I need time away from you as well. You can take as much time as you need to find a place. You really don't have a choice but to remain my friend, since Calvin and Jermaine consider themselves brothers," Camille said, smiling. She rose to her feet then leaned over and kissed Ann on the cheek, then April. "Now, if you guys will excuse me, I'm going for a walk."

Camille's Dilemma

Camille grabbed her jacket and walked back over to her old stomping grounds, the playground, where she took a seat on a green bench. She waved at a couple of guys who were sitting a few benches over that she went to high school with. They were laughing and guzzling down what appeared to be a forty-ounce of beer inside a brown paper bag.

Camille looked up into the sky that had become a little cloudy. She heard one of the guys say, "Man, it's getting ready to rain. Dog, let's go sit on my porch."

Camille took a deep breath and felt soft drizzles of rain on her face. The first image in Camille's head was Louise. She smiled. She closed her eyes, stashed her hands into her jacket pockets, and took a deep breath. When she exhaled and opened her eyes, stretched across the sky was a rainbow. Camille always felt that each color in the rainbow represented a saved soul. And the reason a rainbow appeared thin was because of all the lost souls. She didn't know which color represented Louise but was sure one belonged to her.

As the rain began to pour out of what now was a sunny but colorful sky, something told Camille that life had something good in store for her. An angelic voice whispered, "Don't go looking for it; let it come to you." Camille rose from the bench and buried her hands deep into her jacket pockets then smiled all the way home.

The next day, April moved back home with her family. Two weeks later, after Ann's husband admitted himself into a drug rehab, she went back home.

D.C. Johnson

Camille then called Corrine and told her that she wasn't ending their friendship but needed time to be alone. That she would explain it to her later. Camille then planned a trip for her and Calvin to go to Disney World.

THE END

Printed in the United States
21569LVS00004B/52-111